Prudence of the Parsonage

Ethel Hueston

Contents

PRUDENCE OF
THE PARSONAGE

BY

Ethel Hueston

*TO MY MOTHER
WHO DEVOTED HER LIFE TO REARING
A WHOLE PARSONAGE-FULL OF ROLLICKING
YOUNG METHODISTS*

CHAPTER I
INTRODUCING HER

None but the residents consider Mount Mark, Iowa, much of a town, and those who are honest among them admit, although reluctantly, that Mount Mark can boast of far more patriotism than good judgment! But the *very most* patriotic of them all has no word of praise for the ugly little red C., B. & Q. railway station. If pretty is as pretty does, as we have been told so unpleasantly often, then the station is handsome enough, but as an ornament to the commonwealth it is a dismal failure,--low, smoky and dust-grimed. In winter its bleakness and bareness add to the chill of the rigorous Iowa temperature, and in summer the sap oozing through the boards is disagreeably suggestive of perspiration. The waiting-room itself is "cleaned" every day, and yet the same dust lies in the corners where it has lain for lo, these many years. And as for the cobwebs, their chief distinction lies in their ripe old age. If there were only seven spiders in the ark, after the subsiding of the waters, at least a majority of them must have found their way to Mount Mark station in South-eastern Iowa.

Mount Mark is anything but proud of the little station. It openly scoffs at it, and sniffs contemptuously at the ticket agent who bears the entire C., B. & Q. reputation upon his humble shoulders. At the same time, it certainly does owe the railroad and the state a debt of gratitude for its presence there. It is the favorite social rendezvous for the community! Only four passenger trains daily pass through Mount Mark,--not including the expresses, which rush haughtily by with no more than a scornful whistle for the sleepy town, and in return for this indignity, Mount Mark cherishes a most unchristian antipathy toward those demon fliers.

But the "passengers"--ah, that is a different matter. The arrival of a passenger train in Mount Mark is an event--something in the nature of a C., B. & Q. "At

Home," and is always attended by a large and enthusiastic gathering of "our best people." All that is lacking are the proverbial "light refreshments!"

So it happened that one sultry morning, late in the month of August, there was the usual flutter of excitement and confusion on the platform and in the waiting-room of the station. The habitues were there in force. Conspicuous among them were four gaily dressed young men, smoking cigarettes and gazing with lack-luster eyes upon the animated scene, which evidently bored them. All the same, they invariably appeared at the depot to witness this event, stirring to others no doubt, but incapable of arousing the interest of these life-weary youths. They comprised the Slaughter-house Quartette, and were the most familiar and notorious characters in all the town.

The Daily News reporter, in a well-creased, light gray suit and tan shoes, and with eye-glasses scientifically balanced on his aquiline nose, was making pointed inquiries into the private plans of the travelers. *The Daily News* reporters in Mount Mark always wear well-creased, light gray suits and tan shoes, and always have eye-glasses scientifically balanced on aquiline noses. The uninitiated can not understand how it is managed, but there lies the fact. Perhaps *The News* includes these details in its requirements of applicants. Possibly it furnishes the gray suits and the tan shoes, and even the eye-glasses. Of course, the reporters can practise balancing them scientifically,--but how does it happen that they always have aquiline noses? At any rate, that is the Mount Mark type. It never varies.

The young woman going to Burlington to spend the week-end was surrounded with about fifteen other young women who had come to "see her off." She had relatives in Burlington and went there very often, and she used to say she was glad she didn't have to exchange Christmas presents with all the "friends" who witnessed her arrivals and departures at the station. Mount Mark is a very respectable town, be it understood, and girls do not go to the station without an excuse!

The Adams Express wagon was drawn close to the track, and the agent was rushing about with a breathless energy which seemed all out of proportion to his accomplishments. The telegraph operator was gazing earnestly out of his open window, and his hands were busily moving papers from one pigeon-hole to another, and back again. Old Harvey Reel, who drove the hotel bus, was discussing politics with the man who kept the restaurant, and the baggage master, superior and supremely dirty, was checking baggage with his almost unendurably lordly air.

This was one of the four daily rejuvenations that gladdened the heart of Mount Mark.

A man in a black business suit stood alone on the platform, his hands in his pockets, his eyes wandering from one to another of the strange faces about him. His plain white ready-made tie proclaimed his calling.

"It's the new Methodist preacher," volunteered the baggage master, crossing the platform, ostensibly on business bound, but really to see "who all" was there. "I know him. He's not a bad sort."

"They say he's got five kids, and most of 'em girls," responded the Adams Express man. "I've ordered me a dress suit to pay my respects in when they get here. I want to be on hand early to pick me out a girl."

"Yah," mocked the telegraph operator, bobbing his head through the window, "you need to. They tell me every girl in Mount Mark has turned you down a'ready."

But the Methodist minister, gazing away down the track where a thin curl of smoke announced the coming of Number Nine, and Prudence,--heard nothing of this conversation. He was not a handsome man. His hair was gray at the temples, his face was earnest, only saved from severity by the little clusters of lines at his eyes and mouth which proclaimed that he laughed often, and with relish.

"Train going east!"

The minister stood back from the crowd, but when the train came pounding in a brightness leaped into his eyes that entirely changed the expression of his face. A slender girl stood in the vestibule, leaning dangerously outward, and waving wildly at him a small gloved hand. When the train stopped she leaped lightly from the steps, ignoring the stool placed for her feet by the conductor.

"Father!" she cried excitedly and small and slight as she was, she elbowed her way swiftly through the gaping crowd. "Oh, father!" And she flung her arms about him joyously, unconscious of the admiring eyes of the Adams Express man, and the telegraph operator, and old Harvey Reel, whose eyes were always admiring when girls passed by. She did not even observe that the Slaughterhouse Quartette looked at her unanimously, with languid interest from out the wreaths of smoke they had created.

Her father kissed her warmly. "Where is your baggage?" he asked, a hand held out to relieve her.

"Here!" And with a radiant smile she thrust upon him a box of candy and a gaudy-covered magazine.

"Your suit-case," he explained patiently.

"Oh!" she gasped. "Run, father, run! I left it on the train!"

Father did run, but Prudence, fleeter-footed, out-distanced him and clambered on board, panting.

When she rejoined her father her face was flushed. "Oh, father," she said quite snappily, "isn't that just like me?"

"Yes, very like," he agreed, and he smiled. "Where is your umbrella?"

Prudence stopped abruptly. "I don't know," she said, with a stony face. "I can't remember a blessed thing about the old umbrella. Oh, I guess I didn't bring it, at all." She breathed long in her relief. "Yes, that's it, father, I left it at Aunt Grace's. Don't you worry about it. Fairy'll bring it to-morrow. Isn't it nice that we can count on Fairy's remembering?"

"Yes, very nice," he said, but his eyes were tender as he looked down at the little figure beside him.

"And so this is Mount Mark! Isn't it a funny name, father? Why do they call it Mount Mark?"

"I don't know. I hadn't thought to inquire. We turn here, Prudence; we are going north now. This is Main Street. The city part of the town--the business part--is to the south."

"It's a pretty street, isn't it?" she cried. "Such nice big maples, and such shady, porchy houses. I love houses with porches, don't you? Has the parsonage a porch?"

"Yes, a big one on the south, and a tiny one in front. The house faces west. That is the college there. It opens in three weeks, and Fairy can make freshmen all right, they tell me. I wish you could go, too. You haven't had your share of anything--any good thing, Prudence."

"Well, I have my share of you, father," she said comfortingly. "And I've always had my share of oatmeal and sorghum molasses,--though one wouldn't think it to look at me. Fairy gained a whole inch last week at Aunt Grace's. She was so disgusted with herself. She says she'll not be able to look back on the visit with any pleasure at all, just because of that inch. Carol said she ought to look back with more pleasure, because there's an inch more of her to do it! But Fairy says she did not gain the inch in her eyes! Aunt Grace laughed every minute we were there. She says she is all sore up and down, from laughing so much."

"We have the house fixed up pretty well, Prudence, but of course you'll have to go over it yourself and arrange it as you like. But remember this: You are not allowed to move the heavy furniture. I forbid it emphatically. There isn't enough of you for that."

"Yes, I'll remember,--I think I will. I'm almost certain to remember some things, you know."

"I must go to a trustees' meeting at two o'clock, but we can get a good deal done before then. Mrs. Adams is coming to help you this afternoon. She is one of our Ladies, and very kind. There, that is the parsonage!"

Prudence gazed in silence. Many would not have considered it a beautiful dwelling, but to Prudence it was heavenly. Fortunately the wide, grassy, shaded lawn greeted one first. Great spreading maples bordered the street, and clustering rose-bushes lined the walk leading up to the house. The walk was badly worn and broken to be sure,--but the roses were lovely! The grass had been carefully cut,-- the father-minister had seen to that. The parsonage, to Prudence's gratified eyes, looked homey, and big, and inviting. In fact, it was very nearly gorgeous! It needed painting badly, it is true. The original color had been a peculiar drab, but most of it had disappeared long before, so it was no eyesore on account of the color. There were many windows, and the well-known lace curtains looked down upon Prudence tripping happily up the little board walk,--or so it seemed to her.

"Two whole stories, and an attic besides! Not to mention the bathroom! Oh, father, the night after you wrote there was a bathroom, Constance thanked God for it when she said her prayers. And I couldn't reprove her, for I felt the same way about it myself. It'll be so splendid to have a whole tub to bathe in! I spent half the time bathing this last week at Aunt Grace's. A tub is so bountiful! A pan is awfully insufficient, father, even for me! I often think what a trouble it must be to Fairy! And a furnace, too! And electric lights! Don't you think there is something awe-inspiring in the idea of just turning a little knob on the wall, and flooding a whole room with light? I do revel in electric lights, I tell you. Oh, we have waited a long time for it, and we've been very patient indeed, but, between you and me, father, I am most mightily glad we've hit the luxury-land at last. I'm sure we'll all feel much more religious in a parsonage that has a bathroom and electric lights! Oh, father!"

He had thrown open the door, and Prudence stood upon the threshold of her new home. It was not a fashionable building, by any means. The hall was narrow and long, and the staircase was just a plain businesslike staircase, with no room for cushions, and flowers, and books. The doors leading from the hall were open, and Prudence caught a glimpse of three rooms furnished, rather scantily, in the old familiar furniture that had been in that other parsonage where Prudence was born, nineteen years before.

Together she and her father went from room to room, up-stairs and down, moving a table to the left, a bed to the right,--according to her own good pleasure. Afterward they had a cozy luncheon for two in the "dining-room."

"Oh, it is so elegant to have a dining-room," breathed Prudence happily. "I always pretended it was rather fun, and a great saving of work, to eat and cook and study and live in one room, but inwardly the idea always outraged me. Is that the school over there?"

"Yes, that's where Connie will go. There is only one high school in Mount Mark, so the twins will have to go to the other side of town,--a long walk, but in good weather they can come home for dinner.--I'm afraid the kitchen will be too cold in winter, Prudence,--it's hardly more than a shed, really. Maybe we'd----"

"Oh, father, if you love me, don't suggest that we move the stove in here in winter! I'm perfectly willing to freeze out there, for the sake of having a dining-room. Did I ever tell you what Carol said about that kitchen-dining-room-living-room combination at Exminster? Well, she asked us a riddle, 'When is a dining-room not a dining-room?' And she answered it herself, 'When it's a little pig-pen.' And I felt so badly about it, but it did look like a pig-pen, with stove here, and cupboard there, and table yonder, and--oh, no, father, please let me freeze!"

"I confess I do not see the connection between a roomful of furniture and a pig-pen, but Carol's wit is often too subtle for me."

"Oh, that's a lovely place over there, father!" exclaimed Prudence, looking from the living-room windows toward the south. "Isn't it beautiful?"

"Yes. The Avery family lives there. The parents are very old and feeble, and the daughters are all--elderly--and all school-teachers. There are four of them, and the youngest is forty-six. It is certainly a beautiful place. See the orchard out behind, and the vineyard. They are very wealthy, and they are not fond of children outside of school hours, I am told, so we must keep an eye on Connie.--Dear me, it is two o'clock already, and I must go at once. Mrs. Adams will be here in a few minutes, and you will not be lonely."

But when Mrs. Adams arrived at the parsonage, she knocked repeatedly, and in vain, upon the front door. After that she went to the side door, with no better result. Finally, she gathered her robes about her and went into the back yard. She peered into the woodshed, and saw no one. She went into the barn-lot, and found it empty. In despair, she plunged into the barn--and stopped abruptly.

In a shadowy corner was a slender figure kneeling beside an overturned nail keg, her face buried in her hands. Evidently this was Prudence engaged in prayer,--and in the barn, of all places in the world!

"A--a--a--hem!" stammered Mrs. Adams inquiringly.

"Amen!" This was spoken aloud and hurriedly, and Prudence leaped to her feet. Her fair hair clung about her face in damp babyish tendrils, and her face was flushed and dusty, but alight with friendly interest. She ran forward eagerly, thrusting forth a slim and grimy hand.

"You are Mrs. Adams, aren't you? I am Prudence Starr. It is so kind of you to come the very first day," she cried. "It makes me love you right at the start."

"Ye--yes, I am Mrs. Adams." Mrs. Adams was embarrassed. She could not banish from her mental vision that kneeling figure by the nail keg. Interrogation was written all over her ample face, and Prudence promptly read it and hastened to reply.

"I do not generally say my prayers in the barn, Mrs. Adams, I assure you. I suppose you were greatly surprised. I didn't expect to do it myself, when I came out here, but--well, when I found this grand, old, rambling barn, I was so thankful I couldn't resist praying about it. Of course, I didn't specially designate the barn, but God knew what I meant, I am sure."

"But a barn!" ejaculated the perplexed "member." "Do you call that a blessing?"

"Yes, indeed I do," declared Prudence. Then she explained patiently: "Oh, it is on the children's account, you know. They have always longed for a big romantic barn to play in. We've never had anything but a shed, and when father went to Conference this year, the twins told him particularly to look out for a good big barn. They said we'd be willing to put up with any kind of a parsonage, if only we might draw a barn for once. You can't imagine how happy this dear old place will make them, and I was happy on their account. That's why I couldn't resist saying my prayers,--I was so happy I couldn't hold in."

As they walked slowly toward the house, Mrs. Adams looked at this parsonage girl in frank curiosity and some dismay, which she strongly endeavored to conceal from the bright-eyed Prudence. The Ladies had said it would be so nice to have a grown girl in the parsonage! Prudence was nineteen from all account, but she looked like a child and--well, it was not exactly grown-up to give thanks for a barn, to say the very least! Yet this girl had full charge of four younger children, and was further burdened with the entire care of a minister-father! Well, well! Mrs. Adams sighed a little.

"You are tired," said Prudence sympathetically. "It's so hot walking, isn't it? Let's sit on the porch until you are nicely rested. Isn't this a lovely yard? And the children will be so happy to have this delicious big porch. Oh, I just adore Mount Mark already."

"This is a fine chance for us to get acquainted," said the good woman with eagerness.

Now if the truth must be told, there had been some ill feeling in the Ladies' Aid Society concerning the reception of Prudence. After the session of Conference, when the Reverend Mr. Starr was assigned to Mount Mark, the Ladies of the church had felt great interest in the man and his family. They inquired on every hand, and learned several interesting items. The mother had been taken from the family five years before, after a long illness, and Prudence, the eldest daughter, had taken charge of the household. There were five children. So much was known, and being women, they looked forward with eager curiosity to the coming of Prudence, the young mistress of the parsonage.

Mr. Starr had arrived at Mount Mark a week ahead of his family. The furniture had been shipped from his previous charge, and he, with the assistance of a strong and willing negro, had "placed it" according to the written instructions of Prudence, who had conscientiously outlined just what should go in every room. She and the other children had spent the week visiting at the home of their aunt, and Prudence had come on a day in advance of the others to "wind everything up," as she had expressed it.

But to return to the Ladies,--the parsonage girls always capitalized the Ladies of their father's church, and indeed italicized them, as well. And the irrepressible Carol had been heard to remark, "I often feel like exclamation-pointing them, I promise you." But to return once more.

"One of us should go and help the dear child," said Mrs. Scott, the president of the Aids, when they assembled for their business meeting, "help her, and welcome her, and advise her."

"I was thinking of going over," said one, and another, and several others.

"Oh, that will not do at all," said the president; "she would be excited meeting so many strangers, and could not properly attend to her work. That will never do, never, never! But one of us must go, of course."

"I move that the president appoint a committee of one to help Miss Prudence get settled, and welcome her to our midst," said Mrs. Barnaby, secretly hoping that in respect for her making this suggestion honoring the president, the president would have appreciation enough to appoint Mrs. Barnaby herself as committee.

The motion was seconded, and carried.

"Well," said Mrs. Scott slowly, "I think in a case like this the president herself should represent the society. Therefore, I will undertake this duty for you."

But this called forth a storm of protest and it became so clamorous that it was unofficially decided to draw cuts! Which was done, and in consequence of that drawing of cuts, Mrs. Adams now sat on the front porch of the old gray parsonage, cheered by the knowledge that every other Lady of the Aid was envying her!

"Now, just be real sociable and tell me all about yourself, and the others, too," urged Mrs. Adams. "I want to know all about every one of you. Tell me everything."

"There isn't much to tell," said Prudence, smiling. "There are five of us; I am the oldest, I am nineteen. Then comes Fairy, then the twins, and then the baby."

"Are the twins boys, or a boy and a girl?"

"Neither," said Prudence, "they are both girls."

"More girls!" gasped Mrs. Adams. "And the baby?"

"She is a girl, too." And Prudence laughed. "In short, we are all girls except father. He couldn't be, of course,--or I suppose he would, for our family does seem to run to girls."

"Prudence is a very nice name for a minister's daughter," said Mrs. Adams suggestively.

"Yes,--for some ministers' daughters," assented Prudence. "But is sadly unsuitable for me. You see, father and mother were very enthusiastic about the first baby who hadn't arrived. They had two names all picked out months ahead,--Prudence and John Wesley. That's how I happen to be Prudence. They thought, as you do, that it was an uplifting name for a parsonage baby.--I was only three years old when Fairy was born, but already they realized that they had made a great mistake. So they decided to christen baby number two more appropriately. They chose Frank and Fairy,--both light-hearted, happy, cheerful names.--It's Fairy," Prudence smiled reflectively. "But things went badly again. They were very unlucky with their babies. Fairy is Prudence by nature, and I am Fairy. She is tall and a little inclined to be fat. She is steady, and industrious, and reliable, and sensible, and clever. In fact, she is an all-round solid and worthwhile girl. She can do anything, and do it right, and is going to be a college professor. It is a sad thing to think of a college professor being called Fairy all her life, isn't it? Especially when she is so dignified and grand. But one simply can't tell beforehand what to expect, can one?

"Father and mother were quite discouraged by that time. They hardly knew what to do. But anyhow they were sure the next would be a boy. Every one predicted a boy, and so they chose a good old Methodist name,--Charles. They hated to give it John Wesley, for they had sort of dedicated that to me, you know,--only I happened to be Prudence. But Charles was second-best. And they were very happy about it, and--it was twin girls! It was quite a blow, I guess. But they rallied swiftly, and called them Carol and Lark. Such nice musical names! Father and mother were both good singers, and mother a splendid pianist. And Fairy and I showed musical symptoms early in life, so they thought they couldn't be far wrong that time. It was a bitter mistake. It seemed to turn the twins against music right from the start. Carol can carry a tune if there's a strong voice beside her, but Lark can hardly tell the difference between *Star Spangled Banner* and *Rock of Ages*.

"The neighbors were kind of amused by then, and mother was very sensitive about it. So the next time she determined to get ahead of Fate. 'No more nonsense, now,' said mother. 'It's almost certain to be a boy, and we'll call him William after father,--and Billy for short.' We all liked the name Billy, mother especially. But she couldn't call father anything but William,--we being parsonage people, you know. But she kept looking forward to little Billy,--and then they changed it in a hurry to Constance. And after that, father and mother gave the whole thing up as a bad job. There aren't any more of us. Connie settled the baby business in our family."

Mrs. Adams wiped her eyes, and leaned weakly back in her chair, gasping for breath. "Well, I swan!" was all she could say at that moment.

While giving herself time to recover her mental poise she looked critically at this young daughter of the parsonage. Then her eyes wandered down to her clothes, and lingered, in silent questioning, on Prudence's dress. It was a very peculiar color. In fact, it was no color at all,--no named color. Prudence's eyes had followed Mrs. Adams' glance, and she spoke frankly.

"I suppose you're wondering if this dress is any color! Well, I think it really is, but it isn't any of the regular shades. It is my own invention, but I've never named it. We couldn't think of anything appropriate. Carol suggested 'Prudence Shade,' but I couldn't bring myself to accept that. Of course, Mrs. Adams, you understand how parsonage people do with clothes,--handing them down from generation unto generation. Well, I didn't mind it at first,--when I was the biggest. But all of a sudden Fairy grew up and out and around, and one day when I was so nearly out of clothes I hardly felt that I could attend church any more, she suggested that I cut an old one of hers down for me! At first I laughed, and then I was insulted. Fairy is three years younger than I, and before then she had got my handed-downs. But now the tables were turned. From that time on, whenever anything happened to Fairy's clothes so a gore had to be cut out, or the bottom taken off,--they were cut down for me. I still feel bitter about it. Fairy is dark, and dark blues are becoming to her. She handed down this dress,--it was dark blue then. But I was not wanting a dark blue, and I thought it would be less recognizable if I gave it a contrasting color. I chose lavender. I dyed it four times, and this was the result."

"Do the twins dress alike?" inquired Mrs. Adams, when she could control her voice.

"Yes,--unfortunately for Connie. They do it on purpose to escape the handed-downs! They won't even have hair ribbons different. And the result is that poor Connie never gets one new thing except shoes. She says she can not help thanking the Lord in her prayers, that all of us outwear our shoes before we can outgrow them.--Connie is only nine. Fairy is sixteen, and the twins are thirteen. They are a very clever lot of girls. Fairy, as I told you, is just naturally smart, and aims to be a college professor. Lark is an intelligent studious girl, and is going to be an author. Carol is pretty, and lovable, and kind-hearted, and witty,--but not deep. She is going to be a Red Cross nurse and go to war. The twins have it all planned out. Carol is going to war as a Red Cross nurse, and Lark is going, too, so she can write a book about it, and they are both going to marry soldiers,--preferably dashing young generals! Now they can hardly wait for war to break out. Connie is a sober, odd, sensitive little thing, and hasn't decided whether she wants to be a foreign missionary, or get married and have ten children.--But they are all clever, and I'm proud of every one of them."

"And what are you going to be?" inquired Mrs. Adams, looking with real affection at the bright sweet face.

But Prudence laughed. "Oh, dear me, Mrs. Adams, seems to me if I just get the others raised up properly, I'll have my hands full. I used to have aims, dozens of them. Now I have just one, and I'm working at it every day."

"You ought to go to school," declared Mrs. Adams. "You're just a girl yourself."

"I don't want to go to school," laughed Prudence. "Not any more. I like it, just taking care of father and the girls,--with Fairy to keep me balanced! I read, but I do not like to study.--No, you'll have to get along with me just the way I am, Mrs. Adams. It's all I can do to keep things going now, without spending half the time dreaming of big things to do in the future."

"Don't you have dreams?" gasped Mrs. Adams. "Don't you have dreams of the future? Girls in books nowadays dream----"

"Yes, I dream," interrupted Prudence, "I dream lots,--but it's mostly of what Fairy and the others will do when I get them properly raised. You'll like the girls, Mrs. Adams, I know you will. They really are a gifted little bunch,--except me.

But I don't mind. It's a great honor for me to have the privilege of bringing up four clever girls to do great things,--don't you think? And I'm only nineteen myself! I don't see what more a body could want."

"It seems to me," said Mrs. Adams, "that I know more about your sisters than I do about you. I feel more acquainted with them right now, than with you."

"That's so, too," said Prudence, nodding. "But they are the ones that really count, you know. I'm just common little Prudence of the Parsonage,--but the others!" And Prudence flung out her hands dramatically.

CHAPTER II
THE REST OF THE FAMILY

It was Saturday morning when the four young parsonage girls arrived in Mount Mark. The elderly Misses Avery, next door, looked out of their windows, pending their appearance on Main Street, with interest and concern. It was a serious matter, this having a whole parsonage-full of young girls so close to the old Avery mansion. To be sure, the Averys had a deep and profound respect for ministerial households, but they were Episcopalians themselves, and in all their long lives they had never so much as heard of a widower-rector with five daughters, and no housekeeper. There was something blood-curdling in the bare idea.

The Misses Avery considered Prudence herself rather a sweet, silly little thing.

"You have some real nice people in the Methodist church," Miss Dora had told her. "I dare say you will find a few of them very likeable."

"Oh, I will like them all," said Prudence quickly and seriously.

"Like them all!" echoed Miss Dora. "Oh, impossible!"

"Not for us," said Prudence. "We are used to it, you know. We always like people."

"That is ridiculous," said Miss Dora. "It is absolutely impossible. One can't! Of course, as Christians, we must tolerate, and try to help every one. But Christian tolerance and love are----"

"Oh, excuse me, but--really I can't believe there is such a thing as Christian tolerance," said Prudence firmly. "There is Christian love, and--that is all we need." Then leaning forward: "What do you do, Miss Avery, when you meet people you dislike at very first sight?"

"Keep away from them," was the grim reply.

"Exactly! And keep on disliking them," said Prudence triumphantly. "It's very different with us. When we dislike people at first sight, we visit them, and talk to them, and invite them to the parsonage, and entertain them with our best linen and silverware, and keep on getting friendlier and friendlier, and--first thing you know, we like them fine! It's a perfectly splendid rule, and it has never failed us once. Try it, Miss Avery, do! You will be enthusiastic about it, I know."

So the Misses Avery concluded that Prudence was very young, and couldn't seem to quite outgrow it! She was not entirely responsible. And they wondered, with something akin to an agony of fear, if the younger girls "had it, too!" Therefore the Misses Avery kept watch at their respective windows, and when Miss Alice cried excitedly, "Quick! Quick! They are coming!" they trooped to Miss Alice's window with a speed that would have done credit to the parsonage girls themselves. First came the minister, whom they knew very well by this time, and considered quite respectable. He was lively, as was to be expected of a Methodist minister, and told jokes, and laughed at them! Now, a comical rector,--oh, a very different matter,--it wasn't done, that's all! At any rate, here came the Methodist minister, laughing, and on one side of him tripped a small earnest-looking maiden, clasping his hand, and gazing alternately up into his face, and down at the stylish cement sidewalk beneath her feet. On the other side, was Fairy. The Misses Avery knew the girls by name already,--having talked much with Prudence.

"Such a Fairy!" gasped Miss Millicent, and the others echoed the gasp, but wordlessly.

For Fairy for very nearly as tall as her father, built upon generous lines, rather commanding in appearance, a little splendid-looking. Even from their windows they could discern something distinctly Juno-like in this sixteen-year-old girl, with the easy elastic stride that matched her father's, and the graceful head, well carried. A young goddess,--named Fairy!

Behind them, laughing and chattering, like three children, as they were,--came the twins with Prudence, each with an arm around her waist. And Prudence was very little taller than they. When they reached the fence that bordered the parsonage, the scene for a moment resembled a miniature riot. The smaller girls jumped and exclaimed, and clasped their hands. Fairy leaned over the fence, and stared intently at this, their parsonage home. Then the serious little girl scrambled under the fence, followed closely by the lithe-limbed twins. A pause, a very short one,-- and then Prudence, too, was wriggling beneath the fence.

"Hold the wire up for me, papa," cried Fairy, "I'm too fat." And a second later she was running gracefully across the lawn toward the parsonage. The Method- ist minister laughed boyishly, and placing his hands on the fence-post, he vaulted lightly over, and reached the house with his daughters. Then the Misses Avery, school-teachers, and elderly, looked at one another.

"Did you ever?" whispered the oldest Miss Avery, and the others slowly shook their heads.

Now, think! Did you ever see a rector jumping a three-wire fence, and run- ning full speed across his front yard, in pursuit of a flying family? It may possibly have occurred,--we have never seen it. Neither had the Misses Avery. Nor did they ever expect to. And if they had seen it, it is quite likely they would have joined the backsliders at that instant.

But without wasting much time on this gruesome thought, they hurried to a window commanding the best view of the parsonage, and raised it. Then they clustered behind the curtains, and watched, and listened. There was plenty to hear! From the parsonage windows came the sound of scampering feet and banging doors. Once there was the unmistakable clatter of a chair overturned. With it all, there was a constant chorus of "Oh, look!" "Oh! Oh!" "Oh, how sweet!" "Oh, papa!" "Oh, Prudence!" "Look, Larkie, look at this!"

Then the thud of many feet speeding down the stairs, and the slam of a door, and the slam of a gate. The whole parsonage-full had poured out into the back yard, and the barn-lot. Into the chicken coop they raced, the minister ever close upon their heels. Over the board fence they clambered to the big rambling barn, and the wide door swung closed after them. But in a few seconds they were out once more, by the back barn door, and over the fence, and on to the "field." There they closed ranks, with their arms recklessly around whoever was nearest, and made a thorough tour of the bit of pasture-land. For some moments they leaned upon the dividing fence and gazed admiringly into the rich orchard and vineyard of the Avery estate. But soon they were skipping back to the parsonage again, and the kitchen door banged behind them.

Then the eldest Miss Avery closed the window overlooking the parsonage and confronted her sisters.

"We must just make the best of it," she said quietly.

But next door, the gray old ugly parsonage was full to overflowing with satisfaction and happiness and love.

The Starrs had never had an appointment like this before. They had just come from the village of Exminster, of five hundred inhabitants. There the Reverend Mr. Starr had filled the pulpits of three small Methodist churches, scattered at random throughout the country,--consideration, five hundred dollars. But here,--why, Mount Mark had a population of fully three thousand, and a business academy, and the Presbyterian College,--small, to be sure, but the name had a grand and inspiring sound. And Mr. Starr had to fill only one pulpit! It was heavenly, that's what it was. To be sure, many of his people lived out in the country, necessitating the upkeep of a horse for the sake of his pastoral work, but that was only an advantage. Also to be sure, the Methodists in Mount Mark were in a minority, and an inferiority,-- Mount Mark being a Presbyterian stronghold due to the homing there of the trim and orderly little college. But what of that? The salary was six hundred and fifty dollars and the parsonage was adorable! The parsonage family could see nothing at all wrong with the world that day, and the future was rainbow-tinted.

Every one has experienced the ecstatic creepy sensation of sleeping in a brand-new home. The parsonage girls reveled in the memory of that first night for many days. "It may be haunted for all we know," cried Carol deliciously. "Just think, Connie, there may be seven ghosts camped on the head of your bed, waiting----"

"Carol!"

When the family gathered for worship on that first Sabbath morning, Mr. Starr said, as he turned the leaves of his well-worn Bible, "I think it would be well for you girls to help with the morning worship now. You need practise in praying aloud, and--so we will begin to-day. Connie and I will make the prayers this morning, Prudence and Carol to-morrow, and Fairy and Lark the next day. We will keep that system up for a while, anyhow. When I finish reading the chapter, Connie, you will make the first prayer. Just pray for whatever you wish as you do at night for yourself. I will follow you."

Connie's eyes were wide with responsibility during the reading of the chapter, but when she began to speak her voice did not falter. Connie had nine years of good

Methodist experience back of her!

"Our Father, who art in Heaven, we bow ourselves before Thy footstool in humility and reverence. Thou art our God, our Creator, our Saviour. Bless us this day, and cause Thy face to shine upon us. Blot out our transgressions, pardon our trespasses. Wash us, that we may be whiter than snow. Hide not Thy face from the eyes of Thy children, turn not upon us in wrath. Pity us, Lord, as we kneel here prostrate before Thy majesty and glory. Let the words of our mouths and the meditations of our hearts, be acceptable in Thy sight, O Lord, our strength and our Redeemer. And finally save us, an unbroken family around Thy throne in Heaven, for Jesus' sake. Amen."

This was followed by an electric silence. Prudence was biting her lips painfully, and counting by tens as fast as she could. Fairy was mentally going over the prayer, sentence by sentence, and attributing each petition to the individual member in the old church at Exminster to whom it belonged. The twins were a little amazed, and quite proud. Connie was an honor to the parsonage,--but they were concerned lest they themselves should do not quite so well when their days came.

But in less than a moment the minister-father began his prayer. His voice was a little subdued, and he prayed with less fervor and abandon than usual, but otherwise things went off quite nicely. When he said, "Amen," Prudence was on her feet and half-way up-stairs before the others were fairly risen. Fairy stood gazing intently out of the window for a moment, and then went out to the barn to see if the horse was through eating. Mr. Starr walked gravely and soberly out the front door, and around the house. He ran into Fairy coming out the kitchen door, and they glanced quickly at each other.

"Hurry, papa," she whispered, "you can't hold in much longer! Neither can I!"

And together, choking with laughter, they hurried into the barn and gave full vent to their feelings.

So it was that the twins and Connie were alone for a while.

"You did a pretty good job, Connie," said Carol approvingly.

"Yes. I think I did myself," was the complacent answer. "But I intended to put in, 'Keep us as the apple of Thy eye, hold us in the hollow of Thy hand,' and I forgot it until I had said 'Amen.' I had a notion to put in a post-script, but I believe that isn't done."

"Never mind," said Carol, "I'll use that in mine, to-morrow."

It can not be said that this form of family worship was a great success. The twins were invariably stereotyped, cut and dried. They thanked the Lord for the beautiful morning, for kind friends, for health, and family, and parsonage. Connie always prayed in sentences extracted from the prayers of others she had often heard, and every time with nearly disastrous effect.

But the days passed around, and Prudence and Carol's turn came again. Carol was a thoughtless, impetuous, impulsive girl, and her prayers were as nearly "verbal repetitions" as any prayers could be. So on this morning, after the reading of the chapter, Carol knelt by her chair, and began in her customary solemn voice:

"Oh, our Father, we thank Thee for this beautiful morning." Then intense silence. For Carol remembered with horror and shame that it was a dreary, dismal morning, cloudy, ugly and all unlovely. In her despair, the rest of her petition scattered to the four winds of heaven. She couldn't think of another word, so she gulped, and stammered out a faint "Amen."

But Prudence could not begin. Prudence was red in the face, and nearly suffocated. She felt all swollen inside,--she couldn't speak. The silence continued. "Oh, why doesn't father do it?" she wondered. As a matter of fact, father couldn't. But Prudence did not know that. One who laughs often gets in the habit of laughter,--and sometimes laughs out of season, as well as in. Finally, Prudence plunged in desperately, "Dear Father"--as she usually began her sweet, intimate little talks with God,--and then she paused. Before her eyes flashed a picture of the "beautiful morning," for which Carol had just been thankful! She tried again. "Dear Father,"--and then she whirled around on the floor, and laughed. Mr. Starr got up from his knees, sat down on his chair, and literally shook. Fairy rolled on the lounge, screaming with merriment. Even sober little Connie giggled and squealed. But Carol could not get up. She was disgraced. She had done a horrible, disgusting, idiotic thing. She had insulted God! She could never face the family again. Her shoulders rose and fell convulsively.

Lark did not laugh either. With a rush she was on her knees beside Carol, her arms around the heaving shoulders. "Don't you care, Carrie," she whispered. "Don't you care. It was just a mistake,--don't cry, Carrie."

But Carol would not be comforted. She tried to sneak unobserved from the room, but her father stopped her.

"Don't feel so badly about it, Carol," he said kindly, really sorry for the stricken child,--though his eyes still twinkled, "it was just a mistake. But remember after this, my child, to speak to God when you pray. Remember that you are talking to Him. Then you will not make such a blunder.--So many of us," he said reflectively, "ministers as well as others, pray into the ears of the people, and forget we are talking to God."

After that, the morning worship went better. The prayers of the children changed,--became more personal, less flowery. They remembered from that time on, that when they knelt they were at the feet of God, and speaking direct to Him.

It was the hated duty of the twins to wash and dry the dishes,--taking turns about with the washing. This time was always given up to story-telling, for Lark had a strange and wonderful imagination, and Carol listened to her tales with wonder and delight. Even Connie found dish-doing hours irresistible, and could invariably be found, face in her hands, both elbows on the table, gazing with passionate earnestness at the young story-teller. Now, some of Lark's stories were such weird and fearful things that they had seriously interfered with Connie's slumbers, and Prudence had sternly prohibited them. But this evening, just as she opened the kitchen door, she heard Lark say in thrilling tones:

"She crept down the stairs in the deep darkness, her hand sliding lightly over the rail. Suddenly she stopped. Her hand was arrested in its movement. Ice-cold fingers gripped hers tightly. Then with one piercing shriek, she plunged forward, and fell to the bottom of the stairs with a terrific crash, while a mocking laugh----"

The kitchen door slammed sharply behind Prudence as she stepped into the kitchen, and Connie's piercing shriek would surely have rivaled that of Lark's unfortunate heroine. Even Carol started nervously, and let the plate she had been solemnly wiping for nine minutes, fall to the floor. Lark gasped, and then began sheepishly washing dishes as though her life depended on it. The water was cold, and little masses of grease clung to the edges of the pan and floated about on the surface of the water.

"Get fresh hot water, Lark, and finish the dishes. Connie, go right up-stairs to bed. You twins can come in to me as soon as you finish."

But Connie was afraid to go to bed alone, and Prudence was obliged to accompany her. So it was in their own room that the twins finally faced an indignant Prudence.

"Carol, you may go right straight to bed. And Lark--I do not know what in the world to do with you. Why don't you mind me, and do as I tell you? How many times have I told you not to tell weird stories like that? Can't you tell nice, interesting, mild stories?"

"Prudence, as sure as you live, I can't! I start them just as mild and proper as can be, but before I get half-way through, a murder, or death, or mystery crops in, and I can't help it."

"But you must help it, Lark. Or I shall forbid your telling stories of any kind. They are so silly, those wild things, and they make you all nervous, and excitable, and-- Now, think, Larkie, and tell me how I shall punish you."

Lark applied all the resources of her wonderful brain to this task, and presently suggested reluctantly: "Well, you might keep me home from the ice-cream social to-morrow night." But her face was wistful.

"No," said Prudence decidedly, to Lark's intense relief. "I can't do that. You've been looking forward to it so long, and your class is to help with the serving. No, not that, Larkie. That would be too mean. Think of something else."

"Well,--you might make me wash and dry the dishes all alone--for a week, Prudence, and that will be a bad punishment, too, for I just despise washing dishes by myself. Telling stories makes it so much--livelier."

"All right, then," said Prudence, relieved in turn, "that is what I will do. And Carol and Connie must not even stay in the kitchen with you."

"I believe I'll go to bed now, too," said Lark, with a thoughtful glance at her two sisters, already curled up snugly and waiting for the conclusion of the administering of justice. "If you don't mind, Prudence."

Prudence smiled a bit ruefully. "Oh, I suppose you might as well, if you like. But remember this, Lark: No more deaths, and murders, and mysteries, and highway robberies."

"All right, Prudence," said Lark with determination. And as Prudence walked slowly down-stairs she heard Lark starting in on her next story:

"Once there was a handsome young man, named Archibald Tremaine,--a very respectable young fellow. He wouldn't so much as dream of robbing, or murdering, or dying."

Then Prudence smiled to herself in the dark and hurried down.

The family had been in the new parsonage only three weeks, when a visiting minister called on them. It was about ten minutes before the luncheon hour at the time of his arrival. Mr. Starr was in the country, visiting, so the girls received him alone. It was an unfortunate day for the Starrs. Fairy had been at college all morning, and Prudence had been rummaging in the attic, getting it ready for a rainy-day and winter playroom for the younger girls. She was dusty, perspirey and tired.

The luncheon hour arrived, and the girls came in from school, eager to be up and away again. Still the grave young minister sat discoursing upon serious topics with the fidgety Prudence,--and in spite of dust and perspiration, she was good to look upon. The Reverend Mr. Morgan realized that, and could not tear himself away. The twins came in, shook hands with him soberly, glancing significantly at the clock as they did so. Connie ran in excitedly, wanting to know what was the matter with everybody, and weren't they to have any luncheon? Still Mr. Morgan remained in his chair, gazing at Prudence with frank appreciation. Finally Prudence sighed.

"Do you like sweet corn, Mr. Morgan?"

This was entirely out of the line of their conversation, and for a moment he faltered. "Sweet corn?" he repeated.

"Yes, roasting-ears, you know,--cooked on the cob."

Then he smiled. "Oh, yes indeed. Very much," he said.

"Well," she began her explanation rather drearily, "I was busy this morning and did not prepare much luncheon. We are very fond of sweet corn, and I cooked an enormous panful. But that's all we have for luncheon,--sweet corn and butter. We haven't even bread, because I am going to bake this afternoon, and we never eat it with sweet corn, anyhow. Now, if you care to eat sweet corn and butter, and canned peaches, we'd just love to have you stay for luncheon with us."

The Reverend Mr. Morgan was charmed, and said so. So Prudence rushed to the kitchen, opened the peaches in a hurry, and fished out a clean napkin for their guest. Then they gathered about the table, five girls and the visiting minister. It was really a curious sight, that table. In the center stood a tall vase of goldenrod.

On either side of the vase was a great platter piled high with sweet corn, on the cob! Around the table were six plates, with the necessary silverware, and a glass of water for each. There was also a small dish of peaches at each place, and an individual plate of butter. That was all,--except the napkins. But Prudence made no apologies. She was a daughter of the parsonage! She showed the Reverend Mr. Morgan to his place as graciously and sweetly as though she were ushering him in to a twenty-seven course banquet.

"Will you return thanks, Mr. Morgan?" she said. And the girls bowed their heads. The Reverend Mr. Morgan cleared his throat, and began, "Our Father, we thank Thee for this table."

There was more of the blessing, but the parsonage girls heard not one additional phrase,--except Connie, who followed him conscientiously through every word. By the time he had finished, Prudence and Fairy, and even Lark, had composed their faces. But Carol burst into merry laughter, close upon his reverent "Amen,"--and after one awful glare at her sister, Prudence joined in. This gaiety communicated itself to the others and soon it was a rollicking group around the parsonage table. Mr. Morgan himself smiled uncertainly. He was puzzled. More, he was embarrassed. But as soon as Carol could get her breath, she gasped out an explanation.

"You were just--right, Mr. Morgan,--to give thanks--for the table! There's nothing--on it--to be thankful for!"

And the whole family went off once more into peals of laughter.

Mr. Morgan had very little appetite that day. He did not seem to be so fond of sweet corn as he had assured Prudence. He talked very little, too. And as soon as possible he took his hat and walked hurriedly away. He did not call at the parsonage again.

"Oh, Carol," said Prudence reproachfully, wiping her eyes, "how could you start us all off like that?"

"For the table, for the table!" shrieked Carol, and Prudence joined in perforce.

"It was awful," she gasped, "but it was funny! I believe even father would have laughed."

A few weeks after this, Carol distinguished herself again, and to her lasting mortification. The parsonage pasture had been rented out during the summer months before the change of ministers, the outgoing incumbent having kept neither horse nor cow. As may be imagined, the little pasture had been taxed to the utmost, and when the new minister arrived, he found that his field afforded poor grazing for his pretty little Jersey. But a man living only six blocks from the parsonage had generously offered Mr. Starr free pasturage in his broad meadow, and the offer was gratefully accepted. This meant that every evening the twins must walk the six blocks after the cow, and every morning must take her back for the day's grazing.

One evening, as they were starting out from the meadow homeward with the docile animal, Carol stopped and gazed at Blinkie reflectively.

"Lark," she said, "I just believe to my soul that I could ride this cow. She's so gentle, and I'm such a good hand at sticking on."

"Carol!" ejaculated Lark. "Think how it would look for a parsonage girl to go down the street riding a cow."

"But there's no one to see," protested Carol. And this was true. For the parsonage was near the edge of town, and the girls passed only five houses on their way home from the meadow,--and all of them were well back from the road. And Carol was, as she had claimed, a good hand at "sticking on." She had ridden a great deal while they were at Exminster, a neighbor being well supplied with rideable horses, and she was passionately fond of the sport. To be sure, she had never ridden a cow, but she was sure it would be easy.

Lark argued and pleaded, but Carol was firm. "I must try it," she insisted, "and if it doesn't go well I can slide off. You can lead her, Lark."

The obliging Lark boosted her sister up, and Carol nimbly scrambled into place, riding astride.

"I've got to ride this way," she said; "cows have such funny backs I couldn't keep on any other way. If I see any one coming, I'll slide for it."

For a while all went well. Lark led Blinkie carefully, gazing about anxiously to see that no one approached. Carol gained confidence as they proceeded, and chatted with her sister nonchalantly, waving her hands about to show her perfect balance and lack of fear. So they advanced to within two blocks of the parsonage.

"It's very nice," said Carol, "very nice indeed,--but her backbone is rather--well, rather penetrating. I think I need a saddle."

By this time, Blinkie concluded that she was being imposed upon. She shook her head violently, and twitched the rope from Lark's hand,--for Lark now shared her sister's confidence, and held it loosely. With a little cry she tried to catch the end of it, but Blinkie was too quick for her. She gave a scornful toss of her dainty head, and struck out madly for home. With great presence of mind, Carol fell flat upon the cow's neck, and hung on for dear life, while Lark, in terror, started out in pursuit.

"Help! Help!" she cried loudly. "Papa! Papa! Papa!"

In this way, they turned in at the parsonage gate, which happily stood open,--otherwise Blinkie would undoubtedly have gone through, or over. As luck would have it, Mr. Starr was standing at the door with two men who had been calling on him, and hearing Lark's frantic cries, they rushed to meet the wild procession, and had the unique experience of seeing a parsonage girl riding flat on her stomach on the neck of a galloping Jersey, with another parsonage girl in mad pursuit.

Blinkie stopped beside the barn, and turned her head about inquiringly. Carol slid to the ground, and buried her face in her hands at sight of the two men with her father. Then with never a word, she lit out for the house at top speed. Seeing that she was not hurt, and that no harm had been done, the three men sat down on the ground and burst into hearty laughter.

Lark came upon them as they sat thus, and Lark was angry. She stamped her foot with a violence that must have hurt her.

"I don't see anything to laugh at," she cried passionately, "it was awful, it was just awful! Carrie might have been killed! It--it----"

"Tell us all about it, Lark," gasped her father. And Lark did so, smiling a little herself, now that her fears were relieved. "Poor Carol," she said, "she'll never live down the humiliation. I must go and console her."

And a little later, the twins were weeping on each other's shoulders.

"I wouldn't have cared," sobbed Carol, "if it had been anybody else in the world! But--the presiding elder,--and--the president of the Presbyterian College! And I know the Presbyterians look down on us Methodists anyhow, though they wouldn't admit it! And riding a cow! Oh, Larkie, if you love me, go down-stairs and get me the carbolic acid, so I can die and be out of disgrace."

This, however, Lark stoutly refused to do, and in a little while Carol felt much better. But she talked it over with Prudence very seriously.

"I hope you understand, Prudence, that I shall never have anything more to do with Blinkie! She can die of starvation for all I care. I'll never take her to and from the pasture again. I couldn't do it! Such rank ingratitude as that cow displayed was never equaled, I am certain."

"I suppose you'll quit using milk and cream, too," suggested Prudence.

"Oh, well," said Carol more tolerantly, "I don't want to be too hard on Blinkie, for after all it was partly my own fault. So I won't go that far. But I must draw the line somewhere! Hereafter, Blinkie and I meet as strangers!"

CHAPTER III
THE LADIES' AID

I t's perfectly disgusting, I admit, father," said Prudence sweetly, "but you know yourself that it very seldom happens. And I am sure the kitchen is perfectly clean, and the soup is very nice indeed,--if it is canned soup! Twins, this is four slices of bread apiece for you! You see, father, I really feel that this is a crisis in the life of the parsonage----"

"How long does a parsonage usually live?" demanded Carol.

"It wouldn't live long if the ministers had many twins," said Fairy quickly.

"Ouch!" grinned Connie, plagiarizing, for that expressive word belonged exclusively to the twins, and it was double impertinence to apply it to one of its very possessors.

"And you understand, don't you, father, that if everything does not go just exactly right, I shall feel I am disgraced for life? I know the Ladies disapprove of me, and look on me with suspicion. I know they think it wicked and ridiculous to leave the raising of four bright spirits in the unworthy hands of a girl like me. I know they will all sniff and smile and--Of course, twins, they have a perfect right to feel, and act, so. I am not complaining. But I want to show them for once in their lives that the parsonage runs smoothly and sweetly. If you would just stay at home with us, father, it would be a big help. You are such a tower of strength."

"But unfortunately I can not. People do not get married every day in the week, and when they are all ready for it they do not allow even Ladies' Aids to stand in their way. It is a long drive, ten miles at least, and I must start at once. And it will likely be very late when I get back. But if you are all good, and help Prudence, and uphold the reputation of the parsonage, I will divide the wedding fee with you,-- share and share alike." This was met with such enthusiasm that he added hastily,

"But wait! It may be only a dollar!"

Then kissing the various members of the parsonage family, he went out the back door, barnward.

"Now," said Prudence briskly, "I want to make a bargain with you, girls. If you'll stay clear away from the Ladies, and be very good and orderly, I'll give you all the lemonade and cake you can drink afterward."

"Oh, Prudence, I'm sure I can't drink much cake," cried Carol tragically, "I just can't imagine myself doing it!"

"I mean, eat the cake, of course," said Prudence, blushing.

"And let us make taffy after supper?" wheedled Carol.

Prudence hesitated, and the three young faces hardened. Then Prudence relented and hastily agreed. "You won't need to appear at all, you know. You can just stay outdoors and play as though you were model children."

"Yes," said Carol tartly, "the kind the members used to have,--which are all grown up, now! And all moved out of Mount Mark, too!"

"Carol! That sounds malicious, and malice isn't tolerated here for a minute. Now,--oh, Fairy, did you remember to dust the back of the dresser in our bedroom?"

"Mercy! What in the world do you want the back of the dresser dusted for? Do you expect the Ladies to look right through it?"

"No, but some one might drop something behind it, and it would have to be pulled out and they would all see it. This house has got to be absolutely spotless for once,--I am sure it will be the first time."

"And the last, I hope," added Carol sepulchrally.

"We have an hour and a half yet," continued Prudence. "That will give us plenty of time for the last touches. Twins and Connie, you'd better go right out in the field and play. I'll call you a little before two, and then you must go quietly upstairs, and dress--just wear your plain little ginghams, the clean ones of course! Then if they do catch a glimpse of you, you will be presentable.--Yes, you can take some bread and sugar, but hurry."

"You may take," said Fairy.

"Yes, of course, may take is what I mean.--Now hurry."

Then Prudence and Fairy set to work again in good earnest. The house was already well cleaned. The sandwiches were made. But there were the last "rites," and every detail must be religiously attended to.

It must be remembered that the three main down-stairs rooms of the parsonage were connected by double doors,--double doors, you understand, not portieres! The front room, seldom used by the parsonage family, opened on the right of the narrow hallway. Beyond it was the living-room, which it must be confessed the parsonage girls only called "living-room" when they were on their Sunday behavior,--ordinarily it was the sitting-room, and a cheery, homey, attractive place it was, with a great bay window looking out upon the stately mansion of the Averys. To the left of the living-room was the dining-room. The double doors between them were always open. The other pair was closed, except on occasions of importance.

Now, this really was a crisis in the life of the parsonage family,--if not of the parsonage itself. The girls had met, separately, every member of the Ladies' Aid. But this was their first combined movement upon the parsonage, and Prudence and Fairy realized that much depended on the success of the day. As girls, the whole Methodist church pronounced the young Starrs charming. But as parsonage people,--well, they were obliged to reserve judgment. And as for Prudence having entire charge of the household, it must be acknowledged that every individual Lady looked forward to this meeting with eagerness,--they wanted to "size up" the situation. They were coming to see for themselves! Yes, it was undoubtedly a crisis.

"There'll be a crowd, of course," said Fairy. "We'll just leave the doors between the front rooms open."

"Yes, but we'll close the dining-room doors. Then we'll have the refreshments all out on the table, and when we are ready we'll just fling back the doors carelessly and--there you are!"

So the table was prettily decorated with flowers, and great plates of sandwiches and cake were placed upon it. In the center was an enormous punch-bowl, borrowed from the Averys, full of lemonade. Glasses were properly arranged on the trays, and piles of nicely home-laundered napkins were scattered here and there. The girls felt that the dining-room was a credit to them, and to the Methodist Church entire.

From every nook and corner of the house they hunted out chairs and stools, anticipating a real run upon the parsonage. Nor were they disappointed. The twins and Connie were not even arrayed in their plain little ginghams, clean, before the first arrivals were ushered up into the front bedroom, ordinarily occupied by Prudence and Fairy.

"There's Mrs. Adams, and Mrs. Prentiss, and Mrs.----," began Connie, listening intently to the voices in the next room.

"Yes," whispered Carol, "peek through the keyhole, Lark, and see if Mrs. Prentiss is looking under the bed for dust. They say she----"

"You'd better not let Prudence catch you repeating----"

"There's Mrs. Stone, and Mrs. Davis, and----"

"They say Mrs. Davis only belongs to the Ladies' Aid for the sake of the refreshments, and----"

"Carol! Prudence will punish you."

"Well, I don't believe it," protested Carol. "I'm just telling you what I've heard other people say."

"We aren't allowed to repeat gossip," urged Lark.

"No, and I think it's a shame, too, for it's awfully funny. Minnie Drake told me that Miss Varne joined the Methodist church as soon as she heard the new minister was a widower so she----"

"Carol!"

Carol whirled around sharply, and flushed, and swallowed hard. For Prudence was just behind her.

"I--I--I--" but she could get no further.

Upon occasion, Prudence was quite terrible. "So I heard," she said dryly, but her eyes were hard. "Now run down-stairs and out to the field, or to the barn, and play. And, Carol, be sure and remind me of that speech to-night. I might forget it."

The girls ran quickly out, Carol well in the lead.

"No wedding fee for me," she mumbled bitterly. "Do you suppose there can be seven devils in my tongue, Lark, like there are in the Bible?"

"I don't remember there being seven devils in the Bible," said Lark.

"Oh, I mean the--the possessed people it tells about in the Bible,--crazy, I suppose it means. Somehow I just can't help repeating----"

"You don't want to," said Lark, not without sympathy. "You think it's such fun, you know."

"Well, anyhow, I'm sure I won't get any wedding fee to-night. It seems to me Prudence is very--harsh sometimes."

"You can appeal to father, if you like."

"Not on your life," said Carol promptly and emphatically; "he's worse than Prudence. Like as not he'd give me a good thrashing into the bargain. No,--I'm strong for Prudence when it comes to punishment,--in preference to father, I mean. I can't seem to be fond of any kind of punishment from anybody."

For a while Carol was much depressed, but by nature she was a buoyant soul and her spirits were presently soaring again.

In the meantime, the Ladies of the Aid Society continued to arrive. Prudence and Fairy, freshly gowned and smiling-faced, received them with cordiality and many merry words. It was not difficult for them, they had been reared in the hospitable atmosphere of Methodist parsonages, where, if you have but two dishes of oatmeal, the outsider is welcome to one. That is Carol's description of parsonage life.

But Prudence was concerned to observe that a big easy chair placed well back in a secluded corner, seemed to be giving dissatisfaction. It was Mrs. Adams who sat there first. She squirmed quite a little, and seemed to be gripping the arms of the chair with unnecessary fervor. Presently she stammered an excuse, and rising, went into the other room. After that, Mrs. Miller tried the corner chair, and soon moved away. Then Mrs. Jack, Mrs. Norey, and Mrs. Beed, in turn, sat there,--and did not stay. Prudence was quite agonized. Had the awful twins filled it with needles for the reception of the poor Ladies? At first opportunity, she hurried into the secluded corner, intent upon trying the chair for herself. She sat down anxiously. Then she gasped, and clutched frantically at the arms of the chair. For she discovered at once to her dismay that the chair was bottomless, and that only by hanging on for her life could she keep from dropping through. She thought hard for a moment,--but thinking did not interfere with her grasp on the chair-arms,--and then she realized that the wisest thing would be to discuss it publicly. Anything would be better than leaving it unexplained, for the Ladies to comment upon privately.

So up rose Prudence, conscientiously pulling after her the thin cushion which had concealed the chair's shortcoming. "Look, Fairy!" she cried. "Did you take the bottom out of this chair?--It must have been horribly uncomfortable for those who have sat there!--However did it happen?"

Fairy was frankly amazed, and a little inclined to be amused.

"Ask the twins," she said tersely, "I know nothing about it."

At that moment, the luckless Carol went running through the hall. Prudence knew it was she, without seeing, because she had a peculiar skipping run that was quite characteristic and unmistakable.

"Carol!" she called.

And Carol paused.

"Carol!" more imperatively.

Then Carol slowly opened the door,--she was a parsonage girl and rose to the occasion. She smiled winsomely,--Carol was nearly always winsome.

"How do you do?" she said brightly. "Isn't it a lovely day? Did you call me, Prudence?"

"Yes. Do you know where the bottom of that chair has gone?"

"Why, no, Prudence--gracious! That chair!--Why, I didn't know you were going to bring that chair in here--Why,--oh, I am so sorry! Why in the world didn't you tell us beforehand?"

Some of the Ladies smiled. Others lifted their brows and shoulders in a mildly suggestive way, that Prudence, after nineteen years in the parsonage, had learned to know and dread.

"And where is the chair-bottom now?" she inquired. "And why did you take it?"

"Why we wanted to make----"

"You and Lark?"

"Well, yes,--but it was really all my fault, you know. We wanted to make a seat up high in the peach tree, and we couldn't find a board the right shape. So she discovered--I mean, I did--that by pulling out two tiny nails we could get the bottom off the chair, and it was just fine. It's a perfectly adorable seat," brightening, but sobering again as she realized the gravity of the occasion. "And we put the cushion in the chair so that it wouldn't be noticed. We never use that chair, you know, and we didn't think of your needing it to-day. We put it away back in the cold corner of the sitting--er, living-room where no one ever sits. I'm so sorry about it."

Carol was really quite crushed, but true to her parsonage training, she struggled valiantly and presently brought forth a crumpled and sickly smile.

But Prudence smiled at her kindly. "That wasn't very naughty, Carol," she said frankly. "It's true that we seldom use that chair. And we ought to have looked." She glanced reproachfully at Fairy. "It is strange that in dusting it, Fairy--but never mind. You may go now, Carol. It is all right."

Then she apologized gently to the Ladies, and the conversation went on, but Prudence was uncomfortably conscious of keen and quizzical eyes turned her way. Evidently they thought she was too lenient.

"Well, it wasn't very naughty," she thought wretchedly. "How can I pretend it was terribly bad, when I feel in my heart that it wasn't!"

Before long, the meeting was called to order, and the secretary instructed to read the minutes.

"Oh," fluttered Miss Carr excitedly, "I forgot to bring the book. I haven't been secretary very long, you know."

"Only six months," interrupted Mrs. Adams tartly.

"How do you expect to keep to-day's minutes?" demanded the president.

"Oh, I am sure Miss Prudence will give me a pencil and paper, and I'll copy them in the book as soon as ever I get home."

"Yes, indeed," said Prudence. "There is a tablet on that table beside you, and pencils, too. I thought we might need them."

Then the president made a few remarks, but while she talked, Miss Carr was excitedly opening the tablet. Miss Carr was always excited, and always fluttering, and always giggling girlishly. Carol called her a sweet old simpering soul, and so she was. But now, right in the midst of the president's serious remarks, she quite giggled out.

The president stared at her in amazement. The Ladies looked up curiously. Miss Carr was bending low over the tablet, and laughing gaily to herself.

"Oh, this is very cute," she said. "Who wrote it? Oh, it is just real cunning."

Fairy sprang up, suddenly scarlet. "Oh, perhaps you have one of the twins' books, and they're always scribbling and----"

"No, it is yours, Fairy. I got it from among your school-books."

Fairy sank back, intensely mortified, and Miss Carr chirped brightly:

"Oh, Fairy, dear, did you write this little poem? How perfectly sweet! And what a queer, sentimental little creature you are. I never dreamed you were so romantic. Mayn't I read it aloud?"

Fairy was speechless, but the Ladies, including the president, were impatiently waiting. So Miss Carr began reading in a sentimental, dreamy voice that must have been very fetching fifty years before. At the first suggestion of poetry, Prudence sat up with conscious pride,--Fairy was so clever! But before Miss Carr had finished the second verse, she too was literally drowned in humiliation.

"My love rode out of the glooming night,   Into the glare of the morning light. My love rode out of the dim unknown,   Into my heart to claim his own.   My love rode out of the yesterday,   Into the now,--and he came to stay.   Oh, love that is rich, and pure, and true,   The love in my heart leaps out to you.   Oh, love, at last you have found your part,--   To come and dwell in my empty heart."

Miss Carr sat down, giggling delightedly, and the younger Ladies laughed, and the older Ladies smiled.

But Mrs. Prentiss turned to Fairy gravely. "How old are you, my dear?"

And with a too-apparent effort, Fairy answered, "Sixteen!"

"Indeed!" A simple word, but so suggestively uttered. "Shall we continue the meeting, Ladies?"

This aroused Prudence's ire on her sister's behalf, and she squared her shoulders defiantly. For a while, Fairy was utterly subdued. But thinking it over to herself, she decided that after all there was nothing absolutely shameful in a sixteen-year-old girl writing sentimental verses. Silly, to be sure! But all sixteen-year-olds are silly. We love them for it! And Fairy's good nature and really good judgment came to her rescue, and she smiled at Prudence with her old serenity.

The meeting progressed, and the business was presently disposed of. So far, things were not too seriously bad, and Prudence sighed in great relief. Then the Ladies took out their sewing, and began industriously working at many unmentionable articles, designed for the intimate clothing of a lot of young Methodists confined in an orphans' home in Chicago. And they talked together pleasantly and gaily. And Prudence and Fairy felt that the cloud was lifted.

But soon it settled again, dark and lowering. Prudence heard Lark running through the hall and her soul misgave her. Why was Lark going upstairs? What was her errand? And she remembered the wraps of the Ladies, up-stairs, alone and unprotected. Dare she trust Lark in such a crisis? Perhaps the very sight of Prudence and the Ladies' Aid would arouse her better nature, and prevent catastrophe. To be sure, her mission might be innocent, but Prudence dared not run the risk. Fortunately she was sitting near the door.

"Lark!" she called softly. Lark stopped abruptly, and something fell to the floor.

"Lark!"

There was a muttered exclamation from without, and Lark began fumbling rapidly around on the floor talking incoherently to herself.

"Lark!"

The Ladies smiled, and Miss Carr, laughing lightly, said, "She is an attentive creature, isn't she?"

Prudence would gladly have flown out into the hall to settle this matter, but she realized that she was on exhibition. Had she done so, the Ladies would have set her down forever after as thoroughly incompetent,--she could not go! But Lark must come to her.

"Lark!" This was Prudence's most awful voice, and Lark was bound to heed.

"Oh, Prue," she said plaintively, "I'll be there in a minute. Can't you wait just five minutes? Let me run up-stairs first, won't you? Then I'll come gladly! Won't that do?"

Her voice was hopeful. But Prudence replied with dangerous calm:

"Come at once, Lark."

"All right, then," and added threateningly, "but you'll wish I hadn't."

Then Lark opened the door,--a woeful figure! In one hand she carried an empty shoe box. And her face was streaked with good rich Iowa mud. Her clothes were plastered with it. One shoe was caked from the sole to the very top button, and a great gash in her stocking revealed a generous portion of round white leg.

Poor Prudence! At that moment, she would have exchanged the whole parsonage, bathroom, electric lights and all, for a tiny log cabin in the heart of a great forest where she and Lark might be alone together.

And Fairy laughed. Prudence looked at her with tears in her eyes, and then turned to the wretched girl.

"What have you been doing, Lark?"

The heart-break expressed in the face of Lark would have made the angels weep. Beneath the smudges of mud on her cheeks she was pallid, and try as she would, she could not keep her chin from trembling ominously. Her eyes were fastened on the floor for the most part, but occasionally she raised them hurriedly, appealingly, to her sister's face, and dropped them again. Not for worlds would she have faced the Ladies! Prudence was obliged to repeat her question before Lark could articulate a reply. She gulped painfully a few times,--making meanwhile a desperate effort to hide the gash in one stocking by placing the other across it, rubbing it up and down in great embarrassment, and balancing herself with apparent difficulty. Her voice, when she was able to speak, was barely recognizable.

"We--we--we are making--mud images, Prudence. It--it was awfully messy, I know, but--they say--it is such a good--and useful thing to do. We--we didn't expect--the--the Ladies to see us."

"Mud images!" gasped Prudence, and even Fairy stared incredulously. "Where in the world did you get hold of an idea like that?"

"It--it was in that--that Mother's Home Friend paper you take, Prudence." Prudence blushed guiltily. "It--it was modeling in clay, but--we haven't any clay, and--the mud is very nice, but--Oh, I know I look just--horrible. I--I--Connie pushed me in the--puddle--for fun. I--I was vexed about it, Prudence, honestly. I--I was chasing her, and I fell, and tore my stocking,--and--and--but, Prudence, the papers do say children ought to model, and we didn't think of--getting caught." Another appealing glance into her sister's face, and Lark plunged on, bent on smoothing matters if she could. "Carol is--is just fine at it, really. She--she's making a Venus de Milo, and it's good. But we can't remember whether her arm is off at the elbow or below the shoulder----" An enormous gulp, and by furious blinking Lark managed to crowd back the tears that would slip to the edge of her lashes. "I--I'm very sorry, Prudence."

"Very well, Lark, you may go. I do not really object to your modeling in mud, I am sure. I am sorry you look so disreputable. You must change your shoes and stockings at once, and then you can go on with your modeling. But there must be no more pushing and chasing. I'll see Connie about that to-night. Now----"

"Oh! Oh! Oh! What in the world is that?"

This was a chorus of several Ladies' Aid voices,--a double quartette at the very least. Lark gave a sharp exclamation and began looking hurriedly about her on the floor.

"It's got in here,--just as I expected," she exclaimed. "I said you would be sorry, Prue,--Oh, there it is under your chair, Mrs. Prentiss. Just wait,--maybe I can shove it back in the box again."

This was greeted with a fresh chorus of shrieks. There was a hurried and absolute vacation of that corner of the front room. The Ladies fled, dropping their cherished sewing, shoving one another in a most Unladies-Aid-like way.

And there, beneath a chair, squatted the cause of the confusion, an innocent, unhappy, blinking toad!

"Oh, Larkie!"

This was a prolonged wail.

"It's all right, Prue, honestly it is," urged Lark with pathetic solemnity. "We didn't do it for a joke. We're keeping him for a good purpose. Connie found him in the garden,--and--Carol said we ought to keep him for Professor Duke,--he asked us to bring him things to cut up in science, you remember. So we just shoved him into this shoe box, and--we thought we'd keep him in the bath-tub until morning. We did it for a good purpose, don't you see we did? Oh, Prudence!"

Prudence was horribly outraged, but even in that critical moment, justice insisted that Lark's arguments were sound. The professor had certainly asked the scholars to bring him "things to cut up." But a toad! A live one!--And the Ladies' Aid! Prudence shivered.

"I am sure you meant well, Larkie," she said in a low voice, striving hard to keep down the bitter resentment in her heart, "I know you did. But you should not have brought that--that thing--into the house. Pick him up at once, and take him out-of-doors and let him go."

But this was not readily done. In spite of her shame and deep dismay, Lark refused to touch the toad with her fingers.

"I can't touch him, Prudence,--I simply can't," she whimpered. "We shoved him in with the broom handle before."

And as no one else was willing to touch it, and as the Ladies clustered together in confusion, and with much laughter, in the far corner of the other room, Prudence brought the broom and the not unwilling toad was helped to other quarters.

"Now go," said Prudence quickly, and Lark was swift to avail herself of the permission.

Followed a quiet hour, and then the Ladies put aside their sewing and walked about the room, chatting in little groups. With a significant glance to Fairy, Prudence walked calmly to the double doors between the dining-room and the sitting-room. The eyes of the Ladies followed her with interest and even enthusiasm. They were hungry. Prudence slowly opened wide the doors, and--stood amazed! The Ladies clustered about her, and stood amazed also. The dining-room was there, and the table! But the appearance of the place was vastly different! The snowy cloth was draped artistically over a picture on the wall, the lowest edges well above the floor. The plates and trays, napkin-covered, were safely stowed away on the floor in distant corners. The kitchen scrub bucket had been brought in and turned upside down, to afford a fitting resting place for the borrowed punch bowl, full to overflowing with fragrant lemonade.

And at the table were three dirty, disheveled little figures, bending seriously over piles of mud. A not-unrecognizable Venus de Milo occupied the center of the table. Connie was painstakingly at work on some animal, a dog perhaps, or possibly an elephant. And----

The three young modelers looked up in exclamatory consternation as the doors opened.

"Oh, are you ready?" cried Carol. "How the time has flown! We had no idea you'd be ready so soon. Oh, we are sorry, Prudence. We intended to have everything fixed properly for you again. We needed a flat place for our modeling. It's a shame, that's what it is. Isn't that a handsome Venus? I did that!--If you'll just shut the door one minute, Prudence, we'll have everything exactly as you left it. And we're as sorry as we can be. You can have my Venus for a centerpiece, if you like."

Prudence silently closed the doors, and the Ladies, laughing significantly, drew away.

"Don't you think, my dear," began Mrs. Prentiss too sweetly, "that they are a little more than you can manage? Don't you really think an older woman is needed?"

"I do not think so," cried Fairy, before her sister could speak, "no older woman could be kinder, or sweeter, or more patient and helpful than Prue."

"Undoubtedly true! But something more is needed, I am afraid! It appears that girls are a little more disorderly than in my own young days! Perhaps I do not judge advisedly, but it seems to me they are a little--unmanageable."

"Indeed they are not," cried Prudence loyally. "They are young, lively, mischievous, I know,--and I am glad of it. But I have lived with them ever since they were born, and I ought to know them. They are unselfish, they are sympathetic, they are always generous. They do foolish and irritating things,--but never things that are hateful and mean. They are all right at heart, and that is all that counts. They are not bad girls! What have they done to-day? They were exasperating, and humiliating, too, but what did they do that was really mean? They embarrassed and mortified me, but not intentionally! I can't punish them for the effect on me, you know! Would that be just or fair? At heart, they meant no harm."

It must be confessed that there were many serious faces among the Ladies. Some cheeks were flushed, some eyes were downcast, some lips were compressed and some were trembling. Every mother there was asking in her heart, "Did I punish my children just for the effect on me? Did I judge my children by what was in their hearts, or just by the trouble they made me?"

And the silence lasted so long that it became awkward. Finally Mrs. Prentiss crossed the room and stood by Prudence's side. She laid a hand tenderly on the young girl's arm, and said in a voice that was slightly tremulous:

"I believe you are right, my dear. It is what girls are at heart that really counts. I believe your sisters are all you say they are. And one thing I am very sure of,--they are happy girls to have a sister so patient, and loving, and just. Not all real mothers have as much to their credit!"

CHAPTER IV
A SECRET SOCIETY

Carol and Lark, in keeping with their twin-ship, were the dearest of chums and comrades. They resembled each other closely in build, being of the same height and size. They were slender, yet gave a suggestion of sturdiness. Carol's face was a delicately tinted oval, brightened by clear and sparkling eyes of blue. She was really beautiful, bright, attractive and vivacious. She made friends readily, and was always considered the "most popular girl in our crowd"--whatever Carol's crowd at the time might be. But she was not extremely clever, caring little for study, and with no especial talent in any direction. Lark was as nearly contrasting as any sister could be. Her face was pale, her eyes were dark brown and full of shadows, and she was a brilliant and earnest student. For each other the twins felt a passionate devotion that was very beautiful, but ludicrous as well.

To them, the great rambling barn back of the parsonage was a most delightful place. It had a big cow-shed on one side, and horse stalls on the other, with a "heavenly" haymow over all, and with "chutes" for the descent of hay,--and twins! In one corner was a high dark crib for corn, with an open window looking down into the horse stalls adjoining. When the crib was newly filled, the twins could clamber painfully up on the corn, struggle backward through the narrow window, and holding to the ledge of it with their hands, drop down into the nearest stall. To be sure they were likely to fall,--more likely than not,--and their hands were splinter-filled and their heads blue-bumped most of the time. But splinters and bumps did not interfere with their pursuit of pleasure.

Now the twins had a Secret Society,--of which they were the founders, the officers and the membership body. Its name was Skull and Crossbones. Why that name was chosen perhaps even the twins themselves could not explain, but it sounded deep, dark and bloody,--and so was the Society. Lark furnished the brain power for the organization but her sister was an enthusiastic and energetic second. Carol's club name was Lady Gwendolyn, and Lark's was Sir Alfred Angelcourt ordinarily, although subject to frequent change. Sometimes she was Lord Beveling, the villain of the plot, and chased poor Gwendolyn madly through corn-crib, horse stalls and haymow. Again she was the dark-browed Indian silently stalking his unconscious prey. Then she was a fierce lion lying in wait for the approaching damsel. The old barn saw stirring times after the coming of the new parsonage family.

"Hark! Hark!" sounded a hissing whisper from the corn-crib, and Connie, eavesdropping outside the barn, shivered sympathetically.

"What is it! Oh, what is it?" wailed the unfortunate lady.

"Look! Look! Run for your life!"

Then while Connie clutched the barn door in a frenzy, there was a sound of rattling corn as the twins scrambled upward, a silence, a low thud, and an unromantic "Ouch!" as Carol bumped her head and stumbled.

"Are you assaulted?" shouted the bold Sir Alfred, and Connie heard a wild scuffle as he rescued his companion from the clutches of the old halter on which she had stumbled. Up the haymow ladder they hurried, and then slid recklessly down the hay-chutes. Presently the barn door was flung open, and the "Society" knocked Connie flying backward, ran madly around the barn a few times, and scurried under the fence and into the chicken coop.

A little later, Connie, assailed with shots of corncobs, ran bitterly toward the house. "Peaking" was strictly forbidden when the twins were engaged in Skull and Crossbones activities.

And Connie's soul burned with desire. She felt that this secret society was threatening not only her happiness, but also her health, for she could not sleep for horrid dreams of Skulls and Crossbones at night, and could not eat for envying the twins their secret and mysterious joys. Therefore, with unwonted humility, she applied for entrance. She had applied many times previously, without effect. But this time she enforced her application with a nickel's worth of red peppermint drops, bought for the very purpose. The twins accepted the drops gravely, and told Connie she must make formal application. Then they marched solemnly off to the barn with the peppermint drops, without offering Connie a share. This hurt, but she did not long grieve over it, she was so busy wondering what on earth they meant by "formal application." Finally she applied to Prudence, and received assistance.

The afternoon mail brought to the parsonage an envelope addressed to "Misses Carol and Lark Starr, The Methodist Parsonage, Mount Mark, Iowa," and in the lower left-hand corner was a suggestive drawing of a Skull and Crossbones. The eyes of the mischievous twins twinkled with delight when they saw it, and they carried it to the barn for prompt perusal. It read as follows:

"Miss Constance Starr humbly and respectfully craves admittance into the Ancient and Honorable Organization of Skull and Crossbones."

The twins pondered long on a fitting reply, and the next afternoon the postman brought a letter for Connie, waiting impatiently for it. She had approached the twins about it at noon that day.

"Did you get my application?" she had whispered nervously.

But the twins had stared her out of countenance, and Connie realized that she had committed a serious breach of secret society etiquette.

But here was the letter! Her fingers trembled as she opened it. It was decorated lavishly with skulls and crossbones, splashed with red ink, supposedly blood, and written in the same suggestive color.

"Skull and Crossbones has heard the plea of Miss Constance Starr. If she present herself at the Parsonage Haymow this evening, at eight o'clock, she shall learn the will of the Society regarding her petition."

Connie was jubilant! In a flash, she saw herself admitted to the mysterious Barnyard Order, and began working out a name for her own designation after entrance. It was a proud day for her.

By the time the twins had finished washing the supper dishes, it was dark. Constance glanced out of the window apprehensively. She now remembered that eight o'clock was very, very late, and that the barn was a long way from the house! And up in the haymow, too! And such a mysterious bloody society! Her heart quaked within her. So she approached the twins respectfully, and said in an offhand way:

"I can go any time now. Just let me know when you're ready, and I'll go right along with you."

But the twins stared at her again in an amazing and overbearing fashion, and vouchsafed no reply. Connie, however, determined to keep a watchful eye upon them, and when they started barnward, she would trail closely along in their rear. It was a quarter to eight, and fearfully dark, when she suddenly remembered that they had been up-stairs an unnaturally long time. She rushed up in a panic. They were not there. She ran through the house. They were not to be found. The dreadful truth overwhelmed her,--the twins were already in the haymow, the hour had come, and she must go forth.

Breathlessly, she slipped out of the back door, and closed it softly behind her. She could not distinguish the dark outlines of the barn in the equal darkness of the autumn night. She gave a long sobbing gasp as she groped her way forward. As she neared the barn, she was startled to hear from the haymow over her head, deep groans as of a soul in mortal agony. Something had happened to the twins!

"Girls! Girls!" she cried, forgetting for the moment her own sorry state. "What is the matter? Twins!"

Sepulchral silence! And Connie knew that this was the dreadful Skull and Bones. Her teeth chattered as she stood there, irresolute in the intense and throbbing darkness.

"It's only the twins," she assured herself over and over, and began fumbling with the latch of the barn door,--but her fingers were stiff and cold. Suddenly from directly above her, there came the hideous clanking of iron chains. Connie had read ghost stories, and she knew the significance of clanking chains, but she stood her ground in spite of the almost irresistible impulse to fly. After the clanking, the loud and clamorous peal of a bell rang out.

"It's that old cow bell they found in the field," she whispered practically, but found it none the less horrifying.

Finally she stepped into the blackness of the barn, found the ladder leading to the haymow and began slowly climbing. But her own weight seemed a tremendous thing, and she had difficulty in raising herself from step to step. She comforted herself with the reflection that at the top were the twins,--company and triumph hand in hand. But when she reached the top, and peered around her, she found little comfort,--and no desirable company?

A small barrel draped in black stood in the center of the mow, and on it a lighted candle gave out a feeble flickering ray which emphasized the darkness around it. On either side of the black-draped barrel stood a motionless figure, clothed in somber black. On the head of one was a skull,--not a really skull, just a pasteboard imitation, but it was just as awful to Connie. On the head of the other were cross-bones.

"Kneel," commanded the hoarse voice of Skull, in which Connie could faintly distinguish the tone of Lark.

She knelt,--an abject quivering neophyte.

"Hear the will of Skull and Crossbones," chanted Crossbones in a shrill mono-tone.

Then Skull took up the strain once more. "Skull and Crossbones, great in mer-cy and in condescension, has listened graciously to the prayer of Constance, the Seeker. Hear the will of the Great Spirit! If the Seeker will, for the length of two weeks, submit herself to the will of Skull and Crossbones, she shall be admitted into the Ancient and Honorable Order. If the Seeker accepts this condition, she must bow herself to the ground three times, in token of submission."

"There's no ground here," came a small faint voice from the kneeling Seeker.

"The floor, madam," Skull explained sternly. "If the Seeker accepts the condition,--to submit herself absolutely to the will of Skull and Crossbones for two entire weeks,--she shall bow herself three times."

Constance hesitated. It was so grandly expressed that she hardly understood what they wanted. Carol came to her rescue.

"That means you've got to do everything Lark and I tell you for two weeks," she said in her natural voice.

Then Constance bowed herself three times,--although she lost her balance in the act, and Carol forgot her dignity and gave way to laughter, swiftly subdued, however.

"Arise and approach the altar," she commanded in the shrill voice, which yet gave signs of laughter.

Constance arose and approached.

"Upon the altar, before the Eternal Light, you will find a small black bow, with a drop of human blood in the center. This is the badge of your pledgedom. You must wear it day and night, during the entire two weeks. After that, if all is well; you shall be received into full membership. If you break your pledge to the Order, it must be restored at once to Skull and Crossbones. Take it, and pin it upon your breast."

Constance did so,--and her breast heaved with rapture and awe in mingling.

Then a horrible thing happened. The flame of the "Eternal Light" was suddenly extinguished, and Carol exclaimed, "The ceremony is ended. Return, damsel, to thine abode."

A sound of scampering feet,--and Constance knew that the Grand Officials had fled, and she was alone in the dreadful darkness. She called after them pitifully, but she heard the slam of the kitchen door before she had even reached the ladder.

It was a sobbing and miserable neophyte who stumbled into the kitchen a few seconds later. The twins were bending earnestly over their Latin grammars by the side of the kitchen fire, and did not raise their eyes as the Seeker burst into the room. Constance sat down, and gasped and quivered for a while. Then she looked down complacently at the little black bow with its smudge of red ink, and sighed contentedly.

The week that followed was a gala one for the twins of Skull and Crossbones. Constance swept their room, made their bed, washed their dishes, did their chores, and in every way behaved as a model pledge of the Ancient and Honorable. The twins were gracious but firm. There was no arguing, and no faltering. "It is the will of Skull and Crossbones that the damsel do this," they would say. And the damsel did it.

Prudence did not feel it was a case that called for her interference. So she sat back and watched, while the twins told stories, read and frolicked, and Constance did their daily tasks.

So eight days passed, and then came Waterloo. Constance returned home after an errand downtown, and in her hand she carried a great golden pear. Perhaps Constance would have preferred that she escape the notice of the twins on this occasion, but as luck would have it, she passed Carol in the hall.

"Gracious! What a pear! Where did you get it?" demanded Carol covetously.

"I met Mr. Arnold down-town, and he bought it for me. He's very fond of me. It cost him a dime, too, for just this one. Isn't it a beauty?" And Connie licked her lips suggestively.

Carol licked hers, too, thoughtfully. Then she called up the stairs, "Lark, come here, quick!"

Lark did so, and duly exclaimed and admired. Then she said significantly, "I suppose you are going to divide with us?"

"Of course," said Connie with some indignation. "I'm going to cut it in five pieces so Prudence and Fairy can have some, too."

A pause, while Carol and Lark gazed at each other soberly. Mentally, each twin was figuring how big her share would be when the pear was divided in fives. Then Lark spoke.

"It is the will of Skull and Crossbones that this luscious fruit be turned over to them immediately."

Constance faltered, held it out, drew it back.

"If I do, I suppose you'll give me part of it, anyhow," she said, and her eyes glittered.

"Not so, damsel," said Carol ominously. "The Ancient and Honorable takes,--it never gives."

For a moment Constance wavered. Then she flamed into sudden anger. "I won't do it, so there!" she cried. "I think you're mean selfish pigs, that's what I think! Taking my very own pear, and--but you won't get it! I don't care if I never get into your silly old society,--you don't get a bite of this pear, I can tell you that!" And Constance rushed up-stairs and slammed a door. A few seconds later the door opened again, and her cherished badge was flung down upon Skull and Crossbones.

"There's your old black string smeared up with red ink!" she yelled at them wildly. And again the door slammed.

Carol picked up the insulted badge, and studied it thoughtfully. Lark spoke first.

"It occurs to me, Fair Gwendolyn, that we would do well to keep this little scene from the ears of the just and righteous Prudence."

"Right, as always, Brave Knight," was the womanly retort. And the twins betook themselves to the haymow in thoughtful mood.

A little later, when Prudence and Fairy came laughing into the down-stairs hall, a white-faced Constance met them. "Look," she said, holding out a pear, divided into three parts, just like Gaul. "Mr. Arnold gave me this pear, and here's a piece for each of you."

The girls thanked her warmly, but Prudence paused with her third almost touching her lips. "How about the twins?" she inquired. "Aren't they at home? Won't they break your pledge if you leave them out?"

Constance looked up sternly. "I offered them some half an hour ago, and they refused it," she said. "And they have already put me out of the society!" There was tragedy in the childish face, and Prudence put her arms around this baby-sister.

"Tell Prue all about it, Connie," she said. But Constance shook her head.

"It can't be talked about. Go on and eat your pear. It is good."

"Was it all right?" questioned Prudence. "Did the twins play fair, Connie?"

"Yes," said Constance. "It was all right. Don't talk about it."

But in two days Constance repented of her rashness. In three days she was pleading for forgiveness. And in four days she was starting in on another two weeks of pledgedom, and the desecrated ribbon with its drop of blood reposed once more on her ambitious breast.

For three days her service was sore indeed, for the twins informed her, with sympathy, that she must be punished for insubordination. "But after that, we'll be just as easy on you as anything, Connie," they told her. "So don't you get sore now. In three days, we'll let up on you."

A week passed, ten days, and twelve. Then came a golden October afternoon when the twins sat in the haymow looking out upon a mellow world. Constance was in the yard, reading a fairy story. The situation was a tense one, for the twins were hungry, and time was heavy on their hands.

"The apple trees in Avery's orchard are just loaded," said Lark aimlessly. "And there are lots on the ground, too. I saw them when I was out in the field this morning."

"Some of the trees are close to our fence, too," said Carol slowly. "Very close."

Lark glanced up with sudden interest. "That's so," she said. "And the wires on the fence are awfully loose."

Carol gazed down into the yard where Constance was absorbed in her book. "Constance oughtn't to read as much as she does," she argued. "It's so bad for the eyes."

"Yes, and what's more, she's been getting off too easy the last few days. The time is nearly up."

"That's so," said Lark. "Let's call her up here." This was done at once, and the unfortunate Constance walked reluctantly toward the barn, her fascinating story still in her hand.

"You see, they've got more apples than they need, and those on the ground are just going to waste," continued Carol, pending the arrival of the little pledge. "The chickens are pecking at them, and ruining them."

"It's criminal destruction, that's what it is," declared Lark.

Connie stood before them respectfully, as they had instructed her to stand. The twins hesitated, each secretly hoping the other would voice the order. But Lark as usual was obliged to be the spokesman.

"Damsel," she said, "it is the will of Skull and Crossbones that you hie ye to yonder orchard,--Avery's, I mean,--and bring hither some of the golden apples basking in the sun."

"What!" ejaculated Connie, startled out of her respect.

Carol frowned.

Connie hastened to modify her tone. "Did they say you might have them?" she inquired politely.

"That concerns thee not, 'tis for thee only to render obedience to the orders of the Society. Go out through our field and sneak under the fence where the wires are loose, and hurry back. We're awfully hungry. The trees are near the fence. There isn't any danger."

"But it's stealing," objected Connie. "What will Prudence----"

"Damsel!" And Connie turned to obey with despair in her heart.

"Bring twelve," Carol called after her, "that'll be four apiece. And hurry, Connie. And see they don't catch you while you're about it."

After she had gone, the twins lay back thoughtfully on the hay and stared at the cobwebby roof above them.

"It's a good thing Prudence and Fairy are downtown," said Lark sagely.

"Yes, or we'd catch it," assented Carol. "But I don't see why! The Averys have too many apples, and they are going to waste. I'm sure Mrs. Avery would rather let us have them than the chickens."

They lay in silence for a while. Something was hurting them, but whether it was their fear of the wrath of Prudence, or the twinges of tender consciences,--who can say?

"She's an unearthly long time about it," exclaimed Lark, at last. "Do you suppose they caught her?"

This was an awful thought, and the girls were temporarily suffocated. But they heard the barn door swinging beneath them, and sighed with relief. It was Connie! She climbed the ladder skilfully, and poured her golden treasure before the arch thieves, Skull and Crossbones.

There were eight big tempting apples.

"Hum! Eight," said Carol sternly. "I said twelve."

"Yes, but I was afraid some one was coming. I heard such a noise through the grapevines, so I got what I could and ran for it. There's three apiece for you, and two for me," said Connie, sitting down sociably beside them on the hay.

But Carol rose. "Damsel, begone," she ordered. "When Skull and Crossbones feast, thou canst not yet share the festive board. Rise thee, and speed."

Connie rose, and walked soberly toward the ladder. But before she disappeared she fired this parting shot, "I don't want any of them. Stolen apples don't taste very good, I reckon."

Carol and Lark had the grace to flush a little at this, but however the stolen apples tasted, the twins had no difficulty in disposing of them. Then, full almost beyond the point of comfort, they slid down the hay-chutes, went out the back way, climbed over the chicken coops,--not because it was necessary, but because it was their idea of amusement,--and went for a walk in the field. At the farthest corner of the field they crawled under the fence, cut through a neighboring potato patch, and came out on the street. Then they walked respectably down the sidewalk, turned the corner and came quietly in through the front door of the parsonage.

Prudence was in the kitchen preparing the evening meal. Fairy was in the sitting-room, busy with her books. The twins set the table conscientiously, filled the wood-box, and in every way labored irreproachably. But Prudence had no word of praise for them that evening. She hardly seemed to know they were about the place. She went about her work with a pale face, and never a smile to be seen.

Supper was nearly ready when Connie sauntered in from the barn. After leaving the haymow, she had found a cozy corner in the com-crib, with two heavy lap robes discarded by the twins in their flight from wolves, and had settled down there to finish her story. As she stepped into the kitchen, Prudence turned to her with such a sorry, reproachful gaze that Connie was frightened.

"Are you sick, Prue?" she gasped.

Prudence did not answer. She went to the door and called Fairy. "Finish getting supper, will you, Fairy? And when you are all ready, you and the twins go right on eating. Don't wait for father,--he isn't coming home until evening. Come up-stairs with me, Connie; I want to talk to you."

Connie followed her sister soberly, and the twins flashed at each other startled and questioning looks.

The three girls were at the table when Prudence came into the dining-room alone. She fixed a tray-supper quietly and carried it off up-stairs. Then she came back and sat down by the table. But her face bore marks of tears, and she had no appetite. The twins had felt small liking for their food before, now each mouthful seemed to choke them. But they dared not ask a question. They were devoutly thankful when Fairy finally voiced their interest.

"What is the matter? Has Connie been in mischief?"

"It's worse than that," faltered Prudence, tears rushing to her eyes again.

"Why, Prudence! What in the world has she done?"

"I may as well tell you, I suppose,--you'll have to know it sooner or later. She--went out into Avery's orchard and stole some apples this afternoon. I was back in the alley seeing if Mrs. Moon could do the washing, and I saw her from the other side. She went from tree to tree, and when she got through the fence she ran. There's no mistake about it,--she confessed." The twins looked up in agony, but Prudence's face reassured them. Constance had told no tales. "I have told her she must spend all of her time up-stairs alone for a week, taking her meals there, too. She will go to school, of course, but that is all. I want her to see the awfulness of it. I told her I didn't think we wanted to eat with--a thief--just yet! I said we must get used to the idea of it first. She is heartbroken, but--I must make her see it!"

That was the end of supper. No one attempted to eat another bite. After the older girls had gone into the sitting-room, Carol and Lark went about their work with stricken faces.

"She's a little brick not to tell," whispered Lark.

"I'm going to give her that pearl pin of mine she always liked," said Carol in a hushed voice.

"I'll give her my blue ribbon, too,--she loves blue so. And to-morrow I'll take that quarter I've saved and buy her a whole quarter's worth of candy."

But that night when the twins went up to bed, they were doomed to disappointment. They had no chance of making it up with Constance. For Prudence had moved her small bed out of the twins' room, and had placed it in the front room occupied by herself and Fairy. They asked if they might speak to Constance, but Prudence went in with them to say good night to her. The twins broke down and cried as they saw the pitiful little figure with the wan and tear-stained face. They threw their arms around her passionately and kissed her many times. But they went to bed without saying anything.

Hours later, Lark whispered, "Carol! are you asleep?"

"No. I can't go to sleep somehow."

"Neither can I. Do you think we'd better tell Prudence all about it?"

Carol squirmed in the bed. "I--suppose we had," she said reluctantly.

"But--it'll be lots worse for us than for Connie," Lark added. "We're so much older, and we made her do it."

"Yes, and we ate all the apples," mourned Carol.

"Maybe we'd better just let it go," suggested Lark.

"And we'll make it up to Connie afterwards," said Carol.

"Now, you be careful and not give it away, Carol."

"You see that you don't."

But it was a sorry night for the twins. The next morning they set off to school, with no chance for anything but a brief good morning with Connie,--given in the presence of Prudence. Half-way down the parsonage walk, Carol said:

"Oh, wait a minute, Lark. I left my note-book on the table." And Lark walked slowly while Carol went rushing back. She found Prudence in the kitchen, and whispered:

"Here--here's a note, Prudence. Don't read it until after I've gone to school,--at ten o'clock you may read it. Will you promise?"

Prudence laughed a little, but she promised, and laid the note carefully away to wait the appointed hour for its perusal. As the clock struck ten she went to the mantle, and took it down. This is what Carol had written:

"Oh, Prudence, do please forgive me, and don't punish Connie any more. You can punish me any way you like, and I'll be glad of it. It was all my fault. I made her go and get the apples for me, and I ate them. Connie didn't eat one of them. She said stolen apples would not taste very good. It was all my fault, and I'm so sorry. I was such a coward I didn't dare tell you last night. Will you forgive me? But you must punish me as hard as ever you can. But please, Prudence, won't you punish me some way without letting Lark know about it? Please, please, Prudence, don't let Larkie know. You can tell Papa and Fairy so they will despise me, but keep it from my twin. If you love me, Prudence, don't let Larkie know."

As Prudence read this her face grew very stern. Carol's fault! And she was ashamed to have her much-loved twin know of her disgrace. At that moment, Prudence heard some one running through the hall, and thrust the note hastily into her dress. It was Lark, and she flung herself wildly upon Prudence, sobbing bitterly.

"What is the matter, Lark?" she tried, really frightened. "Are you sick?"

"Heartsick, that's all," wailed Lark. "I told the teacher I was sick so I could come home, but I'm not. Oh, Prudence, I know you'll despise and abominate me all the rest of your life, and everybody will, and I deserve it. For I stole those apples myself. That is, I made Connie go and get them for me. She didn't want to. She begged not to. But I made her. She didn't eat one of them,--I did it. And she felt very badly about it. Oh, Prudence, you can do anything in the world to me,--I don't care how horrible it is; I only hope you will. But, Prudence, you won't let Carol know, will you? Oh, spare me that, Prudence, please. That's my last request, that you keep it from Carol."

Prudence was surprised and puzzled. She drew the note from her pocket, and gave it to Lark. "Carol gave me that before she went to school," she explained. "Read it, and tell me what you are driving at. I think you are both crazy. Or maybe you are just trying to shield poor Connie."

Lark read Carol's note, and gasped, and--burst out laughing! The shame, and bitter weeping, and nervousness, had rendered her hysterical, and now she laughed and cried until Prudence was alarmed again.

In time, however, Lark was able to explain. "We both did it," she gasped, "the Skull and Crossbones. And we both told the truth about it. We made her go and get them for us, and we ate them, and she didn't want to go. I advised Carol not to tell, and she advised me not to. All the way to school this morning, we kept advising each other not to say a word about it. But I intended all the time to pretend I was sick, so I could come and confess alone. I wanted to take the punishment for both of us, so Carol could get out. I guess that's what she thought, too. Bless her little old heart, as if I'd let her be punished for my fault. And it was mostly my fault, too, Prue, for I mentioned the apples first of all."

Prudence laughed,--it was really ludicrous. But when she thought of loyal little Connie, sobbing all through the long night, the tears came to her eyes again. She went quickly to the telephone, and called up the school building next door to the parsonage.

"May I speak to Constance Starr, Mr. Imes?" she asked. "It is very important. This is Prudence, her sister." And when Connie came to the telephone, she cried, "Oh, you blessed little child, why didn't you tell me? Will you forgive me, Connie? I ought to have made you tell me all about it, but I was so sorry, I couldn't bear to talk much about it. The twins have told me. You're a dear, sweet, good little darling, that's what you are."

"Oh, Prudence!" That was all Connie said, but something in her voice made Prudence hang up the receiver quickly, and cry bitterly!

That noon Prudence pronounced judgment on the sinners, but her eyes twinkled, for Carol and Lark had scolded each other roundly for giving things away!

"Connie should have refused to obey you," she said gently, holding Connie in her arms. "She knew it was wrong. But she has been punished more than enough. But you twins! In the first place, I right now abolish the Skull and Crossbones forever and ever. And you can not play in the barn again for a month. And you must go over to the Averys this afternoon, and tell them about it, and pay for the apples. And you must send all of your spending money for the next month to that woman who is gathering up things for the bad little children in the Reform School,--that will help you remember what happens to boys and girls who get in the habit of taking things on the spur of the moment!"

The twins accepted all of this graciously, except that which referred to confessing their sin to their neighbors. That did hurt! The twins were so superior, and admirable! They couldn't bear to ruin their reputations. But Prudence stood firm, in spite of their weeping and wailing. And that afternoon two shamefaced sorry girls crept meekly in at the Averys' door to make their peace.

"But about the Skull and Crossbones, it's mostly punishment for me, Prue," said Connie regretfully, "for the twins have been in it ever since we came to Mount Mark, and I never got in at all! And I wanted them to call me Lady Magdalina Featheringale." And Connie sighed.

CHAPTER V
THE TWINS STICK UP FOR THE BIBLE

Prudence had been calling on a "sick member." Whenever circumstances permitted she gladly served as pastoral assistant for her father, but she always felt that raising the family was her one big job, and nothing was allowed to take precedence of it. As she walked that afternoon down Maple Street,--seemingly so-called because it was bordered with grand old elms,--she felt at peace with all the world. The very sunshine beaming down upon her through the huge skeletons of the leafless elms, was not more care-free than the daughter of the parsonage. Parsonage life had been running smoothly for as much as ten days past, and Prudence, in view of that ten days' immunity, was beginning to feel that the twins, if not Connie also, were practically reared!

"Mount Mark is a dear old place,--a duck of a place, as the twins would say,--and I'm quite sorry there's a five-year limit for Methodist preachers. I should truly like to live right here until I am old and dead."

Then she paused, and bowed, and smiled. She did not recognize the bright-faced young woman approaching, but she remembered just in time that parsonage people are marked characters. So she greeted the stranger cordially.

"You are Miss Starr, aren't you?" the bright-faced woman was saying. "I am Miss Allen,--the principal of the high school, you know."

"Oh, yes," cried Prudence, thrusting forth her hand impulsively, "oh, yes, I know. I am so glad to meet you."

Miss Allen was a young woman of twenty-six, with clear kind eyes and a strong sweet mouth. She had about her that charm of manner which can only be described as winsome womanliness. Prudence gazed at her with open and honest admiration. Such a young woman to be the principal of a high school in a city the size of Mount

Mark! She must be tremendously clever. But Prudence did not sigh. We can't all be clever, you know. There must be some of us to admire the rest of us!

The two walked along together, chatting sociably on subjects that meant nothing to either of them. Presently Miss Allen stopped, and with a graceful wave of her hand, said lightly:

"This is where I am rooming. Are you in a very great hurry this afternoon? I should like to talk to you about the twins. Will you come in?"

The spirits of Prudence fell earthward with a clatter! The twins! Whatever had they been doing now?

She followed Miss Allen into the house and up the stairs with the joy quite quenched in her heart. She did not notice the dainty room into which she was conducted. She ignored the offered chair, and with a dismal face turned toward Miss Allen.

"Oh, please! What have they been doing? Is it very awful?"

Miss Allen laughed gaily. "Oh, sit down and don't look so distressed. It's nothing at all. They haven't been doing anything. I just want to discuss them on general principles, you know. It's my duty to confer with the parents and guardians of my scholars."

Immensely relieved, Prudence sank down in the chair, and rocked comfortably to and fro a few times. General principles,--ah, blessed words!

"I suppose you know that Carol is quite the idol of the high school already. She is the adored one of the place. You see, she is not mixed up in any scholastic rivalry. Lark is one of the very best in her class, and there is intense rivalry between a few of the freshmen. But Carol is out of all that, and every one is free to worship at her shrine. She makes no pretensions to stand first."

"Is she very stupid?" Prudence was disappointed. She did so want both of her twins to shine.

"Stupid! Not a bit of it. She is a very good scholar, much better than the average. Our first pupils, including Lark, average around ninety-six and seven. Then there are others ranging between ninety and ninety-four. Carol is one of them. The fairly good ones are over eighty-five, and the fairly bad ones are over seventy-five, and the hopeless ones are below that. This is a rough way of showing how they stand. Lark is a very fine scholar, really the best in the class. She not only makes good grades, she grasps the underlying significance of her studies. Very few freshmen, even among the best, do that. She is quite exceptional. We hope to make something very big and fine of Larkie."

Prudence's eyes shone with motherly pride. She nodded, striving to make her voice natural and matter-of-fact as she answered, "Yes, she is bright."

"She certainly is! Carol is quite different, but she is so sweet-spirited, and vivacious, and--un-snobbish, if you know what that means--that every one in high school, and even the grammar-grade children, idolize her. She is very witty, but her wit is always innocent and kind. She never hurts any one's feelings. And she is never impertinent. The professors are as crazy about her as the scholars,--forgive the slang. Did the twins ever tell you what happened the first day of school?"

"No,--tell me." Prudence was clearly very anxious.

"I shall never forget it. The freshmen were sent into the recitation room to confer with Professor Duke about text-books, etc. Carol was one of the first in the line, as they came out. She sat down in her seat in the first aisle, with one foot out at the side. One of the boys tripped over it. 'Carol,' said Miss Adams gently, 'you forgot yourself, didn't you?' And Carol's eyes twinkled as she said, 'Oh, no, Miss Adams, if I had I'd still be in the recitation room.'" Miss Allen laughed, but Prudence's eyes were agonized.

"How hateful of her!"

"Don't the twins tell you little things that happen at school,--like that, for instance?"

"Never! I supposed they were perfectly all right."

"Well, here's another. Twice a week we have talks on First Aid to the Injured. Professor Duke conducts them. One day he asked Carol what she would do if she had a very severe cold, and Carol said, 'I'd soak my feet in hot water and go to bed. My sister makes me.'" Miss Allen laughed again, but Prudence was speechless.

"Sometimes we have talks on normal work, practical informal discussions. Many of our scholars will be country school-teachers, you know. Miss Adams conducts these normal hours. One day she asked Carol what she would do if she had applied for a school, and was asked by the directors to write a thesis on student discipline, that they might judge of her and her ability by it? Carol said, 'I'd get Lark to write it for me.'"

Even Prudence laughed a little at this, but she said, "Why don't you scold her?"

"We talked it all over shortly after she entered school. Miss Adams did not understand Carol at first, and thought she was a little impertinent. But Professor Duke and I stood firm against even mentioning it to her. She is perfectly good-natured about it. You know, of course, Miss Starr, that we really try to make individuals of our scholars. So many, many hundreds are turned out of the public schools all cut on one pattern. We do not like it. We fight against it. Carol is different from others by nature, and we're going to keep her different if possible. If we crush her individuality, she will come out just like thousands of others,--all one pattern! Miss Adams is as fond of Carol now as any one of us. You understand that we could not let impudence or impertinence pass unreproved, but Carol is never guilty of that. She is always respectful and courteous. But she is spontaneous and quick-witted, and we are glad of it. Do you know what the scholars call Professor Duke?"

"Professor Duck," said Prudence humbly. "But they mean it for a compliment. They really admire and like him very much. I hope he does not know what they call him."

"He does! One day he was talking about the nobility system in England. He explained the difference between dukes, and earls, and lords, etc., and told them who is to be addressed as Your Majesty, Your Highness, Your Grace and so on. Then he said, 'Now, Carol, if I was the king's eldest son, what would you call me?' And Carol said, 'I'd still call you a Duck, Professor,--it wouldn't make any difference to me.'"

Prudence could only sigh.

"One other time he was illustrating phenomena. He explained the idea, and tried to get one of the boys to mention the word,--phenomenon, you know. The boy couldn't think of it. Professor gave three or four illustrations, and still the boy couldn't remember it. 'Oh, come now,' professor said, finally, 'something unusual, something very much out of the ordinary! Suppose you should see a blackbird running a race down the street with a sparrow, what would you call it?' The boy couldn't imagine, and professor said, 'What would you call that, Carol?' Carol said, 'A bad dream.'"

Prudence smiled wearily.

"Sometimes we have discussions of moral points. We take turns about conducting them, and try to stimulate their interest in such things. We want to make them think, every one for himself. One day Professor Duke said, 'Suppose a boy in this town has a grudge against you,--unjust and unfair. You have tried one thing after another to change his attitude. But he continues to annoy and inconvenience and even hurt you, on every occasion. Remember that you have tried every ordinary way of winning his good will. Now what are you going to do as a last resort?' Carol said, 'I'll tell papa on him.'" Miss Allen laughed again, heartily. "It does have a disturbing effect on the class, I admit, and often spoils a good point, but Professor Duke calls on Carol every time he sees her eyes twinkle! He does it on purpose. And Miss Adams is nearly as bad as he. One day she said, 'Suppose you have unintentionally done something to greatly irritate and inconvenience a prominent man in town. He knows you did it, and he is very angry. He is a man of sharp temper and disagreeable manners. You know that he will be extremely unpleasant and insulting if you go to him with explanations and apologies. What are you going to do?' 'I think I'll just keep out of his way for a few weeks,' said Carol soberly."

"I hope she doesn't talk like that to you, Miss Allen."

Instantly Miss Allen was grave. "No, she does not, I am so sorry." Leaning forward suddenly, she said, "Miss Starr, why do the twins dislike me?"

"Dislike you!" echoed Prudence. "Why, they do not dislike you! What in the world makes you think----"

"Oh, yes indeed they do,--both of them. Now, why? People generally like me. I have always been popular with my students. This is my second year here. Last year the whole high school stood by me as one man. This year, the freshmen started as usual. After one week, the twins changed. I knew it instantly. Then other freshmen changed. Now the whole class comes as near snubbing me as they dare. Do you mean to say they have never told you about it?"

"Indeed they have not. And I am sure you are mistaken. They do like you. They like everybody."

"Christian tolerance, perhaps," smiled Miss Allen ruefully. "But I want them to like me personally and intimately. I can help the twins. I can do them good, I know I can. But they won't let me. They keep me at arm's length. They are both dear, and I love them. But they freeze me to death! Why?"

"I can't believe it!"

"But it is true. Don't they talk of their professors at home at all?"

"Oh, often."

"What do they say of us?"

"Why, they say Miss Adams is a perfectly sweet old lamb,--they do not mean to be disrespectful. And they say Professor Duke is the dearest duck! They almost swear by 'Professor Duck'!"

"And what do they say of me?"

Prudence hesitated, thinking hard.

"Come now, what do they say? We must get to the bottom of this."

"Why, they have said that you are very pretty, and most unbelievably smart."

"Oh! Quite a difference between sweet old lamb, and the dearest duck, and being very pretty and smart! Do you see it?"

"Yes," confessed Prudence reluctantly, "but I hadn't thought of it before."

"Now, what is wrong? What have I done? Why, look here. The twins think everything of Professor Duke, and I am sure Carol deliberately neglects her science lessons in order to be kept in after school by him. But though she hates mathematics,--my subject,--she works at it desperately so I can't keep her in. She sits on Mr. Duke's table and chats with him by the hour. But she passes me up with a curt, 'Good night, Miss Allen.'"

"And Larkie, too?"

"Lark is worse than Carol. Her dislike is deeper-seated. I believe I could win Carol in time. Sometimes I waylay her when she is leaving after school, and try my best. But just as she begins to thaw, Lark invariably comes up to see if she is ready to go home, and she looks at both of us with superior icy eyes. And Carol freezes in a second. Ordinarily, she looks at me with a sort of sympathetic pity and wonder, but Lark is always haughty and nearly contemptuous. It is different with the rest of the class. It is nothing important to them. The twins are popular in the class, you know, and the others, realizing that they dislike me, hold aloof on their account."

"I can't fathom it," said Prudence.

"Now, Professor Duke is very brilliant and clever and interesting. And he does like Carol tremendously,--Larkie, too. He says she is the cleverest girl he ever knew. But Carol is his favorite. But he does not like teaching, and he has not the real interests of the scholars at heart. Next year, he is to begin some very wonderful research work at a big salary. That is what he loves. That is where his interests lie. But this year, being idle, and his uncle being on the school board here, he accepted this place as a sort of vacation in the meanwhile. That is all it means to him. But I love teaching, it is my life-work. I love the young people, and I want to help them. Why won't the twins give me a chance? Surely I am as attractive as Professor Duke. They are even fond of Miss Adams, whom most people consider rather a sour old maid. But they have no use for me. I want you to find out the reason, and tell me. Will you do it? They will tell you if you ask them, won't they?"

"I think so. It is partly my fault. I am very strict with them about saying hateful things about people. I do not allow it. And I insist that they like everybody,--if they don't, I make them. So they have just kept it to themselves. But I will do my best."

One would have thought that Prudence carried the responsibility for the entire public-school system of the United States upon her shoulders that night, so anxious were her eyes, so grave her face. Supper over, she quietly suggested to Fairy that she would appreciate the absence of herself and Connie for a time. And Fairy instantly realized that the twins must be dealt with seriously for something. So she went in search of Connie, and the two set out for a long walk. Then Prudence went to the kitchen where the twins were washing the dishes, and as usual, laughing immoderately over something.

Prudence sat down and leaned her elbows on the table, her chin in her palms. "I met Miss Allen to-day," she said, closely observing the faces of the twins. A significant glance flashed between them, and they stiffened instantly.

"She's very pretty and sweet, isn't she?" continued Prudence.

"Yes, very," agreed Lark without any enthusiasm.

"Such pretty hair," added Carol dispassionately.

"She must be very popular with the scholars," suggested Prudence.

"Yes, most of them are fond of her," assented Lark.

"She has rather winsome manners, I think," said Carol.

"Which of your professors do you like best?" queried Prudence.

"Duck," they answered unanimously, and with brightening faces. "Why?"

"Because he is a duck," said Carol, and they all laughed. But Prudence returned to the charge without delay.

"Do you like Miss Allen?" She was going through these questions with such solemnity that the twins' suspicions had been aroused right at the start. What had Miss Allen told their sister? Again that significant flash from twin to twin.

"She certainly has very likeable ways," said Lark shrewdly.

"But do you like her?" insisted Prudence.

"I would like her very much under ordinary circumstances," admitted Carol.

"What is unusual about the circumstances?" Prudence wanted to know.

"Look here, Prudence, what did Miss Allen tell you? Was she complaining about us? We've been very nice and orderly, I'm sure." Lark was aggrieved.

"She wasn't complaining. She likes you both. But she says you do not like her. I want to know why."

"Well, if you must know, Miss Allen is a heretic," snapped Lark.

Then Prudence leaned back in her chair and gazed at the flushed faces of the twins for two full minutes.

"A--a--a what?" she ejaculated, when power of speech returned to her.

"Heretic," said Carol with some relish. "A heretic! You know what heresy is, don't you? We'll tell you all about it if you like, now you've got things started."

"We didn't tell you before because we thought you and father would feel badly about sending us to school to a heretic. But don't you worry,--Miss Allen hasn't influenced us any."

"We haven't given her a chance," said Carol, with her impish smile.

"Go on," begged Prudence. "Tell me. You're both crazy, I see that. But tell me!"

"Well," began Lark, for Carol always relegated the story-telling to her more gifted twin, "we've suspected Miss Allen right from the start. They used to have Bible reading every morning in school, one chapter, you know, and then the Lord's prayer. After the first week, Miss Allen dropped it. We thought that was a--a suspicious circumstance."

"Phenomenally so," said Carol darkly.

"But we kept our suspicions to ourselves, and we didn't come across anything else for several days. We wouldn't condemn anybody on--on circumstantial evidence, Prue. We're very fair-minded, you know."

"In spite of being twins," added Carol.

"What's that got to do with it?" Prudence inquired, frowning at Carol.

"Oh, nothing," admitted Carol, driven into a corner. "I just wanted to make it emphatic."

"Go on, Lark."

"Well, there's a girl at school named Hattie Simpson. You do not know her, Prue. We don't associate with her. Oh, yes, we like her very well, but she isn't parsonage material."

"She's a goat," put in Carol. "You needn't frown, Prue, that's Bible! Don't you remember the sheep and the goats? I don't know now just what it was they did, but I know the goats were very--very disreputable characters!"

"Go on, Lark."

"Well, her folks are atheists, and she's an atheist, too. You know what an atheist is, don't you? You know, Prue, Mount Mark is a very religious town, on account of the Presbyterian College, and all, and it seems the Simpsons are the only atheists here. Hattie says people look down on her terribly because of it. She says the church folks consider them, the Simpsons, that is, the dust on their shoes, and the crumbs off the rich man's table. She got that terribly mixed up, but I didn't correct her."

"I think she did very well for an atheist," said Carol, determined not to be totally overlooked in this discussion.

"What has all this to do with Miss Allen?"

"Well, one day Hattie was walking home from school with us, and she was telling us about it,--the dust on their shoes, etc.,--and she said she liked Miss Allen better than anybody else in town. I asked why. She said Miss Allen believed the same things the Simpsons believe, only Miss Allen daren't say so publicly, or they would put her out of the school. She said Miss Allen said that most church members were hypocrites and drunkards and--and just generally bad, and the ones outside the church are nearly always good and moral and kind. She said Miss Allen joined the Presbyterian church here because most of the school board are Presbyterians. She said Miss Allen said she didn't care if people were Catholics or Jews or atheists or--or just ordinary Protestants, so long as they were kind to one another, and went about the world doing good works. And that's why Miss Allen wouldn't read the

Bible and say the Lord's prayer in school."

"What do you think of that?" demanded Carol. "Isn't that heresy? She's as bad as the priest and Levite, isn't she?"

"Did you ask Miss Allen about it?"

"No, indeed, we've just ignored Miss Allen ever since. We have watched her as closely as we could since then, to see if we could catch her up again. Of course she has to be careful what she says in school, but we found several strong points against her. It's a perfectly plain case, no doubt about it."

"And so you went among the other freshmen influencing them, and telling tales, and criticizing your----"

"No indeed, Prue, we wouldn't! But you know it says in the Bible to beware of false doctrines and the sowers of bad seed,--or something like that--"

"And we bewared as hard as we could!" grinned Carol.

"We have tried to explain these things to the other freshmen so Miss Allen could not lead them into--into error. Oh, that's Christian Science, isn't it? Well, Minnie Carlson is a Christian Scientist and she talks so much about falling into error that--honestly----"

"We can't tell error from truth any more," interjected Carol neatly. "And so I hope you won't punish us if we accidentally vary from the truth once in a while."

This was quite beyond Prudence's depth. She knew little of Christian Science save that it was a widely accepted creed of recent origin. So she brought the twins back to Miss Allen again. "But, twins, do you think it was kind, and Christian, and--and like parsonage girls, to accept all this against Miss Allen without giving her a chance to defend herself?"

"As I told you, Prue, we have watched her very close since then. She has never come right out in the open,--she wouldn't dare,--but she has given herself away several times. Nothing can get by us when we're on the watch, you know!"

Prudence knew. "What did Miss Allen say?"

The twins thought seriously for a while.

"Oh, yes, Lark," suggested Carol finally, "don't you remember she said the Bible was an allegory?"

"What?"

"Yes, she did. She was explaining to the English class what was meant by allegory, and she said the purpose of using allegory was to teach an important truth in a homely impressive way that could be remembered. She mentioned several prominent allegories, and said the Bible was one. And you know yourself Prue, that the Bible is Gospel truth, and--I mean, it is so! I mean----"

"What she means," said Lark helpfully, "is that the Bible is not just a pretty way of teaching people to be good, but it's solid fact clear through."

"That's very well expressed, Lark,"--Prudence herself could not have expressed it half so well! "But how do you twins understand all these things so thoroughly?"

"Oh, you know Mrs. Sears is our Sunday-school teacher, and she's always hot on the trail of the higher critics and heretics. She explained all about the--the nefarious system to us one Sunday. She says the higher critics try to explain away the Bible by calling it allegory. So we were ready for Miss Allen there. And whenever anything came up at school, we would ask Mrs. Sears about it on Sunday,--without mentioning names of course. She's very much gratified that we are so much interested in such things. She thinks we're sure to be deaconesses, at the very least. But Carol said she wouldn't be a deaconess,--she was going to be a Red Cross nurse and go to war. That stumped Mrs. Sears for a while, and then she said we could be Red Cross Deaconess nurses."

"I won't," said Carol, "because the deaconess uniforms aren't as stylish as the Red Cross nurses'. I think I'll look pretty fine in a white uniform with a stiff little cap and a red cross on my arm. Red crosses make a very pretty decoration, don't you think they do, Lark?"

"What else did Miss Allen say at school?" Prudence demanded, leading the twins back to the subject.

"Well, one day she said,--you know she gives uplifting little moral talks quite often, Prue. Sometimes she tells us stories with inspiring points. She's really a moral person, I believe."

"And I'm honestly sorry she's a heretic," said Carol, "for I do want to be friendly enough with her to ask if she uses anything on her complexion to keep it so rose-leafy. If she does, I'll have some of it, if it takes all my next year's clothes!"

Lark laughed. "A rose-leaf complexion will be a poor substitute for----"

"Oh, for goodness' sake, twins, come back to Miss Allen. I am going right up to her house this minute, to ask her about it, and explain----"

"She's the one to do the explaining, seems to me," said Carol belligerently. "We've got to stick up for the Bible, Prue,--it's our business."

"And I don't think you should tell her,--it may hurt her feelings," urged Lark.

"Have heretics feelings?" queried Carol. "I suppose it's a feeling of----"

"Carol! Will you quit talking for a minute! This is a serious matter. If she believes all that nonsense, she's no proper teacher and--and she'll have to be put out of the high school. And if she doesn't believe it, she's a martyr! I'm going to find out about it at once. Do you want to come with me?"

"I should say not," said the twins promptly.

"I think you're very foolish to go at all," added Lark.

"I wouldn't go for a dollar," declared Carol. "It'd be very interesting to see how a heretic feels, but I don't care to know how ordinary Christians feel when they fall into their hands. I'm not aching to see Miss Allen to-night."

So Prudence set forth, conscientiously, in the darkness. A brave and heroic thing for Prudence to do, for she was a cowardly creature at heart.

Miss Allen heard her voice in the lower hall, and came running down-stairs to meet her. "Come up," she cried eagerly, "come on up."

And before Prudence was fairly inside the door, she demanded, "What is it? Did you find out? Is it my fault?"

Then Prudence blushed and stammered, "Why--it sounds--silly but--they think you are a--heretic."

Miss Allen gasped. Then she laughed. Then she walked to her dressing-table and picked up a long hatpin. "Will you kindly jab this into me?" she said. "I'm having a nightmare."

Prudence explained in detail. At first Miss Allen laughed, it must be confessed. Then she grew very sober. "It is really my fault," she said, "for I should have remembered that young people read a ton of meaning into a pound of words. Of course, I am not guilty, Miss Starr. Professor Duke and Miss Adams can swear to that. They call me Goody-goody. They say I am an old-fashioned apostle, and they accuse me of wanting to burn them both at the stake! Now, sit down and let me explain."

Prudence sat down. She was glad, so glad, that this sweet-faced, bright-eyed woman was an "ordinary Christian," and not a "priest and a Levite!"

"About the allegory business, it is very simple. What I said was this,--'The Bible is full of allegory.' I did not say, 'The Bible is allegory.' I said the Bible is full of allegory, and so it is. The parables, for instance,--what are they? Do you see the difference?--But it is really more serious about poor little Hattie Simpson. As the twins told you, her parents are atheists. Her father is a loud-voiced, bragging, boastful, coarse-hearted fellow. Hattie herself does not know what her parents believe, and what they do not. She simply follows blindly after them. She thinks she is an eyesore in Mount Mark because of it. She resents it bitterly, but she feels the only decent thing for her to do is to stand by her folks. Let me tell you about our conversation. I tried to make friends with her, for I truly pity her. She has no friends, she slinks about as though constantly ashamed of herself. She trusts no one, herself least of all. I tried to draw her out, and with partial success. She told me how she feels about it all. I said, 'Hattie, won't you let some one--some minister, who knows how--tell you about Christianity, and explain to you what Christians really believe?' 'No,' she said passionately, 'I'll stand by my folks.' Then I saw she was not ready yet. I said, 'Well, perhaps it is just as well for the present, for you are too young now to take any definite stand for yourself. It is true,' I told her, 'that many church members are not Christians, and are bad immoral people,--as your father says. They are not Christians. And it is true that many outside of the church are good moral people,--but they are not Christians, either.' And then I said, 'Don't worry your head just now about whether people are Catholics or Jews or Protestants, or what they are. Just try to love everybody, and try to grow up to be such a sweet, kind, loving woman that you will be a blessing to the world. And what is more,' I said, 'do not puzzle your head now about why some believe the Bible, and some do not. Just wait. When you are older, you shall go into things for yourself, and make your own decision.'"

Prudence nodded. "I think you were very sweet about it," she said.

"I wanted to win her confidence in the hope that some time, a little later, I myself may show her what Christ is to us, and why we love the Bible. But I did fight shy of the real point, for fear I might anger her and put a barrier between us. I just tried to win her confidence and her love, to pave the way for what I may be able to do later on. Do you see? I have had several talks with her, but she is not ready. She is just a child, stubbornly determined to stand with her folks, right or wrong. I am trying now to cultivate the ground, I say nothing to make her dislike or distrust me. I did not think of her telling it to others,--and telling it wrong! Surely no one but the twins could have read so much into it!"

"Well," and Prudence smiled, "you know we are parsonage people! We have to stick up for the Bible, as Carol says."

"Oh, and about the Bible reading," said Miss Allen suddenly, "I have nothing to do with that. As you know, there are Jews and Catholics and Christian Scientists and every branch of Protestant represented in our little school. The Jews and Christian Scientists are in a minority. The Jews, have always objected to Bible reading, but they were too few to be influential. With a Catholic teacher, the Catholics were quite willing to have it. With a Protestant teacher, the Protestants were strong for it. But there was always friction--one side objecting--so the school board ruled it out entirely. I did not explain this to the scholars. I did not want our young people to know of the petty bickering and scrapping going on among the elders in the town. So I simply said that hereafter we would dispense with the Bible reading. But it was the direct order of the board. I argued against it, so did Professor Duke, so did Miss Adams. But as it happens, we are all three Presbyterians! It did no good."

Then as Prudence rose to go home, she asked eagerly, "Do you think the twins will like me now?"

"I don't see how in the world they can help it," declared Prudence, smiling; "indeed, they admitted they were only too anxious to love you, but couldn't honestly do so because they had to stick up for the Bible! I am so glad and relieved! This is the first time I have gone heresy-hunting, and I was quite bowed down with the weight of it. And if ever I can help with poor little Hattie, will you let me know? I must have the twins invite her to spend some Saturday with us. That's the way I make the girls like people,--by being with them a great, great deal."

Just before she said good night, Prudence murmured hopefully, "I am sorry it happened, but it will be a good lesson for the twins. I am sure that after this, they will be less ready to listen to gossip, and more ready to give one the benefit of a doubt. It's a great responsibility, this raising a family, Miss Allen--and especially twins!"

CHAPTER VI
AN ADMIRER

It must be remembered that Prudence did not live in a sheltered and exclusive city home, where girls are rigidly withheld from all unchaperoned intercourse with young men and old. We know how things are managed in the "best homes" of the big cities,--girls are sheltered from innocent open things, and, too often, indulge in really serious amusements on the quiet. But this was the Middle West, where girls are to be trusted. Not all girls, of course, but as a matter of fact, the girls who need watching, seldom get enough of it to keep them out of mischief. Out in Iowa, girls and boys are allowed to like each other, and revel in each other's company. And it is good for both.

Prudence was not a sentimental girl. Perhaps this was partly due to the fact that at the age when most girls are head-full of boy, Prudence was hands-full of younger sisters! And when hands are full to overflowing, there is small likelihood of heads being full of nonsense. Prudence liked boys as she liked girls,--that was the end of it. Romance was to her a closed book, and she felt no inclination to peep between the covers. Soul-stirring had not come to her yet.

But Prudence was attractive. She had that indescribable charm that carries a deep appeal to the eyes, and the lips, and the hearts of men. Happily Prudence herself did not realize this. The first young man of Mount Mark to yield to the charms of Prudence was a serious-minded lawyer, nearly ten years her senior. This was just the type of man to become enraptured with Prudence. He gazed across at her solemnly during the church service. He waited patiently after the benediction until she finished her Methodist practise of hand-shaking, and then walked joyously home with her. He said little, but he gazed in frank enchantment at the small womanly girl beside him.

"He's not half bad, Fairy," Prudence would confide to her sister when they were snug in their bed. "He's not half bad at all. But at heart, he doesn't approve of me. He doesn't know that himself, and I certainly can't believe it is my duty to tell him. But I am convinced that it is true. For instance, he thinks every one, especially women, should have a mission in life, a serious, earnest mission. I told him I didn't believe anything of the kind,--I think we are just supposed to live along from day to day and do what we can, and be happy, and not say mean things about one another. But he said he considered that I was fulfilling the noblest mission a woman could have. Now what do you reckon he meant by that, Fairy? I've been puzzling my brain over it for days and days. Anybody can tell I am not the sort of girl to have a mission! Maybe he just said it to encourage me,--he's a very encouraging sort of man. He's very nice,--oh, very nice, indeed! But isn't it a nuisance to have him tagging along home with me, when I might be having such a good time with you and the twins, or father? Can a girl tell a man she prefers to go home with her family, without hurting his feelings? Is there any way to turn a person down without letting him know it? He's so nice I wouldn't hurt his feelings for anything, but--it's such a bother! I'm too young for beaus, and since I'm never going to get married it's just a waste of time."

And Fairy screamed with laughter, but told Prudence she must solve her own love problems! And Prudence, unwilling to give offense, and preferring self-sacrifice, endured his company until a gay young college lad slipped in ahead of him. "First come, first served," was the motto of heartless Prudence, and so she tripped comfortably away with "Jimmy," laughing at his silly college stories, and never thinking to give more than a parting smile at the solemn face she left behind.

After Jimmy came a grocery clerk named Byron Poe Smith, and after him somebody else, and somebody else, and somebody else. And Prudence continued to laugh, and thought it "awfully amusing, Fairy, but I keep wondering what you and the twins are laughing about!"

But it was Fairy herself who brought a real disturbing element into the life of Prudence. One of the lightest-minded of the many light-minded college men, had been deeply smitten by the charms of dignified Fairy. He walked with her, and talked with her,--this young man was a great deal of a talker, as so pathetically many college men are! He planned many little expeditions and entertainments for her amusement, and his own happiness. His name was Eugene Babler.

"Oh, he talks a lot," said Fairy coolly, "but he certainly shows one a good time, and that's the point, you know!"

She came in from college one afternoon and rattled off this little tale to Prudence.

"A few of us were on the campus to-day, and we decided to go down the creek to-morrow afternoon and take our suppers. There'll be Ellen Stark, and Georgia Prentiss, and myself. And the boys will be Tom Angell, and Frank Morris, and Eugene Babler. And Professor Rayburn was there when we were talking about it, and so we asked him to go along, but we told him he must take a girl. And he said, 'I wonder if your sister wouldn't go? I have only met her once, but perhaps on your recommendation, Miss Fairy----' and he paused with his breath in the air, inquiringly. So I said, 'Do you mean Prudence, or one of the twins?' He smiled very kindly and said, 'I mean Prudence.' I said I was sure you would go, and so you'll have to do it. It's a great honor, Prue, for all the upper-class girls, and even the un-married women on the Fac. are crazy about him. He's so aloof, you know, and very intelligent. I swelled with pride at the public tribute to the parsonage!"

"Professor Rayburn! Of the Fac.!" gasped Prudence. "Oh, I'm sure he didn't mean me, Fairy. You must have misunderstood him. Why, I wouldn't know what to say to a professor, you know! What is his line?"

"Bugs!" cried Fairy. "He's the biology man. And this is his first year here, and he's very brilliant,--they say! I'm no authority on bugs myself. But anyhow every one just raves about him, and he showed very plainly that he was anxious to get acquainted with you, so you'll have to go."

"But bugs!" wailed Prudence. "What do I know about bugs! Will he expect me to know how to divide them,--separate them, you know--"

"I suppose you mean dissect them, you poor child," screamed Fairy. "Divide bugs! If professor could hear you now, Prue, he would be sadly disillusioned. You must just trot up-stairs and get one of the twins' biology books and cram up a little. He won't expect you to be an advanced buggist. He can give you points himself. Men do love to have girls appeal to their superior knowledge, and be admiring and deferent. Maybe he will 'divide one' for you if you ask him 'please.'"

"I won't do it," declared Prudence. "I don't like bugs anyhow, and--why, the very pictures of them in the twins' books make me nervous. I won't do it. You can just tell him I don't feel qualified to go."

"You've got to go," said Fairy sternly, "for I said you would, and he's counting on it. He's going to phone you this afternoon and ask you himself. You've got to go."

At that instant, the telephone rang.

"There's professor!" cried Fairy. "You tell him you are just delighted to go, and that you are so interested in bugs!"

With a flushed face, Prudence took down the receiver. "Hello," she said, "this is the parsonage."

And then, a second later, she said, "Yes, this is Prudence."

After that she stood silent for some little time, with Fairy crouched beside her, trying to hear.

Then spoke Prudence. "Yes, Fairy has been telling me. And it's very kind of you, indeed, and I know I would enjoy it. But as I was telling Fairy, I don't know a thing about bugs, and I don't like them anyhow, so I'm afraid you would find me rather stupid."

Fairy was striving to get a hand over her sister's lips to stem the words, but Prudence eluded her. They were both somewhat astounded at the great peal of laughter which came over the telephone.

"Good! That's just what I was hoping for! You couldn't have said anything that would give me greater pleasure. Then shall I come around with Babler, for you and your sister, about one o'clock?--Oh, that is very kind of you, Miss Starr. Good-by! Don't cultivate an interest in bugs between now and to-morrow, for my sake!"

The girls looked at each other doubtfully when the receiver was once more on its hook.

"I'm afraid he's laughing at me," said Prudence questioningly.

"I should hope so," cried Fairy. "What in the world did you say that for? Couldn't you have pretended to be interested? Professor likes women to be dignified and intellectual and deep, and----"

"Then why on earth did he ask me to go?" demanded Prudence. "Any one could tell to look at me that I'm not dignified and intellectual and deep, and----"

"And I know he admired you, for he was so eager when he asked about you.

Think how grand it would be to speak of 'my sister, Mrs. Professor Rayburn,' and----"

"Don't be silly, Fairy. If I was going to marry anybody, which I am not, I hope you do not think for one minute that I'd marry a buggist! Gracious! Goodness! I've a notion not to go a step! I'll call him up and----"

But Fairy only laughed.

And after all, Prudence looked forward to the little outing in the glorious October woods with eager anticipation. It was seldom indeed that she indulged in merry-making away from the parsonage. Yet she was fond of gaiety. Long before one o'clock on that eventful day, she was ready. And her face was so bright, and her eyes so starry, that placid self-satisfied Fairy felt a twinge of something like envy.

"You look like a creature from another world, Prue," she said. "If Professor Rayburn has any sense in his bones, he will fall dead in love with you,--bugs or no bugs!"

"People do not have sense in their bones, Fairy, and--and--shall I say professor, or just plain Mister?"

"Professor, I suppose,--every one calls him professor."

"Then I shall say Mister," said Prudence. "It will be so hard to enjoy myself if I keep remembering that he teaches bugs! I might as well be at school. I shall say Mister."

And she did say "Mister," and she said it so sweetly, and looked up into Professor Rayburn's face so brightly, and with happiness so evident and so girlish, that the staid professor felt a quick unaccountable throbbing down somewhere beneath his coat. He did look eager! There was no doubt of it. And he looked at Prudence, continuously.

"Just like ordinary men, isn't he?" whispered Fairy to Eugene Babler,--called "Babbie," for short and for humiliation,--for he enjoyed the reputation of being a "talker" even among college men!

The three young couples struck off briskly down the road, creek-ward, and Prudence followed sedately with her professor.

"Fairy says it was perfectly disgusting of me to tell you I didn't know anything about bugs," she said comfortably. "But I thought maybe, you were one of those professors who like one thing so much they can't be interested in anything else.

And I wanted to warn you. But I guess you aren't that kind, after all?"

"Oh, no, indeed," he assured her fervently, looking deep into her blue eyes. "I like bugs, it is true. But really I like other things, one thing at least, much better."

"Is it a riddle?" she inquired. "Am I supposed to guess?"

"It isn't a riddle, but you may guess. Think hard, now! It's a serious matter. Please don't say 'food.'"

"If I get below seventy will I be put down a grade?" she asked. Then with intense solemnity, "I guess girls."

They laughed together, youthfully. "You are right," he said.

And with a sigh of relief, Prudence answered, "That's the first time I ever got a hundred in anything in my life. I was very much accustomed to eighties when I was in school. I am very common and unbrilliant," she assured him. "Fairy says you are perfectly horribly clever----"

She glanced up when she heard his exclamation, and laughed at his rueful face. "Oh, that isn't Fairy's expression. She thinks brilliant and clever people are just adorable. It is only I who think them horrible." Even Prudence could see that this did not help matters. "I--I do not mean that," she stammered. "I am sure you are very nice indeed, and we are going to be good friends, aren't we? But I am such a dunce myself that I am afraid of real clever people. They are so superior. And so uninteresting, and--oh, I do not mean that either." Then Prudence laughed at her predicament. "I may as well give it up. What I really mean is that you are so nice and friendly and interesting, that I can hardly believe you are so clever. You are the nicest smart person I ever saw,--except my own family, I mean." She smiled up at him deliciously. "Does that make it square?"

"More than square," he said. "You are too complimentary. But the only thing that really counts to-day is whether we are going to be real good friends, as you suggested. We are, aren't we? The very best and closest of friends?"

"Yes," agreed Prudence, dimpling. "I like men to be my friends,--nice men, I mean. But it isn't always safe. So many start out to be good friends, and then want to be silly. So a girl has to be very careful. But it's perfectly safe with you, and so we can be the very best of friends. I won't need to be watchful for bad symptoms."

"Do you think me so unmanly that I couldn't fall in love?" he asked, and his voice was curious, as though she had hurt him.

"Oh, of course, you'll fall in love," laughed Prudence. "All nice men do.--But not with me,--that was what I meant I couldn't imagine a buggy professor--oh, I beg your pardon! But the twins are so silly and disrespectful, and they thought it was such a joke that I should even look at a professor of biology that they began calling you the buggy professor. But they do not mean any harm by it, not the least in the world. They're such nice sweet girls, but--young, you know. Are your feelings hurt?" she asked anxiously.

"Not a bit! I think the twins and I will be tremendously good friends. I'm quite willing to be known as the buggy professor. But you were trying to explain why I couldn't fall in love with you. I suppose you mean that you do not want me to."

"Oh, not that at all," she hastened to assure him. Then she stopped. "Yes," she said honestly, "that is true, too. But that isn't what I was trying to say. I was just saying that no one realizes any more than I how perfectly impossible it would be for a clever, grown-up, brilliant professor to fall in love with such an idiot as I am. That's all. I meant it for a compliment," she added, seeing he was not well pleased.

He smiled, but it was a sober smile. "You said it was true that you did not wish me to be--fond of you. Why? Don't you like me then, after all?"

Now, he realized that this was a perfectly insane conversation, but for the life of him, he couldn't help it. Prudence was so alluring, and the sky was so warmly blue, the sunshine so mild and hazy, and the roadside so gloriously gay with colors! Who could have sense on such a day, with such a girl as this?

"Oh, I do like you very much indeed," declared Prudence. "It's a big relief, too, for I didn't expect to--oh, I beg your pardon again, but--well, I was scared when Fairy told me how remarkable you are. I didn't want to disgrace the parsonage, and I knew I would. But--why, the reason I do not want you to fall in love with me,--that's very different from being fond of me, I do want you to be that,--but when people fall in love, they get married. I'm not going to get married, so it would be silly to fall in love, wouldn't it?"

He laughed heartily at the matter-of-factness with which this nineteen-year-old girl disposed of love and marriage. "Why aren't you going to be married?" he inquired, foolishly happy, and showing more foolishness than happiness, just as we all do on such occasions.

"Well, it will be ten or eleven years before Connie is fairly raised."

"Yes, but you won't be a Methuselah, in eleven years," he smiled.

"No, but you forget father."

"Forget father! Are you raising him, too?"

"No, I'm not raising him, but I'm managing him." But when he laughed, she hastened to add, "That is, I take care of him, and keep house for him, and remind him of things he forgets." Then with girlish honesty, she added, "Though I must confess that he has to remind me of things I forget, oftener than I do him. I inherited my forgetfulness from father. I asked him once if he inherited his from grandfather, and he said he forgot whether grandfather was forgetful or not! Father is very clever. So's Fairy. And the twins are the smartest little things you ever saw,--and Connie, too. Connie is the oddest, keenest child. She's wonderful. They all are,--but me. It's kind of humiliating to be the only stupid one in a family of smart folks. I suppose you've no idea how it feels, and I can't explain it. But sometimes I think maybe I ought to go off and die, so the whole family can shine and sparkle together. As it is, there's just a dull glow from my corner, quite pale and ugly compared with the brilliant gleams the others are sending out."

Said Professor Rayburn, "Ah, Prudence, the faint, sweet mellow glows are always beautiful. Not sparkling, perhaps, not brilliant! But comforting, and cheering, and--always to be trusted. It's just these little corner-glows, like yours, that make life worth living."

This was rather deep for Prudence, but she felt instinctively that he was complimenting her. She thanked him sweetly, and said, "And after all, I do not really mind being the stupid one. I think it's rather fun, for then I can just live along comfortably, and people do not expect much of me. It would wear me all out to be as clever as Fairy, or as witty as Carol, or as studious as Lark. But I am most tremendously proud of them, I assure you."

If Professor Rayburn had continued along this interesting and fruitful line of conversation, all would have been well.

"But it came just like a clap of thunder in the sunshine," said Prudence to Fairy dramatically, as they sat in their room talking things over that night. "We were having a perfectly grand time, and I was just thinking he was as nice and interesting as if he didn't know one thing to his name, when--Crash! That's how it happened."

Fairy wiped her eyes, and lay back weakly on the bed. "Go on," she urged. "What happened?"

"He stopped right in the middle of a sentence about me, something real nice, too, that I was awfully interested in, and said, 'Look, Miss Starr!' Then he got down on his knees and began cautiously scraping away the sticks and leaves. Then he fished out the most horrible, woolly, many-legged little animal I ever saw in my life. He said it was a giminythoraticus billyancibus, and he was as tickled over it as though he had just picked up a million-dollar diamond. And what do you suppose the weird creature did with it? He wrapped it in a couple of leaves, and put his handkerchief around it and put it in his pocket!--Do you remember when we were eating by the creek, and I got jam on my fingers? He offered me his handkerchief to wipe it off? Do you remember how I shoved him away, and shuddered? I saw you look reprovingly at me! That's why! Do you suppose I could wipe my fingers with a handkerchief that had been in one of his pockets?"

"It wasn't the one that had the giminy billibus, was it?"

"No, but goodness only knows what had been in this one,--an alligator, maybe, or a snake. He's very fond of snakes. He says some of them are so useful. I try to be charitable, Fairy, and I believe I would give even Satan credit for any good there was in him,--but it is too much to ask me to be fond of a man who is fond of snakes. But that is not the worst. He put the giminy thing in his pocket,--his left pocket! Then he came on walking with me, on my right side. On my right side, Fairy, do you understand what that means? It means that the giminy billibus, as you call it-- oh, I wouldn't swear to the name, Fairy, I do not claim to be smart, but I know how it looked! Well, anyhow, name and all, it was on the side next to me. I stopped to look at a little stick, and switched around on the other side. Then he stooped to look at a bunch of dirt, and got on the wrong side again. Then I stopped, and then he did, and so we kept zig-zagging down the road. A body would have thought we were drunk, I suppose. Four times that man stopped to pick up some wriggling little animal, and four times he deposited his treasure in one of his various pockets. Don't ask why it is impossible for me to be friends with such a being,--spare me that humiliation!"

But the fair daughter of the parsonage proved irresistibly attractive to the unfortunate professor, and he was not to be lightly shunted aside. He forsook the Presbyterian church, of which he was a member, and attended the Methodist meetings with commendable assiduity. After each service, he accompanied Prudence home, and never failed to accept her invitations, feebly given, to "come in a minute." He called as often during the week as Propriety, in the voice of Prudence, deemed fitting. It was wholly unnatural for Prudence to cater to Propriety, but Professor Rayburn did not know this. Weeks passed, a month slipped away, and another. Professor Rayburn was considered a fixture in the parsonage household by all except Prudence herself, who chafed under her bondage.

"I can't just blurt out that I think he's a nuisance," she mourned to Fairy. "Oh, if he'd just do something disgusting so I could fire him off,--Pop! Just like that. Wouldn't it be glorious?"

But the professor did not indulge in disgusting things, and Prudence continued to worry and fret. Then came a blessed evening when the minister and Fairy were away from home, and the twins and Connie were safely in their beds. Professor Rayburn sat with Prudence in the cozy living-room, and Prudence was charming, though quiet, and the professor was only human. Prudence had made tea, and as she rose to relieve him of his empty cup, he also rose to return it to the table. Laughing, they put it down on the tray, each holding one side of the saucer. Then when it was safely disposed of, Prudence turned toward him, still laughing at the silliness of it,--very alluring, very winsome. And Mr. Rayburn, unexpectedly to himself as to her, put his arms around her and kissed her. He was aghast at himself, once it was over, and Prudence,--well, let us say frankly that Prudence was only relieved, for it came to her in a flash that this was the "disgusting thing" for which she had so fervently longed.

"Mr. Rayburn!"

"That was very stupid and unpardonable of me, Prudence," he said quickly, "I really did not think what I was doing. But you were so sweet, and--I'm awfully fond of you, Prudence, you know that."

Prudence looked at him thoughtfully. She felt that this hardly gave her the desired opening. So she waited, hoping he would commit himself further. More humbled by her unnatural silence, he did go on.

"You know, Prudence, when a man cares for a girl as I care for you, it isn't always easy for him to be sober and sensible. You shouldn't have been so--so dear."

Prudence sighed happily. She was content. This gave her the long-desired cue.

"Mr. Rayburn," she said gently but decidedly, "I think you ought not to come here any more."

He walked over to her quickly, and stood beside the chair into which she had dropped when he kissed her.

"Don't say that, Prudence," he said in a hurried low voice.

"It is true," she persisted, feeling somehow sorry, though she did not understand why she should feel so. "I--I--well, you know I--you remember what I told you that first day, don't you? About getting married, and falling in love, and such things. It is true. I don't want to love anybody, and I don't want to get married, and Fairy says--it is--remotely possible--that you might get--very fond of me."

He smiled rather grimly. "Yes, I think it is--remotely possible."

"Then that settles it," she said comfortably. "And besides, I have such a lot to do that I can't--well, bother--spending so much time outside as I have with you. I've been neglecting my work, and it isn't right. I haven't the time."

"Which is your way of saying that you do not like me, isn't it?"

Prudence stood up impulsively. "Oh, I like you, but--" she threw out her hands expressively. He took them in his, tenderly, firmly.

"But, Prudence," he argued, "that is because the woman in you isn't awake. You may never love me--a dismal possibility, but it is true. But don't you think it only fair that you should give me a chance to try?"

"Oh, but that's just the point," she cried. "I do not want you to try. I do not want to run any risk, at all. I wouldn't marry you if I did love you--I told you that right in the beginning."

He still held her hands in one of his, caressing them slowly with the other. "What is there about me that you do not like?" he demanded suddenly. "There is something, I know."

And with her awful unbelievable honesty. Prudence told him. "Yes," she said, "that is true. I hated to mention it, but there is something! Mr. Rayburn, I just can't stand the bugs!"

"Good heavens! The what?"

"The bugs! I can't bear for you to be near me, because I keep wondering if there are bugs and things in your pocket. I'm afraid they'll get over on me. Even now it makes me shiver when you hold my hands, because I know you've been handling the horrible little creatures with yours." He dropped her hands abruptly, and stared at her. "And after you leave, I get down on my hands and knees and look over the floor, and examine the chairs, to see if any have crawled off! It's a terrible feeling, Mr. Rayburn. You know I told you I hated bugs.--I'm afraid I've hurt your feelings," she said sadly.

"Where in the world did you get such an idea as that?" he demanded rather angrily. "Do you think I have pet bugs to carry around with me for company?"

"No,--but don't you remember the picnic,--and how you kept gathering them up in your handkerchiefs and putting them in your pockets? And how I kept squirming around to get on the other side,--I was trying to get away from the bugs!"

"But, my heavens, Prudence, those were my field clothes. I don't put bugs in these pockets,--these are my Sunday togs!" He smiled a little. "And I always wash my hands, you know." He found it humorous, and yet it hurt him. Such a little thing to prejudice a girl so strongly,--and one he liked so marvelously well!

"You might forget, and put them in these pockets,--it's a kind of habit with you, I suppose. And just plain washing won't take the idea of bugs off your hands."

"Prudence, you are only a girl,--a childish girl, but a very sweet one. I want you to like me. When you grow up, you are going to be a wonderfully good and lovely woman. I--I am going to want you then. I know it. Let's just be friends now, can't we--until later--for a long time yet? I'll promise on my word of honor never to put another bug in my pockets, or my handkerchiefs. But I can't promise not to touch them, for I have to do it in class. That's how I earn my living! But I will wash my hands with Ivory soap and sapolio, and rub them with cold cream, and powder them, and perfume them, before I ever come near you again. Won't that do?"

Prudence shook her head. "I know you are laughing at me," she said, "but I always told you I was just a silly simpleton. And--it isn't the bugs altogether. I--I like it better to be with my sisters than----"

"Than with me? I see. As I said, the woman of you is still sleeping. Well, we are young, and I will wait. I won't bother you any more for a long time, Prudence, but I shan't forget you. And some day I will come back to you again." He stared at her moodily. Then he put his hands beneath her elbows, and looked into her eyes searchingly. "You are a strange girl, Prudence. In some ways, you are so womanly, and in other ways so--pitifully girlish! All the woman in your heart seems to be given to your sisters and your father, and-- But you will waken, and I won't hurry you." Then he put his arms around her again, and whispered in her ear, "But I love you, Prudence, and--if some one else should do the awakening--it would hurt!" Then he kissed her, and went away.

But Prudence ran up-stairs, singing happily. "Oh, I feel like a caged-up bird that has broken loose," she cried to her reflection in the mirror jubilantly. "Oh, what fun it will be to come home from church with Fairy and the twins, the way I used to do!"

CHAPTER VII
LESSONS IN ETIQUETTE

Connie was lying flat on her back near the register. The twins were sitting on the floor near her, hearing each other conjugate Latin verbs. And Prudence, with her darning basket, was earnestly trying to solve a domestic problem,--how to get three pairs of wearable stockings out of eleven hosiery remnants. So Fairy found them as she came in, radiant and glowing.

"Glorious day," she said, glancing impartially at her sisters. "Just glorious! Why are you all hugging the register, may I ask? It is perfect weather. Connie, you should be out-of-doors this minute, by all means. Twins, aren't you grown-up enough to sit on chairs, or won't your footies reach the floor?--Babbie, Eugene Babler, you know, is coming to spend the evening, Prudence."

"What is going on to-night?" queried Prudence.

"Nothing is going on. That's why he is coming. It's too cold to meander around outdoors these nights, and so we shall have to amuse ourselves inside as best we can."

The whole family came to attention at this.

"Oh, goody!" cried Connie. "Let's make taffy, shall we, Fairy?"

"Certainly not. This isn't a children's party. You'll go to bed at eight o'clock as usual, Connie mine.--Now, we must have something to eat. The question is, What shall it be?"

"Yes," agreed Carol with enthusiasm,--Carol was always enthusiastic on the subject of something to eat. "Yes, indeed, that is the question. What shall we have?"

"You will likely have pleasant dreams, Carol," was the cool retort. "Babbie did not invite himself to spend the evening with you, I believe."

"Do you mean to suggest," demanded Lark with withering scorn, "that it is your intention to shut yourself up alone with this--this creature, excluding the rest of us?"

"Yes, and have refreshments for just you two?" cried Carol.

"That is my intention most certainly. The twins and Connie will not put in appearance at all. Prue will serve the refreshments, and will eat with us. Babbie and I shall spend the evening in the front room."

"The front room?" echoed Prudence. "This room is much cheerier, and more homelike."

"Well, Babbie isn't a member of the family, you know," said Fairy.

"You are doing your best," sniffed Carol.

"Now, you girls must understand right off, that things are different here from what they were at Exminster. When boys came to the house there they came to have a good time with the whole family. But here it is very different. I've been looking around, and I've got on to the system. The proper thing is to receive callers privately, without the family en masse sitting by and superintending. That's etiquette, you know. And one must always serve refreshments. More etiquette. Men are such greedy animals, they do not care to go places where the eats aren't forthcoming."

"Men! Are you referring to this Babbling creature now?" interposed Carol.

"Ouch!" said Lark.

"But won't it be rather--poky--just sitting in the front room by yourselves all evening?" asked Prudence doubtfully, ignoring the offended twins.

"Oh, I dare say it will. But it's the proper thing to do," said Fairy complacently.

"What are you going to do all evening?" Connie wanted to know. "Just sit and look at each other and admire yourselves?"

The twins thought this very clever of Connie, so they both said "Ouch!" approvingly.

"Why, no, baby dear," said Fairy good-naturedly. "We shall talk. Feast our souls with a flow of reason, you know. We shall converse. We shall hold pleasant intercourse."

"Wouldn't it be more fun to have the girls in for a little while?" This from Prudence.

"Oh, it might,--but it wouldn't be the proper thing at all. College men do not care to be entertained by babies."

"No," snapped Lark, "the wisdom of babies is too deep for these--these--these men in embryo."

This was so exquisitely said that Lark was quite restored to amiability by it. "In embryo," had been added to her vocabulary that very day in the biology class. It was only the sheerest good fortune which gave her the opportunity of utilizing it so soon. And Carol said "Ouch!" with such whole-souled admiration that Lark's spirit soared among the clouds. She had scored!

"And what shall we serve them?" urged Prudence. "I suppose it would hardly do to--pop corn, would it?"

"No, indeed. Popping corn is very nice for the twins and the little boys in the neighborhood." Fairy smiled with relish as she saw the twins wince at this thrust. "But Babbie and I-- Oh, never! It wouldn't do at all. Now, oyster stew and crackers,--I mean wafers,----"

"Oysters are fearfully expensive, Fairy," objected the frugal Prudence.

"Oh, we can stand it for once," said Fairy easily. "This is the first time, and we must do something extra. Babbie is all the rage at school, and the girls are frantic with jealousy because I have cut everybody else out. To be honest about it, I can't understand it myself. Babbie's such a giddy scatter-brained youngster, you'd think he'd prefer----"

"Do you like him, Fairy? Don't you think he's tiresome? He talks so much, it seems to me."

"To be sure I like him. He's great fun. He's always joking and never has a sensible thought, and hates study. He's an amusing soul, I must say. He's going to attend here a couple of years, and then study pharmacy. His father is a druggist in Ottumwa, and quite well off. The only reason Babbie came here instead of going to a big college in the East is because his father is a trustee. Trustees are in honor bound to send their offspring to the college they trustee,--just as ministers are obliged to trade with the members when possible."

"Even if they short-weight and long-charge you," put in Carol.

"Carol!" exclaimed Prudence reprovingly. "Well, we'll serve oyster stew then.

Will you eat in the dining-room?"

"No, we'll eat on the little table in the front room,--informally, you know. You must get it ready, and arrange it nicely on the big tray. Then you must come to the door and say, 'Wouldn't you like a little oyster stew?' Say it carelessly, as if we always have something to eat before going to bed. And I'll say, 'Oh, yes, Prudence, bring it right in.' Then you bring it in, and we'll all eat together.--That's the way to do it! Babbie's had dates with the very swellest girls in school, and he knows about such things. We must do it up brown!"

"Swell!" mocked Lark. "Do it up brown! Oh, you'll be a record-breaker of a college professor all right. I'm sure this young Babler is just the type of man to interest the modern college professor! Swell! Do it up brown!"

"Ouch!" grinned Carol.

"Now, will you twins run down-town for the oysters?" asked Prudence briskly.

"Who? Us?" demanded Lark, indignantly and ungrammatically. "Do you think we can carry home oysters for the--the--personal consumption of this Babbling young prince? Not so! Let Fairy go after the oysters! She can carry them home tenderly and appreciatively. Carol and I can't! We don't grasp the beauty of that man's nature."

"Oh, yes, twinnies, I think you'll go, all right. Hurry now, for you must be back in time to help me get supper. Fairy'll have to straighten the front room, and we won't have time. Run along, and be quick."

For a few seconds the twins gazed at each other studiously. Neither spoke. Without a word, they went up-stairs to prepare for their errand.

They whispered softly going through the upper hall.

"We'd better make a list," said Carol softly.

So with heads close together they wrote out several items on a piece of paper.

"It'll cost quite a lot," objected Carol. "Thirty cents, anyhow. And Prudence'll make us pay for the oysters, sure. Remember that."

"We'd better let Connie in, too," suggested Lark.

Connie was hastily summoned, and the twins whispered explanations in her willing ears. "Good!" she said approvingly. "It'll serve 'em right."

"But it'll cost money," said Carol. "How much have you got?"

Then Connie understood why she had been consulted. The twins always invited her to join their enterprises when money was required.

"A quarter," she faltered.

"Well, we'll go shares," said Lark generously. "We'll pay a dime apiece. It may not take that much. But if Prudence makes us pay for the oysters, you'll have to pay a third. Will you do that?"

"Yes, indeed." Connie was relieved. She did not always get off so easily!

"Twins! You must hurry!" This was Prudence at the bottom of the stairs. And the twins set off quite hurriedly. Their first tall was at the meat market.

"A pint of oysters," said Lark briefly.

When he brought them to her, she smelled them suspiciously. Then Carol smelled.

"Are these rotten oysters?" she demanded hopefully.

"No," he answered, laughing. "Certainly not."

"Have you got any rotten ones?"

"No, we don't keep that kind." He was still laughing.

The twins sighed and hurried next door to the grocer's.

"A nickel's worth of pepper--the strongest you have."

This was quickly settled--and the grave-faced twins betook themselves to the corner drug store.

"We--we want something with a perfectly awful smell," Lark explained soberly.

"What kind of a smell?"

"We don't care what kind, but it must be perfectly sickening. Like something rotten, or dead, if you have it. Something that will stay smelly for several hours,--but it mustn't be dangerous, of course."

"What do you want it for?"

"We want it to put in a room to give it a horrible smell for an hour or so." Lark winked at him solemnly. "It's a joke," she further elucidated.

"I see." His eyes twinkled. "I think I can fix you up." A moment later he handed her a small bottle. "Just sprinkle this over the carpet. It won't do any harm, and it smells like thunder. It costs a quarter."

Carol frowned. "I suppose we'll have to take it," she said, "but it's pretty expensive. I hate to have druggists get such a lot of money."

He laughed aloud. "I hate to have you get a good licking to-morrow, too,--but you'll get it just the same, or I miss my guess."

When the twins arrived home, Fairy was just cutting the candy she had made. "It's delicious," she said to Prudence. "Here's a nice dishful for you and the girls.--Pitch in, twins, and help yourselves. It's very nice."

The twins waved her haughtily away. "No, thank you," they said. "We couldn't eat that candy with relish. We are unworthy."

"All right," Prudence put in quickly, as Fairy only laughed. "I'll put it in the cupboard, and Fairy and I will eat it to-morrow. It's perfectly fine,--simply delicious."

But the twins were not to be tempted. Before they went up-stairs, Lark inquired sarcastically:

"I suppose, Fairy, you'll don your best blue silk in honor of this event?"

"Oh, no," was the ready answer, "I'll just wear my little green muslin. It's old, but very nice and comfortable--just right for an evening at home."

"Yes," scoffed Carol, "and of course you are remembering that every one says it is the most becoming dress you have."

"Oh, yes," laughed Fairy, "I'm remembering that, all right."

Then the twins went up-stairs, but not to their own room at once. Instead they slipped noiselessly into the front bedroom, and a little later Carol came out into the hall and stood listening at the head of the stairs, as though on guard.

"Be sure and leave quite a few stitches in, Lark," she whispered once. "We want it to hang together until Babbie gets here."

That was all. Presently Lark emerged, and their own door closed behind them.

"It's a good thing father has to go to the trustees' meeting to-night, isn't it?" asked Carol. And Lark agreed, absently. She was thinking of the oysters.

As soon as they finished supper, Lark said, "Don't you think we'd better go right to bed, Prue? We don't want to taint the atmosphere of the parsonage. Of course, Fairy will want to wash the dishes herself to make sure they are clean and shining."

"Oh, no," disclaimed Fairy, still good-naturedly. "I can give an extra rub to the ones we want to use,--that is enough. I do appreciate the thought, though, thanks very much.”

So the twins plunged in, carefully keeping Connie beside them. “She has such a full-to-overflowing look,” said Carol. “If we don’t keep hold of her, she’ll let something bubble over.” Connie had a dismal propensity for giving things away,--the twins had often suffered from it. To-night, they were determined to forestall such a calamity.

Then they all three went to bed. To be sure it was ridiculously early, but they were all determined.

“We feel weak under this unusual strain. Our nerves can’t stand the tension. We really must retire to rest. Maybe a good night’s sleep will restore us to normal,” Lark explained gravely.

Fairy only laughed. “Good!” she cried. “Do go to bed. The only time I am sure of you is when you are in your beds. Do you mind if I tie you in, to make assurance doubly sure?”

But the twins and Connie had disappeared.

“You keep your eyes open, Fairy,” Prudence whispered melodramatically. “Those girls do not look right. Something is hanging over our heads.” And she added anxiously, “Oh, I’ll be so disappointed if things go badly. This is the first time we’ve ever lived up to etiquette, and I feel it is really a crisis.”

Fairy was a little late getting up-stairs to dress, but she took time to drop into her sisters’ room. They were all in bed, breathing heavily. She walked from one to another, and stood above them majestically.

“Asleep!” she cried. “Ah, Fortune is kind. They are asleep. How I love these darling little twinnies,--in their sleep!”

An audible sniff from beneath the covers, and Fairy, smiling mischievously, went into the front room to prepare for her caller.

The bell rang as she was dressing. Prudence went to the door, preternaturally ceremonious, and ushered Mr. Babler into the front room. She turned on the electric switch as she opened the door. She was too much impressed with the solemnity of the occasion to take much note of her surroundings, and she did not observe that the young man sniffed in a peculiar manner as he entered the room.

“I’ll call Fairy,” she said demurely.

"Tell her she needn't primp for me," he answered, laughing. "I know just how she looks already."

But Prudence was too heavily burdened to laugh. She smiled hospitably, and closed the door upon him. Fairy was tripping down the stairs, very tall, very handsome, very gay. She pinched her sister's arm as she passed, and the front room door swung behind. But she did not greet her friend. She stood erect by the door, her head tilted on one side, sniffing, sniffing.

"What in the world?" she wondered. Then she blushed. Perhaps it was something he had used on his hair! Or perhaps he had been having his suit cleaned! "Oh, I guess it's nothing, after all," she stammered. But Eugene Babler was strangely quiet. He looked about the room in a peculiar questioning way.

"Shall I raise a window?" he suggested finally. "It's rather--er--hot in here."

"Yes, do," she urged. "Raise all of them. It's--do you--do you notice a--a funny smell in here? Or am I imagining it? It--it almost makes me sick!"

"Yes, there is a smell," he said, in evident relief. "I thought maybe you'd been cleaning the carpet with something. It's ghastly. Can't we go somewhere else?"

"Come on." She opened the door into the sitting-room. "We're coming out here if you do not mind, Prue." And Fairy explained the difficulty.

"Why, that's very strange," said Prudence, knitting her brows. "I was in there right after supper, and I didn't notice anything. What does it smell like?"

"It's a new smell to me," laughed Fairy, "but something about it is strangely suggestive of our angel-twins."

Prudence went to investigate, and Fairy shoved a big chair near the table, waving her hand toward it lightly with a smile at Babbie. Then she sank into a low rocker, and leaned one arm on the table. She wrinkled her forehead thoughtfully.

"That smell," she began. "I am very suspicious about it. It was not at all natural----"

"Excuse me, Fairy," he said, ill at ease for the first time in her knowledge of him. "Did you know your sleeve was coming out?"

Fairy gasped, and raised her arm.

"Both arms, apparently," he continued, smiling, but his face was flushed.

"Excuse me just a minute, will you?" Fairy was unruffled. She sought her sister. "Look here, Prue,--what do you make of this? I'm coming to pieces! I'm hanging by a single thread, as it were."

Her sleeves were undoubtedly ready to drop off at a second's notice! Prudence was shocked. She grew positively white in the face.

"Oh, Fairy," she wailed. "We are disgraced."

"Not a bit of it," said Fairy coolly. "I remember now that Lark was looking for the scissors before supper. Aren't those twins unique? This is almost bordering on talent, isn't it? Don't look so distressed, Prue. Etiquette itself must be subservient to twins, it seems. Don't forget to bring in the stew at a quarter past nine, and have it as good as possible,--please, dear."

"I will," vowed Prudence, "I'll--I'll use cream. Oh, those horrible twins!"

"Go in and entertain Babbie till I come down, won't you?" And Fairy ran lightly up the stairs, humming a snatch of song.

But Prudence did a poor job of entertaining Babbie during her sister's absence. She felt really dizzy! Such a way to introduce Etiquette into the parsonage life. She was glad to make her escape from the room when Fairy returned, a graceful figure in the fine blue silk! She went back to the dining-room, and painstakingly arranged the big tray for the designated moment of its entrance,--according to etiquette. Fairy and Babbie in the next room talked incessantly, laughing often and long, and Prudence, hearing, smiled in sympathy. She herself thought it would be altogether stupid to be shut up in a room alone with "just a man" for a whole evening,--but etiquette required it. Fairy knew about such things, of course.

A little after nine, she called out dismally, "Fairy!" And Fairy, fearing fresh disaster, came running out.

"What now? What----"

"I forget what you told me to say," whispered Prudence wretchedly, "what was it? The soup is ready, and piping hot,--but what is it you want me to say?"

Fairy screamed with laughter. "You goose!" she cried. "Say anything you like. I was just giving you a tip, that was all. It doesn't make any difference what you say."

"Oh, I am determined to do my part just right," vowed Prudence fervently, "according to etiquette and all. What was it you said?"

Fairy stifled her laughter with difficulty, and said in a low voice, "Wouldn't you like a little nice, hot, oyster stew?" Prudence repeated it after her breathlessly.

So Fairy returned once more, and soon after Prudence tapped on the door. Then she opened it, and thrust her curly head inside. "Wouldn't you like a little nice, hot, oyster stew?" she chirped methodically. And Fairy said, "Oh, yes indeed, Prudence,--this is so nice of you."

The stew was steaming hot, and the three gathered sociably about the table. Prudence was talking. Fairy was passing the "crackers,"--Prudence kicked her foot gently beneath the table, to remind her that etiquette calls them "wafers." So it happened that Babbie was first to taste the steaming stew. He gasped, and gulped, and swallowed some water with more haste than grace. Then he toyed idly with spoon and wafer until Prudence tasted also. Prudence did not gasp. She did not cry out. She looked up at her sister with wide hurt eyes,--a world of pathos in the glance. But Fairy did not notice.

"Now, please do not ask me to talk until I have finished my soup," she was saying brightly, "I simply can not think and appreciate oyster stew at the same time."

Then she appreciated it! She dropped her spoon with a great clatter, and jumped up from the table. "Mercy!" she shrieked. "It is poisoned!"

Babbie leaned back in his chair and laughed until his eyes were wet. Prudence's eyes were wet, too, but not from laughter! What would etiquette think of her, after this?

"What did you do to this soup, Prudence?" demanded Fairy.

"I made it,--nothing else," faltered poor Prudence, quite crushed by this blow. And oysters forty cents a pint!

"It's pepper, I think," gasped Babbie. "My insides bear startling testimony to the presence of pepper."

And he roared again, while Prudence began a critical examination of the oysters. She found them literally stuffed with pepper, there was no doubt of it. The twins had done deadly work! Their patience, at least, was commendable,--it seemed that not one oyster had escaped their attention. The entire pint had been ruined by the pepper.

"Revenge, ye gods, how sweet," chanted Fairy. "The twins are getting even with a vengeance,--the same twins you said were adorable, Babbie." It must be said for Fairy that her good nature could stand almost anything. Even this did not seriously disturb her. "Do you suppose you can find us some milk, Prue? And crackers!

I'm so fond of crackers and milk, aren't you, Babbie?"

"Oh, I adore it. But serve a microscope with it, please. I want to examine it for microbes before I taste."

But Prudence did better than that. She made some delicious cocoa, and opened a can of pear preserves, donated to the parsonage by the amiable Mrs. Adams. The twins were very fond of pear preserves, and had been looking forward to eating these on their approaching birthday. They were doomed to disappointment! The three had a merry little feast, after all, and their laughter rang out so often and so unrestrainedly that the twins shook in their beds with rage and disappointment.

Mr. Starr came in while they were eating, and joined them genially. But afterward, when Prudence realized that etiquette called for their retirement, her father still sat complacently by the register, talking and laughing. Prudence fastened her eyes upon him.

"Well, I must honestly go to bed," she said, gazing hypnotically at her father. "I know you will excuse me. I must store up my strength to deal with the twins in the morning."

She got up from her chair, and moved restlessly about the room, still boring her father with her eyes. He did not move. She paused beside him, and slipped her hand under his elbow.

"Now, father," she said gaily, "we must put our heads together, and think out a proper punishment for the awful creatures."

Her hand was uplifting, and Mr. Starr rose with it. Together they left the room with cordial good nights, and inviting Mr. Babler to "try the parsonage again." Prudence listened outside the twins' door, and heard them breathing loudly. Then she went to her own room, and snuggling down beneath the covers, laughed softly to herself.

"Etiquette!" she gurgled. "Etiquette! There's no room for such a thing in a parsonage,--I see that!"

It speaks well for the courage of Babbie, and the attractions of Fairy, that he came to the parsonage again and again. In time he became the best of friends with the twins themselves, but he always called them "the adorables," and they never asked him why. The punishment inflicted upon them by Prudence rankled in their memories for many months. Indeed, upon that occasion, Prudence fairly surpassed herself in the ingenuity she displayed. The twins considered themselves very near-ly as grown-up as Fairy, and the fact that she was a young lady, and they were chil-dren, filled their hearts with bitterness. They never lost an opportunity of showing their independence where she was concerned. And with marvelous insight, Pru-dence used Fairy as her weapon of punishment,--in fact, the twins called Fairy the "ducking-stool" for many days.

"The offense was against Fairy," said Prudence, with a solemnity she did not feel, "and the reparation must be done to her. For three weeks, you must do all of her bedroom work, and run every errand she requires. Moreover, you must keep her shoes well cleaned and nicely polished, and must do every bit of her darning!"

The twins would have preferred whipping a thousand times. They felt they had got a whipping's worth of pleasure out of their mischief! But a punishment like this sat heavily upon their proud young shoulders, and from that time on they held Fairy practically immune from their pranks.

But Prudence did not bother her head about etiquette after that experience. "I'm strong for comfort," she declared, "and since the two can not live together in our family, I say we do without etiquette."

And Fairy nodded in agreement, smiling good-naturedly.

CHAPTER VIII
THE FIRST DARK SHADOW OF WINTER

Prudence and Fairy stood in the bay window of the sitting-room, and looked out at the thickly falling snow. Already the ground was whitely carpeted, and the low-branched peach trees just outside the parsonage windows were beginning to bow down beneath their burdens.

"Isn't it beautiful, Prudence?" whispered Fairy. "Isn't it beautiful? Oh, I love it when it snows."

"Yes, and you love it when the sun shines, too," said Prudence, "and when it rains, and when the wind is blowing. You have the soul of a poet, that's what is the matter with you. You are a nature-fiend, as Carol would say."

Fairy turned abruptly from the window. "Don't talk for a minute, Prue,--I want to write."

So Prudence stood quietly in the window, listening to the pencil scratching behind her.

"Listen now, Prue,--how is this?" Fairy had a clear expressive voice, "a bright voice," Prudence called it. And as she read her simple lines aloud, the heart of Prudence swelled with pride. To Prudence, Fairy was a wonderful girl.

"Good night, little baby earth, going to sleep, Tucked in your blankets, all woolly and deep. Close your tired eyelids, droop your tired head, Nestle down sweetly within your white bed. Kind Mother Sky, bending softly above, Is holding you close in her bosom of love. Closely she draws the white coverlets warm, She will be near you to shield you from harm. Soon she will set all her candles alight, To scatter the darkness, and save you from fright. Then she will leave her cloud-doorway ajar, To watch you, that nothing your slumbers may mar. Rest, little baby earth, rest and sleep tight, The winter has come, and we bid you good night."

Fairy laughed, but her face was flushed. "How is that?" she demanded.

"Oh, Fairy," cried Prudence, "it is wonderful! How can you think of such sweet little things? May I have it? May I keep it? Oh, I think it is perfectly dear--I wish I could do that! I never in the world would have thought of baby earth going to sleep and Mother Sky tucking her in white blankets.--I think you are just wonderful, Fairy!"

Fairy's eyes were bright at the praise, but she laughed as she answered. "You always think me and my scribbles perfection, Prue,--even the love verses that shocked the Ladies' Aid. You are a bad critic. But doesn't the snow make you think--pretty things, Prudence? Come now, as you stood at the window there, what were you thinking?"

"I was just wondering if Connie wore her rubbers to school, and if father remembered to take his muffler."

Fairy burst into renewed laughter. "Oh, you precious, old, practical Prudence," she gurgled. "Rubbers and mufflers, with such a delicious snowfall as this! Oh, Prudence, shame upon you."

Prudence was ashamed. "Oh, I know I am a perfect idiot, Fairy," she said. "I know it better than anybody else. I am so ashamed of myself, all the time." Then she added rather shyly, "Fairy, are you ashamed of me sometimes? When the college girls are here, and you are all talking so brilliantly, aren't you kind of mortified that I am so stupid and dull? I do not care if outsiders do think I am inferior to the rest of you, but--really I do not want you to be ashamed of me! I--oh, I know it myself,--that I do not amount to anything, and never will, but--it would hurt if I thought you and the twins were going to find me--humiliating." Prudence was looking at her sister hungrily, her lips drooping, her eyes dark.

For a long instant Fairy stared at her incredulously. Then she sprang to her feet, her face white, her eyes blazing.

"Prudence Starr," she cried furiously, "how dare you say such things of us? Do you think we are as despicable as all that? Oh, Prudence, I never was so insulted in all my life! Ashamed of you! Ashamed--Why, we are proud of you, every one of us, daddy, too! We think you are the finest and dearest girl that ever lived. We think--Oh, I think God Himself must be proud of a girl like you, Prudence Starr!

Ashamed of you!"

And Fairy, bursting into tears, rushed wildly out of the room. For all her po-etical nature, Fairy was usually self-restrained and calm. Only twice before in all her life had Prudence seen her so tempest-tossed, and now, greatly disturbed, yet pleased at the passionate avowals, she hurried away in search of her sister. She needed no more assurance of her attitude.

So the twins and Connie came into an empty room, and chattered away to themselves abstractedly for an hour. Then Prudence came down. Instantly Connie was asked the all-important question:

"Are your feet wet?"

Connie solemnly took three steps across the room. "Hear me sqush," she said proudly. She did sqush, too!

"Constance Starr, I am ashamed of you! This is positively wicked. You know it is a law of the Medes and Persians that you change your shoes and stockings as soon as you come in when your feet are wet. Do it at once. I'll get some hot water so you can soak your feet, too. And you shall drink some good hot peppermint tea, into the bargain. I'll teach you to sit around in wet clothes! Do you think I want an invalid on my hands?"

"Oh, don't be so fussy," said Connie fretfully, "wet feet don't do any harm." But she obligingly soaked her feet, and drank the peppermint.

"Are your feet wet, twins?"

"No," said Lark, "we have better judgment than to go splashing through the wet old snow.--What's the matter with you, Carol? Why don't you sit still? Are your feet wet?"

"No, but it's too hot in this room. My clothes feel sticky. May I open the door, Prudence?"

"Mercy, no! The snow is blowing a hurricane now. It isn't very hot in here, Carol. You've been running outdoors in the cold, and that makes it seem hot. You must peel the potatoes now, twins, it's time to get supper. Carol, you run up-stairs and ask papa if he got his feet wet. Between him and Connie, I do not have a min-ute's peace in the winter time!"

"You go, Lark," said Carol. "My head aches."

"Do you want me to rub it?" asked Prudence, as Lark skipped up-stairs for her twin.

"No, it's just the closeness in here. It doesn't ache very bad. If we don't have more fresh air, we'll all get something and die, Prudence.--I tell you that. This room is perfectly stuffy.--I do not want to talk any more." And Carol got up from her chair and walked restlessly about the room.

But Carol was sometimes given to moods, and so, without concern, Prudence went to the kitchen to prepare the evening meal.

"Papa says his feet are not wet, and that you are a big simpleton, and--Oh, did you make cinnamon rolls to-day, Prue? Oh, goody! Carrie, come on out! Look,-- she made cinnamon rolls."

Connie, too, hastened out to the kitchen in her bare feet, and was promptly driven back by the watchful Prudence.

"I just know you are going to be sick, Connie,--I feel it in my bones. And walking out in that cold kitchen in your bare feet! You can just drink some more peppermint tea for that, now."

"Well, give me a cinnamon roll to go with it," urged Connie. "Peppermint is awfully dry, taken by itself."

Lark hooted gaily at this sentiment, but joined her sister in pleading for cinnamon rolls.

"No, wait until supper is ready. You do not need to help peel the potatoes to-night, Carol. Run back where it is warm, and you must not read if your head aches. You read too much anyhow. I'll help Lark with the potatoes. No, do not take the paper, Carol,--I said you must not read."

Then Lark and Prudence, working together, and talking much, prepared the supper for the family. When they gathered about the table, Prudence looked critically at Connie.

"Are you beginning to feel sick? Do you feel like sneezing, or any thing?-- Connie's awfully naughty, papa. Her feet were just oozing water, and she sat there in her wet shoes and stockings, just like a stupid child.--Aren't you going to eat any supper, Carol? Are you sick? What is the matter? Does your head still ache?"

"Oh, it doesn't ache exactly, but I do not feel hungry. No, I am not sick, Prudence, so don't stew about it. I'm just not hungry. The meat is too greasy, and the potatoes are lumpy. I think I'll take a cinnamon roll." But she only picked it to pieces idly. Prudence watched her with the intense suspicious gaze of a frightened mother bird.

"There are some canned oysters out there, Carol. If I make you some soup, will you eat it?"

This was a great concession, for the canned oysters were kept in anticipation of unexpected company. But Carol shook her head impatiently. "I am not hungry at all," she said.

"I'll open some pineapple, or those beautiful pickled peaches Mrs. Adams gave us, or--or anything, if you'll just eat something, Carrie."

Still Carol shook her head. "I said I wasn't hungry, Prudence." But her face was growing very red, and her eyes were strangely bright. She moved her hands with unnatural restless motions, and frequently lifted her shoulders in a peculiar manner.

"Do your shoulders hurt, Carol?" asked her father, who was also watching her anxiously.

"Oh, it feels kind of--well--tight, I guess, in my chest. But it doesn't hurt. It hurts a little when I breathe deep."

"Is your throat still sore, Carol?" inquired Lark. "Don't you remember saying you couldn't swallow when we were coming home from school?"

"It isn't sore now," said Carol. And as though intolerant of further questioning, she left the dining-room quickly.

"Shall I put flannel on her chest and throat, father?" asked Prudence nervously.

"Yes, and if she gets worse we will call the doctor. It's probably just a cold, but we must----"

"It isn't diphtheria, papa, you know that," cried Prudence passionately.

For there were four reported cases of that dread disease in Mount Mark.

But the pain in Carol's chest did grow worse, and she became so feverish that she began talking in quick broken sentences.

"It was too hot!--Don't go away, Larkie!--Her feet were wet, and it kept squshing out.--I guess I'm kind of sick, Prue.--Don't put that thing on my head, it is strangling me!--Oh, I can't get my breath!" And she flung her hand out sharply, as though to push something away from her face.

Then Mr. Starr went to the telephone and hurriedly called the doctor. Prudence meanwhile had undressed Carol, and put on her little pink flannel nightgown.

"Go out in the kitchen, girls, and shut the door," she said to her sisters, who stood close around the precious twin, so suddenly stricken. "Fairy!" she cried. "Go at once. It may be catching. Take the others with you. And keep the door shut."

But Lark flung herself on her knees beside her twin, and burst into choking sobs. "I won't go," she cried. "I won't leave Carrie. I will not, Prudence!"

"Oh, it is too hot," moaned Carol. "Oh, give me a drink! Give me some snow, Prudence. Oh, it hurts!" And she pressed her burning hands against her chest.

"Lark," said her father, stepping quickly to her side, "go out to the kitchen at once. Do you want to make Carrie worse?" And Lark, cowed and quivering, rushed into the kitchen and closed the door.

"I'll carry her up-stairs to bed, Prue," said her father, striving to render his voice natural for the sake of the suffering oldest daughter, whose tense white face was frightening.

Together they carried the child up the stairs. "Put her in our bed," said Prudence. "I'll--I'll--if it's diphtheria, daddy, she and I will stay upstairs here, and the rest of you must stay down. You can bring our food up to the head of the stairs, and I'll come out and get it. They can't take Carol away from the parsonage."

"We will get a nurse, Prudence. We couldn't let you run a risk like that. It would not be right. If I could take care of her properly myself, I----"

"You couldn't, father, and it would be wicked for you to take such chances. What would the--others do without you? But it would not make any difference about me. I'm not important. He can give me anti-toxin, and I'm such a healthy girl there will be no danger. But she must not be shut alone with a nurse. She would die!"

And Carol took up the words, screaming, "I will die! I will die! Don't leave me, Prudence. Don't shut me up alone. Prudence! Prudence!"

Down-stairs in the kitchen, three frightened girls clung to one another, crying bitterly as they heard poor Carol's piercing screams.

"It is pneumonia," said the doctor, after an examination. And he looked at Prudence critically. "I think we must have a nurse for a few days. It may be a little severe, and you are not quite strong enough." Then, as Prudence remonstrated,

"Oh, yes," he granted, "you shall stay with her, but if it is very serious a nurse will be of great service. I will have one come at once." Then he paused, and listened to the indistinct sobbing that floated up from the kitchen. "Can't you send those girls away for the night,--to some of the neighbors? It will be much better."

But this the younger girls stubbornly refused to do. "If you send me out of the house when Carol is sick, I will kill myself," said Lark, in such a strange voice that the doctor eyed her sharply.

"Well, if you will all stay down-stairs and keep quiet, so as not to annoy your sister," he consented grudgingly. "The least sobbing, or confusion, or excitement, may make her much worse. Fix up a bed on the floor down here, all of you, and go to sleep."

"I won't go to bed," said Lark, looking up at the doctor with agonized eyes. "I won't go to bed while Carol is sick."

"Give her a cup of something hot to drink," he said to Fairy curtly.

"I won't drink anything," said Lark. "I won't drink anything, and I won't eat a bite of anything until Carol is well. I won't sleep, either."

The doctor took her hand in his, and deftly pushed the sleeve above the elbow.

"You can twist my arm if you like, but I won't eat, and I won't drink, and I won't sleep."

The doctor smiled. Swiftly inserting the point of his needle in her arm, he released her. "I won't hurt you, but I am pretty sure you will be sleeping in a few minutes." He turned to Fairy. "Get her ready for bed at once. The little one can wait."

An hour later, he came down-stairs again. "Is she sleeping?" he asked of Fairy in a low voice. "That is good. You have your work cut out for you, my girl. The little one here will be all right, but this twin is in nearly as bad shape as the one up-stairs."

"Oh! Doctor! Larkie, too!"

"Oh, she is not sick. But she is too intense. She is taking this too hard. Her system is not well enough developed to stand such a strain very long. Something would give way,--maybe her brain. She must be watched. She must eat and sleep. There is school to-morrow, isn't there?"

"But I am sure Lark will not go, Doctor. She has never been to school a day in her life without Carol. I am sure she will not go!"

"Let her stay at home, then. Don't get her excited. But make her work. Keep her doing little tasks about the house, and send her on errands. Talk to her a good deal. Prudence will have her hands full with the other twin, and you'll have all you can do with this one. I'm depending on you, my girl. You mustn't fail me."

That was the beginning of an anxious week. For two days Carol was in delirium most of the time, calling out, crying, screaming affrightedly. And Lark crouched at the foot of the stairs, hands clenched passionately, her slender form tense and motionless.

It was four in the afternoon, as the doctor was coming down from the sick room, that Fairy called him into the dining-room with a suggestive glance.

"She won't eat," she said. "I have done everything possible, and I had the nurse try. But she will not eat a bite. I--I'm sorry, Doctor, but I can't make her."

"What has she been doing?"

"She's been at the foot of the stairs all day. She won't do a thing I tell her. She won't mind the nurse. Father told her to keep away, too, but she does not pay any attention. When I speak to her, she does not answer. When she hears you coming down, she runs away and hides, but she goes right back again."

"Can your father make her eat? If he commands her?"

"I do not know. I doubt it. But we can try. Here's some hot soup,--I'll call father."

So Lark was brought into the dining-room, and her father came down the stairs. The doctor whispered an explanation to him in the hall.

"Lark," said her father, gently but very firmly, "you must eat, or you will be sick, too. We need all of our time to look after Carol to-day. Do you want to keep us away from her to attend to you?"

"No, father, of course not. I wish you would all go right straight back to Carrie this minute and leave me alone. I'm all right. But I can't eat until Carol is well."

Her father drew a chair to the table and said, "Sit down and eat that soup at once, Larkie."

Lark's face quivered, but she turned away. "I can't, father. You don't understand. I can't eat,--I really can't. Carrie's my twin, and--oh, father, don't you see how it is?"

He stood for a moment, frowning at her thoughtfully. Then he left the room, signing for the doctor to follow. "I'll send Prudence down," he said. "She'll manage some way."

"I must stay here until I see her eat it," said the doctor. "If she won't do it, she must be kept under morphine for a few days. But it's better not. Try Prudence, by all means."

So Prudence, white-faced, eyes black-circled, came down from the room where she had served her sister many weary hours. The doctor was standing in the center of the room. Fairy was hovering anxiously near Lark, rigid at the window.

"Larkie," whispered Prudence, and with a bitter cry the young girl leaped into her sister's arms.

Prudence caressed and soothed her tenderly. "Poor little Larkie," she murmured, "poor little twinnie!--But Carol is resting pretty well now, Lark. She's coming through all right. She was conscious several times to-day. The first time she just looked up at me and smiled and whispered, 'Hard luck, Prue.' Then a little later she said, 'Tell Larkie I'm doing fine, and don't let her worry.' Pretty soon she spoke again, 'You make Lark be sensible, Prue, or she'll be sick, too.' Once again she started to say something about you, but she was too sick to finish. 'Larkie is such a--,' but that was as far as she could go. She was thinking of you all the time, Lark. She is so afraid you'll worry and make yourself sick, too. She would be heartbroken if she was able to see you, and you were too sick to come to her. You must keep up your strength for Carol's sake. If she is conscious to-morrow, we're going to bring you up a while to see her. She can hardly stand being away from you, I know. But you must get out-of-doors, and bring some color to your cheeks, first. It would make her miserable to see you like this."

Lark was still sobbing, but more gently now, and she still clung to her sister.

"To-morrow, Prudence? Honestly, may I go up to-morrow? You're not just fooling me, are you? You wouldn't do that!"

"Of course I wouldn't. Yes, you really may, if you'll be good and make yourself look better. It would be very bad for Carrie to see you so white and wan. She would worry. Have you been eating? You must eat lots, and then take a good run out-of-doors toward bedtime, so you will sleep well. It will be a good tonic for

Carol to see you bright and fresh and rosy."

"Oh, I can't bear to be fresh and rosy when Carrie is sick!"

"It hurts,--but you are willing to be hurt for Carol's sake! You will do it on her account. It will do her so much good. Now sit down and eat your soup, and I'll stay here a while and tell you all about her. I gave her the pansies you bought her,--it was so sweet of you, too, Larkie. It must have taken every cent of your money, didn't it? I suppose you ordered them over the telephone, since you wouldn't leave the house. When I told Carol you got them for her, she took them in her hand and held them under the covers. Of course, they wilted right away, but I knew you would like Carrie to have them close to her.'--Oh, you must eat it all, Lark. It looks very good. I must take a little of it up to Carol,--maybe she can eat some.--And you will do your very best to be strong and bright and rosy--for Carol--won't you?"

"Yes, I will,--I'll go and run across the field a few times before I go to bed. Yes, I'll try my very best." Then she looked up at the doctor, and added: "But I wouldn't do it for you, or anybody else, either."

But the doctor only smiled oddly, and went away up-stairs again, wondering at the wisdom that God has placed in the hearts of women!

Dreary miserable days and nights followed after that. And Prudence, to whom Carol, even in delirium, clung with such wildness that they dare not deny her, grew weary-eyed and wan. But when the doctor, putting his hand on her shoulder, said, "It's all right now, my dear. She'll soon be as well as ever,"--then Prudence dropped limply to the floor, trembling weakly with the great happiness.

Good Methodist friends from all over Mount Mark came to the assistance of the parsonage family, and many gifts and delicacies and knick-knacks were sent in to tempt the appetite of the invalid, and the others as well.

"You all need toning up," said Mrs. Adams crossly, "you've all gone clear under. A body would think the whole family had been down with something!"

Carol's friends at the high school, and the members of the faculty also, took advantage of this opportunity to show their love for her. And Professor Duke sent clear to Burlington for a great basket of violets and lilies-of-the-valley, "For our little high-school song-bird," as he wrote on the card. And Carol dimpled with delight as she read it.

"Now you see for yourself, Prudence," she declared. "Isn't he a duck?"

When the little parsonage group, entire, gathered once more around the table in the "real dining-room," they were joyful indeed. It was a gala occasion! The very best china and silverware were brought out in Carol's honor. The supper was one that would have gratified the heart of a bishop, at the very least!

"Apple pie, with pure cream, Carol," said Lark ecstatically, for apple pie with pure cream was the favorite dessert of the sweet-toothed twins. And Lark added earnestly, "And I don't seem to be very hungry to-night, Carol,--I don't want any pie. You shall have my piece, too!"

"I said I felt it in my bones, you remember," said Prudence, smiling at Carol, "but my mental compass indicated Connie when it should have pointed to Carol! And I do hope, Connie dear, that this will be a lesson to you, and impress upon you that you must always change your shoes and stockings when your feet are wet!"

And for the first time in many days, clear, happy-hearted laughter rang out in the parsonage.

CHAPTER IX
PRACTISING ECONOMY

It was a dull dreary day early in December. Prudence and Fairy were sewing in the bay window of the sitting-room.

"We must be sure to have all the scraps out of the way before Connie gets home," said Prudence, carefully fitting together pieces of a dark, warm, furry material. "It has been so long since father wore this coat, I am sure she will not recognize it."

"But she will ask where we got it, and what shall we say?"

"We must tell her it is goods we have had in the house for a long time. That is true. And I made this fudge on purpose to distract her attention. If she begins to ask questions, we must urge her to have more candy. Poor child!" she added very sympathetically. "Her heart is just set on a brand-new coat. I know she will be bitterly disappointed. If the members would just pay up we could get her one. November and December are such bad months for parsonage people. Coal to buy, feed for the cow and the horse and the chickens, and Carol's sickness, and Larkie's teeth! Of course, those last are not regular winter expenses, but they took a lot of money this year. Every one is getting ready for Christmas now, and forgets that parsonage people need Christmas money, too. November and December are always my bitter months, Fairy,--bitter months!"

Fairy took a pin from her mouth. "The velvet collar and cuffs will brighten it up a good bit. It's really a pretty material. I have honestly been ashamed of Connie the last few Sundays. It was so cold, and she wore only that little thin summer jacket. She must have been half frozen."

"Oh, I had her dressed warmly underneath, very warmly indeed," declared Prudence. "But no matter how warm you are underneath, you look cold if you aren't visibly prepared for winter weather. It's a fortunate thing the real cold weather was so slow in coming. I kept hoping enough money would come in to buy her a coat for once in her life."

"She has been looking forward to one long enough," put in Fairy. "This will be a bitter blow to her. And yet it is not such a bad-looking coat, after all." And she quickly ran up a seam on the machine.

"Here comes Connie!" Prudence hastily swept a pile of scraps out of sight, and turned to greet her little sister with a cheery smile.

"Come on in, Connie," she cried, with a brightness she did not feel. "Fairy and I are making you a new coat. Isn't it pretty? And so warm! See the nice velvet collar and cuffs. We want to fit it on you right away, dear."

Connie picked up a piece of the goods and examined it intently.

"Don't you want some fudge, Connie?" exclaimed Fairy, shoving the dish toward her hurriedly.

Connie took a piece from the plate, and thrust it between her teeth. Her eyes were still fastened upon the brown furry cloth.

"Where did you get this stuff?" she inquired, as soon as she was able to speak.

"Oh, we've had it in the house quite a while," said Prudence, adding swiftly, "Isn't it warm, Connie? Oh, it does look nice, doesn't it, Fairy? Do you want it a little shorter, Connie, or is that about right?"

"About right, I guess. Did you ever have a coat like this, Prudence? I don't seem to remember it.'"

"Oh, no, it wasn't mine. Take some more candy, Connie. Isn't it good?--Let's put a little more fullness in the sleeves, Fairy. It's more stylish this year.--The collar fits very nicely. The velvet gives it such a rich tone. And brown is so becoming to you."

"Thanks," said Connie patiently. "Was this something of yours, Fairy?"

"Oh, no, we've just had it in the house quite a while. It comes in very handy right now, doesn't it? It'll make you such a serviceable, stylish coat. Isn't it about time for the twins to get here, Prudence? I'm afraid they are playing along the road. Those girls get more careless every day of their lives."

"Well, if this didn't belong to one of you, whose was it?" demanded Connie. "I know the twins never had anything like this. It looks kind of familiar to me.

Where did it come from?"

"Out of the trunk in the garret, Connie. Don't you want some more fudge? I put a lot of nuts in, especially on your account."

"It's good," said Connie, taking another piece. She examined the cloth very closely. "Say, Prudence, isn't this that old brown coat of father's?"

Fairy shoved her chair back from the machine, and ran to the window. "Look, Prue," she cried. "Isn't that Mrs. Adams coming this way? I wonder----"

"No, it isn't," answered Connie gravely. "It's just Miss Avery getting home from school.--Isn't it, Prudence? Father's coat, I mean?"

"Yes, Connie, it is," said Prudence, very, very gently. "But no one here has seen it, and it is such nice cloth,--just exactly what girls are wearing now."

"But I wanted a new coat!" Connie did not cry. She stood looking at Prudence with her wide hurt eyes.

"Oh, Connie, I'm just as sorry as you are," cried Prudence, with starting tears. "I know just how you feel about it, dearest. But the people didn't pay father up last month, and nothing has come in for this month yet, and we've had so much extra expense.--I will have to wear my old shoes, too, Connie, and you know how they look! The shoemaker says they aren't worth fixing, so I must wear them as they are.--But maybe after Christmas we can get you a coat. They pay up better then."

"I think I'd rather wear my summer coat until then," said Connie soberly.

"Oh, but you can't, dearest. It is too cold. Won't you be a good girl now, and not make sister feel badly about it? It really is becoming to you, and it is nice and warm. You know parsonage people just have to practise economy, Connie,--it can't be helped. Take some more fudge, dear, and run out-of-doors a while. You'll feel better about it presently, I'm sure."

Connie stood solemnly beside the table, her eyes still fastened on the coat, cut down from her father's. "Can I go and take a walk?" she asked finally.

"May I, you mean," suggested Fairy.

"Yes, may I? Maybe I can reconcile myself to it."

"Yes, do go and take a walk," urged Prudence promptly, eager to get the small sober face beyond her range of vision.

"If I am not back when the twins get home, go right on and eat without me. I'll come back when I get things straightened out in my mind."

When Connie was quite beyond hearing, Prudence dropped her head on the table and wept. "Oh, Fairy, if the members just knew how such things hurt, maybe they'd pay up a little better. How do they expect parsonage people to keep up appearances when they haven't any money?"

"Oh, now, Prue, you're worse than Connie! There's no use to cry about it. Parsonage people have to find happiness in spite of financial misery. Money isn't the first thing with folks like us."

"No, but they have pledged it," protested Prudence, lifting her tear-stained face. "They must know we are counting on the money. Why don't they keep their pledges? They pay their meat bills, and grocery bills, and house rent! Why don't they pay for their religion?"

"Now, Prue, you know how things go. Mrs. Adams is having a lot of Christmas expense, and she thinks her four dollars a month won't really be missed. She thinks she will make it up along in February, when Christmas is over. But she forgets that Mrs. Barnaby with two dollars, and Mrs. Scott with five, and Mr. Walter with seven, and Mr. Holmes with three, and about thirty others with one dollar each, are thinking the same thing! Each member thinks for himself, and takes no account of the others. That's how it happens."

Prudence squirmed uncomfortably in her chair. "I wish you wouldn't mention names, Fairy," she begged. "I do not object to lumping them in a body and wondering about them. But I can't feel right about calling them out by name, and criticizing them.--Besides, we do not really know which ones they are who did not pay."

"I was just giving names for illustrative purposes," said Fairy quickly. "Like as not, the very ones I named are the ones who did pay."

"Well, get this stuff out of the way, and let's set the table. Somehow I can't bear to touch it any more. Poor little Connie! If she had cried about it, I wouldn't have cared so much. But she looked so--heartsick, didn't she, Fairy?"

Connie certainly was heartsick. More than that, she was a little disgusted. She felt herself aroused to take action. Things had gone too far! Go to church in her father's coat she could not! But they hadn't the money. If Connie's father had been at home, perhaps they might have reasoned it out together. But he had left town that morning, and would not be home until Saturday evening,--too late to get a coat in time for Sunday, and Prudence had said that Connie must be coated by Sunday! She walked sturdily down the street toward the "city,"--ironically so called. Her face was stony, her hands were clenched. But finally she brightened. Her lagging steps quickened. She skipped along quite cheerfully. She turned westward as she reached the corner of the Square, and walked along that business street with shining eyes. In front of the First National Bank she paused, but after a few seconds she passed by. On the opposite corner was another bank. When she reached it, she walked in without pausing, and the massive door swung behind her. Standing on tiptoe, she confronted the cashier with a grave face.

"Is Mr. Harold in?" she asked politely.

Mr. Harold was the president of the bank! It was a little unusual.

"Yes, he is in," said the cashier doubtfully, "but he is very busy."

"Will you tell him that Constance Starr wishes to speak to him, privately, and that it is very important?"

The cashier smiled. "The Methodist minister's little girl, isn't it? Yes, I will tell him."

Mr. Harold looked up impatiently at the interruption.

"It's the Methodist minister's little daughter, and she says it is important for her to speak to you privately."

"Oh! Probably a message from her father. Bring her in."

Mr. Harold was one of the trustees of the Methodist church, and prominent among them. His keen eyes were intent upon Connie as she walked in, but she did not falter.

"How do you do, Mr. Harold?" she said, and shook hands with him in the good old Methodist way.

His eyes twinkled, but he spoke briskly. "Did your father send you on an errand?"

"No, father is out of town. I came on business,--personal business, Mr. Harold. It is my own affair."

"Oh, I see," and he smiled at the earnest little face. "Well, what can I do for you, Miss Constance?"

"I want to borrow five dollars from the bank, Mr. Harold?"

"You--did Prudence send you?"

"Oh, no, it is my own affair as I told you. I came on my own account. I thought of stopping at the other bank as I passed, but then I remembered that parsonage people must always do business with their own members if possible. And of course, I would rather come to you than to a perfect stranger."

"Thank you,--thank you very much. Five dollars you say you want?"

"I suppose I had better tell you all about it. You see, I need a winter coat, very badly. Oh, very badly, indeed! The girls were ashamed of me last Sunday, I looked so cold outside, though I was dressed plenty warm enough inside. I've been look-ing forward to a new coat, Mr. Harold. I've never had one yet. There was always something to cut down for me, from Prudence, or Fairy, or the twins. But this time there wasn't anything to hand down, and so I just naturally counted on a new one." Connie paused, and looked embarrassed.

"Yes?" His voice was encouraging.

"Well, I'll tell you the rest, but I hope you won't say anything about it, for I'd feel pretty cheap if I thought all the Sunday-school folks knew about it.--You see, the members need such a lot of money now just before Christmas, and so they didn't pay us up last month, and they haven't paid anything this month. And we had to get coal, and feed, and Larkie's teeth had to be fixed, and Carol was sick, you remember. Seems to me Lark's teeth might have been put off until after Christmas, but Prudence says not.--And so there isn't any money left, and I can't have a coat. But Prudence and Fairy are making me one,--out of an old coat of father's!"

Constance paused dramatically. Mr. Harold never even smiled. He just nodded understandingly. "I don't think I could wear a coat of father's to church,--it's cut down of course, but--there's something painful about the idea. I wouldn't expect father to wear any of my clothes! You can see how it is, Mr. Harold. Just imagine how you would feel wearing your wife's coat!--I don't think I could listen to the sermons. I don't believe I could be thankful for the mercy of wearing father's coat! I don't see anything merciful about it. Do you?"

Mr. Harold did not speak. He gazed at Connie sympathetically, and shook his head.

"It's too much, that's what it is. And so I thought I'd just have to take things into my own hands and borrow the money. I can get a good coat for five dollars. But if the bank is a little short right now, I can get along with four, or even three. I'd rather have the cheapest coat in town, than one made out of father's. Do you think you can let me have it?"

"Yes, indeed we can." He seemed to find his voice with an effort. "Of course we can. We are very glad to lend our money to responsible people. We are proud to have your trade."

"But I must tell you, that it may take me quite a while to pay it back. Father gives me a nickel a week, and I generally spend it for candy. There's another nickel, but it has to go in the collection, so I can't really count that. I don't believe father would let me neglect the heathen, even to pay for a winter coat! But I will give you the nickel every week, and at that rate I can pay it back in a couple of years easy enough. But I'd rather give the nickels as fast as I get them. It's so hard to keep money when you can get your hand on it, you know. Sometimes I have quite a lot of money,--as much as a quarter at a time, from doing errands for the neighbors and things like that. I'll pay you as fast as I can. Will that be all right? And the interest, too, of course. How much will the interest be on five dollars?"

"Well, that depends on how soon you repay the money, Connie. But I'll figure it out, and tell you later."

"All right. I know I can trust you not to cheat me, since you're a trustee. So I won't worry about that."

Mr. Harold drew out a bulky book from his pocket, and handed Connie a crisp new bill. Her eyes sparkled as she received it.

"But, Connie," he continued, "I feel that I ought to give you this. We Methodists have done a wicked thing in forgetting our November payments, and I will just give you this bill to make up for it."

But Connie shook her head decidedly. "Oh, no! I'll have to give it back, then. Father would not stand that,--not for one minute. Of course, parsonage people get things given to them, quite a lot. And it's a good thing, too, I must say! But we don't hint for them, Mr. Harold. That wouldn't be right." She held out the bill toward him, with very manifest reluctance.

"Keep it,--we'll call it a loan then, Connie," he said. "And you may pay me back, five cents at a time, just as is most convenient."

The four older girls were at the table when Connie arrived. She exhaled quiet satisfaction from every pore. Prudence glanced at her once, and then looked away again. "She has reconciled herself," she thought. Dinner was half over before Constance burst her bomb. She had intended waiting until they were quite through, but it was more than flesh and blood could keep!

"Are you going to be busy this afternoon, Prudence?" she asked quietly.

"We are going to sew a little," said Prudence. "Why?"

"I wanted you to go down-town with me after school."

"Well, perhaps I can do that. Fairy will be able to finish the coat alone."

"You needn't finish the coat!--I can't wear father's coat to church, Prudence. It's a--it's a--physical impossibility."

The twins laughed. Fairy smiled, but Prudence gazed at "the baby" with tender pity.

"I'm so sorry, dearest, but we haven't the money to buy one now."

"Will five dollars be enough?" inquired Connie, and she placed her crisp new bill beside her plate. The twins gasped! They gazed at Connie with new respect. They were just wishing they could handle five-dollar bills so recklessly.

"Will you loan me twenty dollars until after Christmas, Connie?" queried Fairy.

But Prudence asked, "Where did you get this money, Connie?"

"I borrowed it,--from the bank," Connie replied with proper gravity. "I have two years to pay it back. Mr. Harold says they are proud to have my trade."

Prudence was silent for several long seconds. Then she inquired in a low voice, "Did you tell him why you wanted it?"

"Yes, I explained the whole situation."

"What did he say?"

"He said he knew just how I felt, because he knew he couldn't go to church in his wife's coat.--No, I said that myself, but he agreed with me. He did not say very much, but he looked sympathetic. He said he anticipated great pleasure in seeing me in my new coat at church next Sunday."

"Go on with your luncheon, twins," said Prudence sternly. "You'll be late to school.--We'll see about going down-town when you get home to-night, Connie. Now, eat your luncheon, and don't talk about coats any more."

When Connie had gone back to school, Prudence went straight to Mr. Harold's bank. Flushed and embarrassed, she explained the situation frankly. "My sympathies are all with Connie," she said candidly. "But I am afraid father would not like it. We are dead set against borrowing. After--our mother was taken, we were crowded pretty close for money. So we had to go in debt. It took us two years to get it paid. Father and Fairy and I talked it over then, and decided we would starve rather than borrow again. Even the twins understood it, but Connie was too little. She doesn't know how heartbreaking it is to keep handing over every cent for debt, when one is just yearning for other things.--I do wish she might have the coat, but I'm afraid father would not like it. She gave me the five dollars for safekeeping, and I have brought it back."

Mr. Harold shook his head. "No, Connie must have her coat. This will be a good lesson for her. It will teach her the bitterness of living under debt! Besides, Prudence, I think in my heart that she is right this time. This is a case where borrowing is justified. Get her the coat, and I'll square the account with your father." Then he added, "And I'll look after this salary business myself after this. I'll arrange with the trustees that I am to pay your father his full salary the first of every month, and that the church receipts are to be turned in to me. And if they do not pay up, my lawyer can do a little investigating! Little Connie earned that five dollars, for she taught one trustee a sorry lesson. And he will have to pass it on to the others in self-defense! Now, run along and get the coat, and if five dollars isn't enough you can have as much more as you need. Your father will get his salary after this, my dear, if we have to mortgage the parsonage!"

CHAPTER X
A BURGLAR'S VISIT

P rue!"

A small hand gripped Prudence's shoulder, and again came a hoarsely whispered:

"Prue!"

Prudence sat up in bed with a bounce.

"What in the world?" she began, gazing out into the room, half-lighted by the moonshine, and seeing Carol and Lark shivering beside her bed.

"Sh! Sh! Hush!" whispered Lark. "There's a burglar in our room!"

By this time, even sound-sleeping Fairy was awake. "Oh, there is!" she scoffed.

"Yes, there is," declared Carol with some heat. "We heard him, plain as day. He stepped into the closet, didn't he, Lark?"

"He certainly did," agreed Lark.

"Did you see him?"

"No, we heard him. Carol heard him first, and she spoke, and nudged me. Then I heard him, too. He was at our dresser, but he shot across the room and into the closet. He closed the door after him. He's there now."

"You've been dreaming," said Fairy, lying down again.

"We don't generally dream the same thing at the same minute," said Carol stormily. "I tell you he's in there."

"And you two great big girls came off and left poor little Connie in there alone with a burglar, did you? Well, you are nice ones, I must say."

And Prudence leaped out of bed and started for the door, followed by Fairy, with the twins creeping fearfully along in the rear.

"She was asleep," muttered Carol.

"We didn't want to scare her," added Lark.

Prudence was careful to turn the switch by the door, so that the room was in full light before she entered. The closet door was wide open. Connie was soundly sleeping. There was no one else in the room.

"You see?" said Prudence sternly.

"I'll bet he took our ruby rings," declared Lark, and the twins and Fairy ran to the dresser to look.

But a sickening realization had come home to Prudence. In the lower hall, under the staircase, was a small dark closet which they called the dungeon. The dungeon door was big and solid, and was equipped with a heavy catch-lock. In this dungeon, Prudence kept the family silverware, and all the money she had on hand, as it could there be safely locked away. But more often than not, Prudence forgot to lock it.

Mr. Starr had gone to Burlington that morning to attend special revival services for three days, and Prudence had fifty whole dollars in the house, an unwonted sum in that parsonage! And the dungeon was not locked. Without a word, she slipped softly out of the room, ran down the stairs, making never a sound in her bare feet, and saw, somewhat to her surprise, that the dungeon door was open. Quickly she flung it shut, pushed the tiny key that moved the "catch," and was rushing up the stairs again with never a pause for breath.

A strange sight met her eyes in the twins' room. The twins themselves were in each other's arms, sobbing bitterly. Fairy was still looking hurriedly through the dresser drawers.

"They are gone," wailed Carol, "our beautiful ruby rings that belonged to grandmother."

"Nonsense," cried Prue with nervous anger, "you've left them in the bathroom, or on the kitchen shelves. You're always leaving them somewhere over the place. Come on, and we'll search the house just to convince you."

"No, no," shrieked the twins. "Let's lock the door and get under the bed."

The rings were really valuable. Their grandmother, their mother's mother, whom they had never seen, had divided her "real jewelry" between her two daughters. And the mother of these parsonage girls, had further divided her portion to make it reach through her own family of girls! Prudence had a small but beautiful chain of tiny pearls. Fairy's share consisted of a handsome brooch, with a "sure-enough diamond" in the center! The twin rubies of another brooch had been reset in rings for Carol and Lark, and were the priceless treasures of their lives! And in the dungeon was a solid gold bracelet, waiting until Connie's arm should be sufficiently developed to do it justice.

"Our rings! Our rings!" the twins were wailing, and Connie, awakened by the noise, was crying beneath the covers of her bed.

"Maybe we'd better phone for Mr. Allan," suggested Fairy. "The girls are so nervous they will be hysterical by the time we finish searching the house."

"Well, let's do the up-stairs then," said Prudence. "Get your slippers and kimonos, and we'll go into daddy's room."

But inside the door of daddy's room, with the younger girls clinging to her, and Fairy looking odd and disturbed, Prudence stopped abruptly and stared about the room curiously.

"Fairy, didn't father leave his watch hanging on that nail by the table? Seems to me I saw it there this morning. I remember thinking I would tease him for being forgetful."

And the watch was not there.

"I think it was Sunday he left it," answered Fairy in a low voice. "I remember seeing it on the nail, and thinking he would need it,--but I believe it was Sunday."

Prudence looked under the bed, and in the closet, but their father's room was empty. Should they go farther? For a moment, the girls stood looking at one another questioningly. Then--they heard a loud thud down-stairs, as of some one pounding on a door. There was no longer any doubt. Some one was in the house! Connie and the twins screamed again and clung to Prudence frantically. And Fairy said, "I think we'd better lock the door and stay right here until morning, Prue."

But Prudence faced them stubbornly. "If you think I'm going to let any one steal that fifty dollars, you are mistaken. Fifty dollars does not come often enough for that, I can tell you."

"It's probably stolen already," objected Fairy.

"Well, if it is, we'll find out who did it, and have them arrested. I'm going down to telephone to the police. You girls must lock the door after me, and stay right here."

The little ones screamed again, and Fairy said: "Don't be silly, Prue, if you go I'm going with you, of course. We'll leave the kiddies here and they can lock the door. They'll be perfectly safe in here."

But the children loudly objected to this. If Prue and Fairy went, they would go! So down the stairs they trooped, a timorous trembling crowd. Prudence went at once to the telephone, and called up the residence of the Allans, their neighbors across the street. After a seemingly never-ending wait, the kind-hearted neighbor left his bed to answer the insistent telephone. Falteringly Prudence explained their predicament, and asked him to come and search the house. He promised to be there in five minutes, with his son to help.

"Now," said Prudence more cheerfully, "we'll just go out to the kitchen and wait. It's quiet there, and away from the rest of the house, and we'll be perfectly safe." To the kitchen, then, they hurried, and found real comfort in its smallness and secureness. Prudence raked up the dying embers of the fire, and Fairy drew the blinds to their lowest limits. The twins and Connie trailed them fearfully at every step.

When the fire was burning brightly, Prudence spoke with great assurance. "I'll just run in to the dungeon and see for sure if the money is there. I do not honestly believe there is a soul in the house, but I can't rest until I know that money is safe."

"You'll do nothing of the sort," said Fairy, "you'll stay right here and wait with us. I do not believe there's any one in the house, either, but if there is, you shan't run into him by yourself. You stay right where you are, and don't be silly. Mr. Allan will do the investigating."

Every breath of wind against the windows drew startled cries from the younger girls, and both Fairy and Prudence were white with anxiety when they heard the loud voices of the Allans outside the kitchen door. Prudence began crying nervously the moment the two angels of mercy appeared before her, and Fairy told their tale of woe.

"Well, there now," Mr. Allan said with rough sympathy, "you just got scared, that's all. Everything's suspicious when folks get scared. I told my wife the other day I bet you girls would get a good fright some time left here alone. Come on, Jim, and we'll go over the house in a jiffy."

He was standing near the dining-room door. He lifted his head suddenly, and seemed to sniff a little. There was undoubtedly a faint odor of tobacco in the house.

"Been any men in here to-night?" he asked. "Or this afternoon? Think, now!"

"No one," answered Prudence. "I was alone all afternoon, and there has been no one in this evening."

He passed slowly through the dining-room into the hall, closely followed by his son and the five girls, already much reassured. As he passed the dungeon door he paused for a moment, listening intently, his head bent.

"Oh, Mr. Allan," cried Prudence, "let's look in the dungeon first. I want to see if the money is safe." Her hand was already on the lock, but he shoved her away quickly.

"Is there any way out of that closet besides this door?" he asked.

"No. We call it the dungeon," laughed Prudence, her self-possession quite recovered. "It is right under the stairs, and not even a mouse could gnaw its way out, with this door shut."

"Who shut that door?" he inquired, still holding Prudence's hand from the lock. Then without waiting for an answer, he went on, "Let's go back in the other room a minute. Come on, all of you." In the living-room, he hurried to the telephone, and spoke to the operator in a low voice. "Call the police headquarters, and have them send two or three men to the Methodist parsonage, right away. We've got a burglar locked in a closet, and they'll have to get him out. Please hurry."

At this, the girls crowded around him again in renewed fear.

"Don't be scared," he said calmly, "we're all right. He's in there safe enough and can't get out for a while. Now, tell me about it. How did you get him in the closet? Begin at the beginning, and tell me all about it."

Carol began the story with keen relish. "I woke up, and thought I heard some one in the room. I supposed it was Prudence. I said, 'Prudence,' and nobody answered, and everything was quiet.' But I felt there was some one in there. I nudged Lark, and she woke up. He moved then, and we both heard him. He was fumbling at the dresser, and our ruby rings are gone. We heard him step across the room and into the closet. He closed the door after him, didn't he, Lark?"

"Yes, he did," agreed Lark. "His hand was on the knob."

"So we sneaked out of bed, and went into Prudence's room and woke her and Fairy." She looked at Connie, and blushed. "Connie was asleep, and we didn't waken her because we didn't want to frighten her. We woke the girls,--and you tell the rest, Prudence."

"We didn't believe her, of course. We went back into their room and there was no one there. But the rings were gone. While they were looking at the dresser, I remembered that I forgot to lock the dungeon door, where we keep the money and the silverware, and I ran down-stairs and slammed the door and locked it, and went back up. I didn't hear a sound down-stairs."

Mr. Allan laughed heartily. "Well, your burglar was in that closet after the money, no doubt, and he didn't hear you coming, and got locked in. Did you make any noise coming down the stairs?"

"No. I was in my bare feet, and I tried to be quiet because if there was any one in the house, I did not want him coming at me in the dark. I ran back up-stairs, and we looked in father's room. I thought father had forgotten to take his watch with him, but it wasn't there.--Do you really think it was Sunday he forgot it, Fairy?"

"No," said Fairy, "it was there this afternoon. The burglar's got it in the dungeon with him, of course.--I just said it was Sunday to keep from scaring the twins."

In a few minutes, they heard footsteps around the house and knew the officers had arrived. Mr. Allan let them into the house, four of them, and led them out to the hall. There could be no doubt whatever that the burglar was in the dungeon. He had been busy with his knife, and the lock was nearly removed. If the officers had been two minutes later, the dungeon would have been empty. The girls were sent up-stairs at once, with the Allan boy as guard,--as guard, without regard for the fact that he was probably more frightened than any one of them.

The chief officer rapped briskly on the dungeon door. Then he clicked his revolver.

"There are enough of us to overpower three of you," he said curtly. "And we have men outside the house, too. If you make any disturbance, we shall all fire the instant the door is opened. If you put your firearms on the floor, and hold both hands over your head, you'll be well treated. If your hands are not up, we fire on sight. Get your revolvers ready, boys."

Then the officer opened the door. Evidently the burglar was wise enough to appreciate the futility of fighting against odds. Perhaps he did not wish to add the charge of manslaughter to that of robbery. Certainly, he did not feel himself called to sudden death. At any rate, his hands were above his head, and in less than a second he was securely manacled.

The chief officer had been eying him closely. "Say!" he exclaimed. "Aren't you Limber-Limb Grant?" The burglar grinned, but did not answer. "By jove!" shouted the officer. "It is! Call the girls down here," he ordered, and when they appeared, gazing at the burglar with mingled admiration, pity and fear, he congratulated them with considerable excitement.

"It's Limber-Limb Grant," he explained. "There's a reward of five hundred dollars for him. You'll get the money, as sure as you're born." Then he turned again to the burglar. "Say, Grant, what's a fellow like you doing on such a fifth-rate job as this? A Methodist parsonage is not just in your line, is it?"

Limber-Limb laughed sheepishly. "Well," he explained good-naturedly, "Chicago got too hot for me. I had to get out in a hurry, and I couldn't get my hands on any money. I had a fine lot of jewels, but I was so pushed I couldn't use them. I came here and loafed around town for a while, because folks said Mount Mark was so fast asleep it did not even wake up long enough to read the daily papers. I heard about this parsonage bunch, and knew the old man had gone off to get more religion. This afternoon at the station I saw a detective from Chicago get off the train, and I knew what that meant. But I needed some cash, and so I wasn't above a little job on the side. I never dreamed of getting done up by a bunch of preacher's kids. I went upstairs to get those family jewels I've heard about, and one of the little ones gave the alarm. I already had some of them, so I came down at once. I stopped in the dungeon to get that money, and first thing I knew the door banged shut. That's all. You're welcome to the five hundred dollars, ladies. Some one was bound to get it sooner or later, and I'm partial to the ladies, every time."

Limber-Limb Grant was a modern thief of the new class. At that moment, in Chicago, he had in storage, a hundred thousand dollars' worth of jewels, which he could not dispose of on the pressure of the moment. The law was crowding him close, and he was obliged to choose between meeting the law, or running away from it. He ran. He reached Mount Mark, and trusted to its drowsiness for concealment for a few weeks. But that afternoon the arrival of a detective gave him warning, and he planned his departure promptly. A parsonage occupied by only five girls held no terrors for him, and with fifty dollars and a few fairly good jewels, a man of his talent could accomplish wonders.

But Mount Mark had aroused from its lethargy. Limber-Limb Grant was in the hands of the law.

Mr. Starr had been greatly interested in the accounts of the evangelistic services being held in Burlington. The workers were meeting with marked success, and Mr. Starr felt he should get in touch with them. So on Thursday morning he took the early east-bound train to Burlington. There he sought out a conveniently located second-class hotel, and took up residence. He attended the services at the tabernacle in the afternoon and evening, and then went to bed at the hotel. He slept late the next morning. When he finally appeared, he noticed casually, without giving it thought, that the clerk behind the desk looked at him with marked interest. Mr. Starr nodded cheerfully, and the clerk came at once from behind the desk to speak to him. Two or three other guests, who had been lounging about, drew near.

"We've just been reading about your girls, sir," said the clerk respectfully. "It's a pretty nervy little bunch! You must be proud of them!"

"My girls!" ejaculated Mr. Starr.

"Haven't you seen the morning paper? You're Mr. Starr, the Methodist minister at Mount Mark, aren't you?"

"I am! But what has happened to my girls? Is anything wrong? Give me the paper!"

Mr. Starr was greatly agitated. He showed it.

But the clerk could not lose this opportunity to create a sensation. It was a chance of a life-time. "Why, a burglar got in the parsonage last night," he began, almost licking his lips with satisfaction. "The twins heard him at their dresser, and when he stepped into the closet they locked him in there, and yelled for the rest of the family. But he broke away from them, and went, down-stairs and climbed down into the dungeon to get the money. Then Prudence, she ran down-stairs alone in the dark, and locked him in the dungeon,--pushed him down-stairs or something like that, I believe,--and then telephoned for the police. And she stayed on guard outside the dungeon until the police got there, so he couldn't get away. And the police got him, and found it was Limber-Limb Grant, a famous gentleman thief, and your girls are going to get five hundred dollars reward for catching him."

Five minutes later, Mr. Starr and his suit-case were in a taxicab speeding toward Union Station, and within eight minutes he was en route for Mount Mark,--white in the face, shaky in the knees, but tremendously proud in spirit.

Arriving at Mount Mark, he was instantly surrounded by an exclamatory crowd of station loungers. "Ride, sir? Glad to take you home for nothing," urged Harvey Reel. Mount Mark was enjoying more notoriety than ever before in the two hundred years of its existence. The name of Prudence was upon every tongue, and her father heard it with satisfaction. In the parsonage he found at least two-thirds of the Ladies' Aid Society, the trustees and the Sunday-school superintendent, along with a miscellaneous assortment of ordinary members, mixed up with Presbyterians, Baptists and a few unclassified outsiders. And Prudence was the center of attraction.

She was telling the "whole story," for perhaps the fifteenth time that morning, but she broke off when her father hurried in and flung her arms about him. "Oh, papa," she cried, "they mustn't praise me. I had no idea there was a burglar in the house when I ran down the stairs, and if I hadn't been careless and left the dungeon unlocked the money would have been in no danger, and if the twins hadn't wakened me I wouldn't have known there was a burglar about the place, and if Fairy hadn't kept me from rushing out to the dungeon to see if the money was safe, he would have got away, and--it took the policemen to get him out. Oh, I know that is not very grammatical, father, but it's just as true as if it were! And I honestly can't see that much credit is due me."

But Mount Mark did not take it so calmly. And as for the Methodist church,--well, the Presbyterian people used to say there was "no living with those Methodists, since the girls caught a burglar in the parsonage." Of course, it was important, from the Methodist point of view. Pictures of the parsonage and the church were in all the papers for miles around, and at their very next meeting the trustees decided to get the piano the Sunday-school had been needing for the last hundred years!

When the five hundred dollars arrived from Chicago, Prudence felt that personally she had no real right to the money. "We must divide it," she insisted, "for

I didn't earn it a bit more than any of the others. But it is perfectly glorious to have five hundred dollars, isn't it? Did you ever have five hundred dollars before? Just take it, father, and use it for whatever we need. It's family money."

But he would not hear of this. "No," he said, "put it in the bank, Prudence, for there will come a time when you will want money very badly. Then you will have it."

"Let's divide it then,--a hundred for each of us," she urged.

Neither the younger girls nor their father would consent to this. But when Prudence stood very firm, and pleaded with them earnestly, they decided to divide it.

"I will deposit two hundred and fifty dollars for the four younger ones," he said, "and that will leave you as much."

So it was settled, and Prudence was a happy girl when she saw it safely put away in the bank.

"We can get it whenever we really need it, you know," she told her father joyfully. "It's such a comfort to know it's there! I feel just like a millionaire, I am sure. Do you think it would be all right to send Limber-Limb Grant a letter of thanks for it? We were horribly scared, but--well, I for one am willing to be horribly scared for such a lot of money as that!"

CHAPTER XI
ROMANCE COMES

Sometimes, Methodists, or Presbyterians or heretics, whatever we may be, we are irresistibly impelled to the conclusion that things were simply bound to happen! However slight the cause,--still that cause was predestined from the beginning of time. A girl may by the sheerest accident, step from the street-car a block ahead of her destination,--an irritating incident. But as she walks that block she may meet an old-time friend, and a stranger. And that stranger,--ah, you can never convince the girl that her stepping from the car too soon was not ordered when the foundations of the world were laid.

Even so with Prudence, good Methodist daughter that she was. We ask her, "What if you had not gone out for a ride that morning?" And Prudence, laughing, answers, "Oh, but I had to go, you see." "Well," we continue, "if you had not met him that way, you could have met him some other way, I suppose." "Oh, no," declares Prudence decidedly, "it had to happen just that way."

After all, down in plain ink on plain paper, it was very simple. Across the street from the parsonage was a little white cottage set back among tall cedars. In this cottage lived a girl named Mattie Moore,--a common, unlovely, unexciting girl, with whom Romance could not apparently be intimately concerned. Mattie Moore taught a country school five miles out from town, and she rode to and from her school, morning and evening, on a bicycle.

Years before, when Prudence was young and bicycles were fashionable, she had been intensely fond of riding. But as she gained in age, and bicycles lost in popularity, she discarded the amusement as unworthy a parsonage damsel.

One evening, early in June, when the world was fair to look upon, it was fore-ordained that Prudence should be turning in at the parsonage gate just as Mattie

Moore whirled up, opposite, on her dusty wheel. Prudence stopped to interchange polite inanities with her neighbor, and Mattie, wheeling the bicycle lightly beside her, came across the street and stood beneath the parsonage maples with Prudence. They talked of the weather, of the coming summer, of Mattie's school, rejoicing that one more week would bring freedom from books for Mattie and the younger parsonage girls.

Then said Prudence, seemingly of her own free will, but really directed by an all-controlling Providence, "Isn't it great fun to ride a bicycle? I love it. Sometime will you let me ride your wheel?"

"Why, certainly. You may ride now if you like."

"No," said Prudence slowly, "I am afraid it would not do for me to ride now. Some of the members might see me, and--well, I am very grown up, you know.--Of course," she added hastily, "it is different with you. You ride for business, but it would be nothing but a frolic with me. I want to get up at six o'clock and go early in the morning when the world is fast asleep. Let me take it to-morrow morning, will you? It is Saturday, and you won't be going to school."

"Yes, of course you may," was the hearty answer. "You may stay out as long as you like. I'm going to sew to-morrow. You make take it in the parsonage now and keep it until morning. I always sleep late on Saturdays."

So Prudence delightedly tripped up the parsonage board walk, wheeling the bicycle by her side. She hid it carefully in the woodshed, for the twins were rash and venturesome. But after she had gone to bed, she confided her plan to Fairy.

"I'm going at six o'clock, and I'll be back in time to get breakfast. But as you know, Fairy, my plans do not always work out as I intend, so if I am a little late, you'll get breakfast for papa and the girls, like a dear, won't you?"

Fairy promised. And early the next morning, Prudence, in a plain gingham house dress, with the addition of a red sweater jacket and cap for warmth, set out upon her secret ride. It was a magnificent morning, and Prudence sang for pure delight as she rode swiftly along the country roads. The country was simply irresistible. It was almost intoxicating. And Prudence rode farther than she had intended. East and west, north and south, she went, apparently guided only by her own caprice. She knew it was growing late, "but Fairy'll get breakfast," she thought comfortably.

Finally she turned in a by-road, leading between two rich hickory groves. Dismounting at the top of a long hill, she gazed anxiously around her. No one was in sight. The nearest house was two miles behind, and the road was long, and smooth, and inviting, and the hill was steep. Prudence yearned for a good, soul-stirring coast, with her feet high up on the framework of the wheel, and the pedals flying around beneath her skirts. This was not the new and modern model of bicycle. The pedals on Mattie Moore's wheel revolved, whether one worked them or not.

It seemed safe. The road sloped down gradually at the bottom, with an incline on the other side. What more could one desire. The only living thing in sight besides birds gossiping in the leafy branches and the squirrel scolding to himself, was a sober-eyed serious mule peacefully grazing near the bottom of the hill.

Prudence laughed gleefully, like a child. She never laughed again in exactly that way. This was the last appearance of the old irresponsible Prudence. The curtain was just ready to drop.

"Here goes!" she cried, and leaping nimbly into the saddle, she pedaled swiftly a few times, and then lifted her feet to the coveted position. The pedals flew around beneath her, just as she had anticipated, and the wind whistled about her in a most exhilarating way.

But as she neared the bottom, a disastrous and totally unexpected thing happened. The placid mule, which had been righteously grazing beside the fence, suddenly stalked into the middle of the road. Prudence screamed, jerked the handlebar to the right, then to the left, and then, with a sickening thud, she landed head first upon some part of the mule's anatomy. She did not linger there, however. She bounced on down to the ground, with a little cry of pain. The bicycle crashed beside her, and the mule, slightly startled, looked around at her with ears raised in silent questioning. Then he ambled slowly across the road, and deliberately continued his grazing.

Prudence tried to raise herself, but she felt sharp pain. She heard some one leaping over the fence near her, and wondered, without moving her head, if it could be a tramp bent on highway robbery. The next instant, a man was leaning over her. "It's not a tramp," she thought, before he had time to speak.

"Are you hurt?" he cried. "You poor child!"

Prudence smiled pluckily. "My ankle is hurt a little, but I am not a child."

The young man, in great relief, laughed aloud, and Prudence joined him rather faintly.

"I'm afraid I can not walk," she said. "I believe I've broken my ankle, maybe my whole leg, for all I know. It--hurts--pretty badly!"

"Lie down like this," he said, helping her to a more comfortable position, "do not move. May I examine your foot?"

She shook her head, but he removed the shoe regardless of her head-shake. "I believe it is sprained. I am sure the bone is not broken. But how in the world will you get home? How far is it to Mount Mark? Is that where you live?"

"Yes," considering, "yes, I live there, and it must be four miles, anyhow. What shall I do?"

In answer, he pulled off his coat, and arranged it carefully by the side of the road on the grass. Then jerking open the bag he had carried, he took out a few towels, and three soft shirts. Hastily rolling them together for a pillow, he added it to the bed pro tem. Then he turned again to Prudence.

"I'll carry you over here, and fix you as comfortably as I can. Then I'll go to the nearest house and get a wagon to take you home."

Prudence was not shy, and realizing that his plan was the wise one, she made no objections when he came to help her across the road. "I think I can walk if you lift me up."

But the first movement sent such a twinge of pain through the wounded ankle that she clutched him frantically, and burst into tears. "It hurts," she cried, "don't touch me."

Without speaking, he lifted her as gently as he could and carried her to the place he had prepared for her. "Will you be warm enough?" he asked, after he had stood looking awkwardly down upon the sobbing girl as long as he could endure it.

"Yes," nodded Prudence, gulping down the big soft rising in her throat.

"I'll run. Do you know which way is nearest to a house? It's been a long time since I passed one coming this way."

"The way I came is the nearest, but it's two miles, I think."

"I'll go as fast as I can, and you will be all right This confounded cross-cut is so out of the way that no one will pass here for hours, I suppose. Now lie as comfortably as you can, and do not worry. I'm going to run."

Off he started, but Prudence, left alone, was suddenly frightened. "Please, oh, please," she called after him, and when he came back she buried her face in shame, deep in the linen towel.

"I'm afraid," she whispered, crying again. "I do not wish to be left alone here. A snake might come, or a tramp."

He sat down beside her. "You're nervous. I'll stay with you until you feel better. Some one may come this way, but it isn't likely. A man I passed on the road a ways back told me to cut through the hickory grove and I would save a mile of travel. That's how I happened to come through the woods, and find you." He smiled a little, and Prudence, remembering the nature of her accident, flushed. Then, being Prudence, she laughed.

"It was my own fault. I had no business to go coasting down like that. But the mule was so stationary. It never occurred to me that he contemplated moving for the next century at least. He was a bitter disappointment." She looked down the roadside where the mule was contentedly grazing, with never so much as a sympathetic glance toward his victim.

"I'm afraid your bicycle is rather badly done up."

"Oh,--whatever will Mattie Moore say to me? It's borrowed. Oh, I see now, that it was just foolish pride that made me unwilling to ride during decent hours. What a dunce I was,--as usual."

He looked at her curiously. This was beyond his comprehension.

"The bicycle belongs to Mattie Moore. She lives across the street from the parsonage, and I wanted to ride. She said I could. But I was ashamed to ride in the daytime, for fear some of the members would think it improper for a girl of the parsonage, and so I got up at six o'clock this morning to do it on the sly. Somehow I never can remember that it is just as bad to do things when you aren't seen as when you are. It doesn't seem so bad, does it? But of course it is. But I never think of that when I need to be thinking of it. Maybe I'll remember after this." She was silent a while. "Fairy'll have to get breakfast, and she always gets father's eggs too hard." Silence again. "Maybe papa'll worry. But then, they know by this time that something always does happen to me, so they'll be prepared."

She turned gravely to the young man beside her. He was looking down at her, too. And as their eyes met, and clung for an instant, a slow dark color rose in his face. Prudence felt a curious breathlessness,--caused by her hurting ankle, undoubtedly.

"My name is Prudence Starr,--I am the Methodist minister's oldest daughter."

"And my name is Jerrold Harmer." He was looking away into the hickory grove now. "My home is in Des Moines."

"Oh, Des Moines is quite a city, isn't it? I've heard quite a lot about it. It isn't so large as Chicago, though, of course. I know a man who lives in Chicago. We used to be great chums, and he told me all about the city. Some day I must really go there,--when the Methodists get rich enough to pay their ministers just a little more salary." Then she added thoughtfully, "Still, I couldn't go even if I had the money, because I couldn't leave the parsonage. So it's just as well about the money, after all. But Chicago must be very nice. He told me about the White City, and the big parks, and the elevated railways, and all the pretty restaurants and hotels. I love pretty places to eat. You might tell me about Des Moines. Is it very nice? Are there lots of rich people there?--Of course, I do not really care any more about the rich people than the others, but it always makes a city seem grand to have a lot of rich citizens, I think. Don't you?"

So he told her about Des Moines, and Prudence lay with her eyes half-closed, listening, and wondering why there was more music in his voice than in most voices. Her ankle did not hurt very badly. She did not mind it at all. In fact, she never gave it a thought. From beneath her lids, she kept her eyes fastened on Jerrold Harmer's long brown hands, clasped loosely about his knees. And whenever she could, she looked up into his face. And always there was that curious catching in her breath, and she looked away again quickly, feeling that to look too long was dangerous.

"I have talked my share now," he was saying, "tell me all about yourself, and the parsonage, and your family. And who is Fairy? And do you attend the college at Mount Mark? You look like a college girl."

"Oh, I am not," said Prudence, reluctant to make the admission for the first time in her life. "I am too stupid to be a college girl. Our mother is not living, and I left high school five years ago and have been keeping house for my father and sisters since then. I am twenty years old. How old are you?"

"I am twenty-seven," and he smiled.

"Jerrold Harmer," she said slowly and very musically. "It is such a nice name. Do your friends call you Jerry?"

"The boys at school called me Roldie, and sometimes Hammie. But my mother always called me Jerry. She isn't living now, either. You call me Jerry, will you?"

"Yes, I will, but it won't be proper. But that never makes any difference to me,--except when it might shock the members! You want me to call you Jerry, don't you?"

"Yes, I do. And when we are better acquainted, will you let me call you Prudence?"

"Call me that now.--I can't be too particular, you see, when I am lying on your coat and pillowed with your belongings. You might get cross, and take them away from me.--Did you go to college?"

"Yes, to Harvard, but I was not much of a student. Then I knocked around a while, looking at the world, and two years ago I went home to Des Moines. I have been there ever since except for little runs once in a while."

Prudence sighed. "To Harvard!--I am sorry now that I did not go to college myself."

"Why? There doesn't seem to be anything lacking about you. What do you care about college?"

"Well, you went to college," she answered argumentatively. "My sister Fairy is going now. She's very clever,--oh, very. You'll like her, I am sure,--much better than you do me, of course." Prudence was strangely downcast.

"I am sure I won't," said Jerrold Harmer, with unnecessary vehemence. "I don't care a thing for college girls. I know a lot of them, and--aw, they make a fellow tired. I like home girls,--the kind that stay at home, and keep house, and are sweet, and comfortable, and all that." Jerrold flipped over abruptly, and lay on the grass, his face on his arms turned toward her face. They were quiet for a while, but their glances were clinging.

"Your eyes are brown, aren't they?" Prudence smiled, as though she had made a pleasant discovery.

"Yes. Yours are blue. I noticed that, first thing."

"Did you? Do you like blue eyes? They aren't as--well, as strong and expressive as brown eyes. Fairy's are brown."

"I like blue eyes best. They are so much brighter and deeper. You can't see clear to the bottom of blue eyes,--you have to keep looking." And he did keep looking.

"Did you play football at college? You are so tall. Fairy's tall, too. Fairy's very grand-looking. I've tried my best to eat lots, and exercise, and make myself bigger, but--I am a fizzle."

"Yes, I played football.--But girls do not need to be so tall as men. Don't you remember what Orlando said about Rosalind,--'just as tall as my heart'? I imagine you come about to my shoulder. We'll measure as soon as you are on your feet again."

"Are you going to live in Mount Mark now? Are you coming to stay?" Prudence was almost quivering as she asked this. It was of vital importance.

"No, I will only be there a few days, but I shall probably be back every week or so. Is your father very strict? Maybe he would object to your writing to me."

"Oh, he isn't strict at all. And he will be glad for me to write to you, I know. I write to two or three men when they are away. But they are--oh, I do not know exactly what it is, but I do not really like to write to them. I believe I'll quit. It's such a bother."

"Yes, it is, that's so. I think I would quit, if I were you. I was just thinking how silly it is for me to keep on writing to some girls I used to know. Don't care two cents about 'em. I'm going to cut it out as soon as I get home. But you will write to me, won't you?"

"Yes, of course." Prudence laughed shyly. "It seems so--well, nice,--to think of getting letters from you."

"I'll bet there are a lot of nice fellows in Mount Mark, aren't there?"

"Why, no. I can't think of any real nice ones! Oh, they are all right. I have lots of friends here, but they are--I do not know what! They do not seem very nice. I wouldn't care if I never saw them again. But they are good to me."

"Yes, I can grasp that," he said with feeling.

"Is Des Moines just full of beautiful girls?"

"I should say not. I never saw a real beautiful girl in Des Moines in my life. Or any place else, for that matter,--until I came--You know when you come right down to it, there are mighty few girls that look--just the way you want them to look."

Prudence nodded. "That's the way with men, too. Of all the men I have seen in my life, I never saw one before that looked just the way I wanted him to."

"Before?" he questioned eagerly.

"Yes," said Prudence frankly. "You look just as I wish you to."

And in the meanwhile, at the parsonage, Fairy was patiently getting breakfast. "Prudence went out for an early bicycle ride,--so the members wouldn't catch her," she explained to the family. "And she isn't back yet. She'll probably stay out until afternoon, and then ride right by the grocery store where the Ladies have their Saturday sale. That's Prudence, all over. Oh, father, I did forget your eggs again, I am afraid they are too hard. Here, twins, you carry in the oatmeal, and we will eat. No use to wait for Prudence,--it would be like waiting for the next comet."

Indeed, it was nearly noon when a small, one-horse spring wagon drove into the parsonage yard. Mr. Starr was in his study with a book, but he heard a piercing shriek from Connie, and a shrill "Prudence!" from one of the twins. He was downstairs in three leaps, and rushing wildly out to the little rickety wagon. And there was Prudence!

"Don't be frightened, father. I've just sprained my ankle, and it doesn't hurt hardly any. But the bicycle is broken,--we'll have to pay for it. You can use my own money in the bank. Poor Mr. Davis had to walk all the way to town, because there wasn't any room for him in the wagon with me lying down like this. Will you carry me in?"

Connie's single bed was hastily brought downstairs, and Prudence deposited upon it. "There's no use to put me up-stairs," she assured them. "I won't stay there. I want to be down here where I can boss the girls."

The doctor came in, and bandaged the swollen purple ankle. Then they had dinner,--they tried to remember to call it luncheon, but never succeeded! After that, the whole parsonage family grouped about the little single bed in the cheery sitting-room.

"Whose coat is this, Prudence?" asked Connie.

"And where in the world did you get these towels and silk shirts?" added Fairy.

Prudence blushed most exquisitely. "They are Mr. Harmer's," she said, and glanced nervously at her father.

"Whose?" chorused the family. And it was plain to be seen that Lark was ready to take mental notes with an eye to future stories.

"If you will sit down and keep still, I will tell you all about it. But you must not interrupt me. What time is it, Fairy?"

"Two o'clock."

"Oh, two. Then I have plenty of time. Well, when I got to that little cross-cut through the hickory grove, about four miles out from town, I thought I would coast down the long hill. Do you remember that hill, father? There was no one in sight, and no animals, except one hoary old mule, grazing at the bottom. It was irresistible, absolutely irresistible. So I coasted. But you know yourself, father, there is no trusting a mule. They are the most undependable animals." Prudence looked thoughtfully down at the bed for a moment, and added slowly, "Still, I have no hard feelings against the mule. In fact, I kind of like him.--Well, anyway, just as I got to the critical place in the hill, that mule skipped right out in front of me. It looked as though he did it on purpose. I did not have time to get out of his way, and it never occurred to him to get out of mine, and so I went Bang! right into him. And it broke Mattie Moore's wheel, and upset me quite a little. But that mule never budged! Jerry--er Harmer,--Mr. Harmer, you know,--said he believed an earthquake could coast downhill on to that mule without seriously inconveniencing him. I was hurt a little, and couldn't get up. And so he jumped over the fence,--No, Connie, not the mule, of course! Mr. Harmer! He jumped over the fence, and put his coat on the ground, and made a pillow for me with the shirts and towels in his bag, and carried me over. Then he wanted to go for a wagon to bring me home, but I was too nervous and scared, so he stayed with me. Then Mr. Davis came along with his cart, and Jerry--er--Harmer, you know, helped put me in, and the cart was so small they both had to walk."

"Where is he now?" "Is he young?" "Is he handsome?" "Did he look rich?"

"Don't be silly, girls. He went to the hotel, I suppose. Anyhow, he left us as soon as we reached town. He said he was in a hurry, and had something to look after. His coat was underneath me in the wagon, and he wouldn't take it out for fear of hurting my ankle, so the poor soul is probably wandering around this town in his shirt-sleeves."

Already, in the eyes of the girls, this Jerry--er--Harmer, had taken unto himself all the interest of the affair.

"He'll have to come for his coat," said Lark. "We're bound to see him."

"Where does he live? What was he doing in the hickory grove?" inquired Mr. Starr with a strangely sinking heart, for her eyes were alight with new and wonderful radiance.

"He lives in Des Moines. He was just walking into town, and took a short cut through the grove."

"Walking! From Des Moines?"

Prudence flushed uncomfortably. "I didn't think of that," she said. "But I do not see why he should not walk if he likes. He's strong and athletic, and fond of exercise. I guess he's plenty able to walk if he wants to. I'm sure he's no tramp, father, if that is what you are thinking."

"I am not thinking anything of the kind, Prudence," he said with dignity. "But I do think it rather strange that a young man should set out to walk from Des Moines to Mount Mark. And why should he be at it so early in the morning? Doesn't he require sleep, as the rest of us do?"

"How should I know? I guess if he likes to be but in the morning when it is fresh and sweet, it is all right. I like the morning myself. He had as much right out early as I had. His clothes were nice, and he is a Harvard graduate, and his shoes were dusty, but not soiled or worn. Anyhow, he is coming at four o'clock. If you want to ask if he is a tramp, you can do it." And Prudence burst into tears.

Dramatic silence in the cheerful sitting-room! Then Fairy began bustling about to bathe the face and throat of "poor little Prudence," and her father said sympathetically:

"You're all nervous and wrought up, with the pain and excitement, Prudence. I'm glad he is coming so we can thank him for his kindness. It was mighty lucky he happened along, wasn't it? A Harvard graduate! Yes, they are pretty strong on athletics at Harvard. You'd better straighten this room a little and have things looking nice when he gets here," said Father Starr, with great diplomacy. And he was rewarded, and startled, by observing that Prudence brightened wonderfully at his words.

"Yes, do," she urged eagerly. "Get some of the roses from the corner bush, and put them on the table there. And when you go up-stairs, Fairy, you'd better bring down that little lace spread in the bottom drawer of our dresser. It'll look very nice on this bed.--Work hard, girls, and get everything looking fine. He'll be here at four, he said. You twins may wear your white dresses, and Connie must put on her blue and wear her blue bows.--Fairy, do you think it would be all right for you to wear your silk dress? Of course, the silk is rather grand for home, but you do look so beautiful in it. Father, will you put on your black suit, or are you too busy? And don't forget to wear the pearl cuff buttons Aunt Grace sent you."

He went up-stairs to obey, with despair in his heart. But to the girls, there was nothing strange in this exactness on the part of Prudence. Jerrold Harmer was the hero of the romance, and they must unite to do him honor. He was probably a prince in disguise. Jerrold Harmer was a perfectly thrilling name. It was really a shame that America allows no titles,--Lord Jerrold did sound so noble, and Lady Prudence was very effective, too. He and Prudence were married, and had a family of four children, named for the various Starrs, before one hour had passed.

"I'll begin my book right away," Lark was saying. She and Carol were in the dining-room madly polishing their Sunday shoes,--what time they were not performing the marriage ceremony of their sister and The Hero.

"Yes, do! But for goodness' sake, don't run her into a mule! Seems to me even Prudence could have done better than that."

"I'll have his automobile break down in the middle of the road, and Prudence can run into it. The carbureter came off, and of course the car wouldn't run an inch without it."

"Yes, that's good," said Carol approvingly. "It must be a sixty cylinder, eight horsepower--er--Ford, or something real big and costly."

"Twins! You won't be ready," warned Prudence, and this dire possibility sent them flying upstairs in a panic.

While the girls, bubbling over with excitement, were dressing for the great event, Mr. Starr went down-stairs to sit with Prudence. Carol called to him on his way down, and he paused on the staircase, looking up at her.

"Lark and I are going to use some of Fairy's powder, father," she said. "We feel that we simply must on an occasion like this. And for goodness' sake, don't mention it before Him! It doesn't happen very often, you know, but to-day we simply must.

Now, don't you say anything about falling in the flour barrel, or turning pale all of a sudden, whatever else you do. We'd be so mortified, father."

Mr. Starr was concerned with weightier matters, and went on down to Prudence with never so much as a reproving shake of the head for the worldly-minded young twins.

"Father," began Prudence, her eyes on the lace coverlet, "do you think it would be all right for me to wear that silk dressing-gown of mother's? I need something over my nightgown, and my old flannel kimono is so ugly. You know, mother said I was to have it, and--I'm twenty now. Do you think it would be all right? But if you do not want me to wear it----"

"I do want you to," was the prompt reply. "Yes, it is quite time you were wearing it. I'll get it out of the trunk myself, and send Fairy down to help you." Then as he turned toward the door, he asked carelessly, "Is he very good-looking, Prudence?"

And Prudence, with a crimson face, answered quickly, "Oh, I really didn't notice, father."

He went on up-stairs then, and presently Fairy came down with the dainty silk gown trimmed with fine soft lace. "I brought my lavender ribbon for your hair, Prudence. It will match the gown so nicely. Oh, you do look sweet, dearest. I pity Jerrold Harmer, I can tell you that. Now I must hurry and finish my own dressing."

But with her foot on the bottom stair, she paused. Her sister was calling after her. "Send father down here, quick, Fairy."

Father ran down quickly, and Prudence, catching hold of his hands, whispered wretchedly, "Oh, father, he--he is good-looking. I--I did notice it. I didn't really mean to lie to you."

"There, now, Prudence," he said, kissing her tenderly, "you mustn't get excited again. I'm afraid you are too nervous to have callers. You must lie very quietly until he comes. That was no lie, child. You are so upset you do not know what you are saying to-day. Be quiet now, Prudence,--it's nearly time for him to come."

"You are a dear good father," she cried, kissing his hands passionately, "but it was a lie. I did know what I was saying. I did it on purpose."

And Mr. Starr's heart was heavy, for he knew that his fears were realized.

CHAPTER XII
ROUSED FROM HER SLUMBER

At twenty minutes to four, the parsonage family clustered excitedly in the sitting-room, which the sunshine flooded cheerily. They were waiting for the hero of Prudence's romance.

"Oh, Larkie, will you run up-stairs and bring my lace handkerchief? It's on our dresser, in the burnt-wood box." And after Lark had departed, she went on, "The flowers are not quite in the center of the table, Fairy,--a little to the right.--If you would move the curtains the least little bit, those torn places would not show." Then she sighed. "How nice you all look. Oh, Connie, won't you turn the clock a little this way, so I can see it? That's better, thank you, precious. Thank you, Lark,--isn't it a pretty handkerchief? I've only carried it three times, and I have never really used it. Would you keep these pearls on, Fairy, or would you take them off?"

"I would keep them on, Prue,--they catch the color of the gown a little, and are just beautiful. You do look so sweet, but your face is very flushed. I am afraid you are feverish. Maybe we had better not let him see Prue to-day, father. Perhaps he can come back to-morrow."

"Fairy!" exclaimed Prudence. "Besides, he must come in to get his coat. We can't expect him to go coatless over Sunday. Listen,--listen, girls! Look, Fairy, and see if that is he! Yes, it is, I know,--I can tell by his walk." Warm rich color dyed her face and throat, and she clasped her hands over her heart, wondering if Connie beside her could hear its tumult.

"I'll go to the door," said Father Starr, and Prudence looked at him beseechingly.

"I--I am sure he is all right, father. I--you will be nice to him, won't you?"

Without answering, Mr. Starr left the room. He could not trust his voice.

"Listen, girls, I want to hear," whispered Prudence. And she smiled as she heard her father's cordial voice.

"You are Mr. Harmer, aren't you? I am Prudence's father. Come right in. The whole family is assembled to do you honor. The girls have already made you a prince in disguise. Come back this way. Prudence is resting very nicely."

When the two men stepped into the sitting-room, Prudence, for once, quite overlooked her father. She lifted her eyes to Jerrold Harmer's face, and waited, breathless. Nor was he long in finding her among the bevy of girls. He walked at once to the bed, and took her hand.

"My little comrade of the road," he said gaily, but with tenderness, "I am afraid you are not feeling well enough for callers to-day."

"Oh, yes, I am," protested Prudence with strange shyness.

He turned to the other girls, and greeted them easily. He was entirely self-possessed. "Miss Starr told me so much about you that I know you all to begin with." He smiled at Fairy as he added, "In fact, she predicted that I am to fall in love with you. And so, very likely, I should,--if I hadn't met your sister first."

They all laughed at that, and then he walked back and stood by Prudence once more. "Was it a bad sprain? Does it pain you very badly? You look tired. I am afraid it was an imposition for me to come this afternoon."

"Oh, don't worry about that," put in Connie anxiously. "She wanted you to come. She's been getting us ready for you ever since the doctor left. I think it was kind of silly for me to wear my blue just for one caller."

The twins glared at her, realizing that she was discrediting the parsonage, but Jerrold Harmer laughed, and Prudence joined him.

"It is quite true," she admitted frankly. "The mule and I disgraced the parsonage this morning, and I wanted the rest of you to redeem it this afternoon." She looked at him inquiringly. "Then you had another coat?"

"No, I didn't. I saw this one in a window this morning, and couldn't resist it. Was the ride very hard on your ankle?"

Mr. Starr was puzzled. Evidently it was not lack of funds which brought this man on foot from Des Moines to Mount Mark,--half-way across the state! He did not look like a man fleeing from justice. What, then, was the explanation?

"You must have found it rather a long walk," he began tentatively, his eyes on the young man's face.

"Yes, I think my feet are a little blistered. I have walked farther than that many times, but I am out of practise now. Sometimes, however, walking is a painful necessity."

"How long did it take you coming from Des Moines to Mount Mark?" inquired Carol in a subdued and respectful voice,--and curious, withal.

"I did not come directly to Mount Mark. I stopped several places on business. I hardly know how long it would take coming straight, through. It would depend on one's luck, I suppose."

"Well," said Lark, "taking it a little at a time it might be done, but for myself, I should never dream of undertaking so much exercise."

"Could you walk from here to Burlington at one stretch?" asked Connie.

He looked rather surprised. "Why, perhaps I could if I was in shape, but-- seven miles was all I cared about this morning."

"Well, I think it was mighty brave of you to walk that far,--I don't care why you did it," announced Connie with emphasis.

"Brave!" he repeated. "I have walked three times seven miles, often, when I was in school."

"Oh, I mean the whole thing--clear from Des Moines," explained Connie.

"From Des Moines," he gasped. "Good heavens! I did not walk from Des Moines! Did you--" He turned to Prudence questioningly. "Did you think I walked clear from Des Moines?"

"Yes." And added hastily, "But I did not care if you did. It did not make any difference how you came."

For a moment he was puzzled. Then he burst out laughing. "I am afraid we had too much to talk about this morning. I thought I had explained my situation, but evidently I did not. I drove from Des Moines in the car, and----"

"The automobile!" gasped Carol, with a triumphant look at Lark.

"Yes, just so. I stopped several places on business as I came through. I drove from Burlington this morning, but I got off the road. The car broke down on me, and I couldn't fix it,--broke an axle. So I had to walk in. That is what I was seeing about to-day,--sending a man out for the car and arranging about the repairs." He smiled again. "What in the world did you think I would walk from Des Moines for?" he asked Prudence, more inquisitive than grammatical.

"I did not think anything about it until they asked, and--I did not know about the car. You did not mention it."

"No. I remember now. We were talking of other things all the time." He turned frankly to Mr. Starr. "Perhaps you have heard of the Harmer Automobile Company, of Des Moines. My father was Harvey Harmer. Two years ago, when I was running around in Europe, he died. It was his desire that I should personally take charge of the business. So I hurried home, and have had charge of the company since then. We are establishing sales agencies here, and in Burlington, and several other towns. I came out for a little trip, and took advantage of the opportunity to discuss the business with our new men. That's what brought me to Mount Mark." To Connie he added laughingly, "So I must sacrifice myself, and do without your praise. I did not walk until the car broke down and compelled me to do so."

For the first time in her life, Prudence distinctly triumphed over her father. She flashed him the glance of a conqueror, and he nodded, understandingly. He liked Jerrold Harmer,--as much as he could like any man who stepped seriously into the life of Prudence. He was glad that things were well. But--they would excuse him, he must look after his Sunday's sermons.

A little later the twins and Connie grew restless, and finally Connie blurted out, "Say, Prue, don't you think we've upheld the parsonage long enough? I want to get some fresh air." The twins would never have been guilty of such social indiscretion as this, but they gladly availed themselves of Connie's "break," and followed her out-of-doors. Then Fairy got up, laughing. "I have done my share, too. I think we'll leave the parsonage in your hands now, Prue. I want to write to Aunt Grace. I'll be just at the head of the stairs, and if Prudence wants me, you will call, won't you, Mr. Harmer? And won't you stay for dinner with us? I'm sure to disgrace the parsonage again, for I am no cook, but you can get along for once, surely. We spend more time laughing when the food is bad, and laughter is very healthful. You will stay, won't you?"

Jerrold Harmer looked very eager, and yet he looked somewhat doubtfully at Prudence. Her eyes were eloquent with entreaties. Finally he laughed, and said, "I should certainly like to stay, but you see I want to come back to-morrow. Now, will I dare to come back to-morrow if I stay for dinner to-night? Wouldn't Connie say that was disgracing the parsonage?"

Fairy laughed delightedly. "That is very good," she said. "Then you will stay. I'll try to fix it up with Connie to save the reputation of the house. Now, do not talk too much, Prue, and--what shall we have for dinner? We only say dinner when we have company, Mr. Harmer. What we have is supper."

Prudence contracted her brows in the earnest endeavor to compose a menu suitable for this occasion. "Mashed potatoes, and--use cream, Fairy. You'd better let Lark do the mashing, for you always leave lumps. And breaded veal cutlet," with a significant glance, "and creamed peas, and radishes, and fruit. Will that be enough for you, Mr. Harmer?"

"Oceans," he said contentedly.

"Well, I'll collect the twins and Connie and we will try to think up a few additions. Where's the money?"

"In the dungeon, and the key is on the nail above the door. And the silverware is there, too," with another significant glance.

After that, Prudence lay back happily on the pillows and smoothed the lace on her mother's silk dressing gown.

"Talk to me," she said, "tell me about where you live, and what you do,--your work, you know, and how you amuse yourself. I want you to amuse me now, Mr. Harmer."

"You called me Jerry this morning."

"Yes, I know. Do you want me to call you Jerry still?"

"Yes, Prudence, I do. Do you mind if I move my chair a little closer?"

"No, put it right here. Now, I am ready."

"But there's nothing interesting about me. Let's talk of----"

"It's interesting to me. Tell me about your business."

"You don't care anything about business, I am sure."

"I care about your business."

"Do you, Prudence?--You look so sweet this afternoon. I nearly blurted it out before the whole family. Wouldn't the twins have laughed? It would have disgraced the parsonage. I think Mr. Starr is awfully lucky to have five girls, and all of them pretty. But isn't it strange that the prettiest and dearest one of them all should be the oldest daughter?"

"Oh, but I'm not really--" Prudence began earnestly. Then she stopped, and added honestly, "But I am glad you think so."

No, they did not quote poetry, they did not discuss the psychological intricacies of spontaneous attraction, they did not say anything deep, or wise, or learned. But they smiled at each other, with pleased investigating eyes. He put his hand on the coverlet, just near enough to touch the lace on the sleeve of her silk dressing gown. And together they found Paradise in the shabby sitting-room of the old Methodist parsonage that afternoon.

"Must you prepare meat for breading half an hour before cooking, or when?" demanded Fairy, from the dining-room door.

"What?--Oh!--Fifteen minutes before. Don't forget to salt and pepper the crumbs, Fairy."

"Perhaps some time your father will let you and a couple of the others come to Des Moines with me in the car. You would enjoy a few days there, I know. I live with my aunt, a dear, motherly little old soul. She will adore you, Prudence, and you will like her, too. Would your father let you spend a week? We can easily drive back and forth in the car."

"Maybe he will,--but who will keep the parsonage while I am away?"

"Fairy, to be sure. She must be a good fairy once in a while. We can take the twins with us, Connie, too, if you like, and then Fairy will only have to mother your father. Do you like riding in a car?"

"Oh, I love it. But I have not ridden very much. Willard Morley took me quite often when he was here, but he is in Chicago now."

"When's he coming back?" suspiciously.

"Prudence, shall we have tea or coffee?" This was Lark from the doorway. "Fairy wants to know."

"What?--Oh!--Which do you want, Jerry?"

"Which does your father prefer?"

"He doesn't drink either except for breakfast."

"I generally drink coffee, but I do not care much for it, so do not bother----"

"Coffee, Lark."

"When's that Morley chap coming back?"

"I do not know." And then, "He is never coming back as far as I am concerned."

Jerrold relented promptly. "You are why he went away, I suppose."

"At any rate, he is gone."

"Did you ever have a lover, Prudence? A real lover, I mean."

"No, I, never did."

"I'm awfully glad of that. I'll----"

"Prudence, do you use half milk and half water for creamed tomato soup, or all milk?"

"What?--Oh!--All milk, Connie, and tell Fairy not to salt it until it is entirely done, or it may curdle."

"What in the world would they ever do without you, Prudence? You are the soul of the parsonage, aren't you?"

"No, I am just the cook and the chambermaid," she answered, laughing. "But don't you see how hard it will be for me to go away?"

"But it isn't fair! Vacation is coming now, and Fairy ought to take a turn. What will they do when you get married?"

"I have always said I would not get married."

"But don't you want to get married,--some time?"

"Oh, that isn't it. I just can't because I must take care of the parsonage, and raise the girls. I can't."

"But you will," he whispered, and his hand touched hers for just a second. Prudence did not answer. She lifted her eyes to his face, and caught in her breath once more.

A little later he said, "Do you mind if I go upstairs and talk to your father a few minutes? Maybe I'd better."

"But do not stay very long," she urged, and she wondered why the brightness and sunshine vanished from the room when he went out. "First door to the right," she called after him.

Mr. Starr arose to greet him, and welcomed him to his combination study and bedroom with great friendliness. But Jerrold went straight to the point.

"Mr. Starr, it's very kind of you to receive a perfect stranger as you have me. But I understand that with a girl like Prudence, you will want to be careful. I can give you the names of several prominent men in Des Moines, Christians, who know me well, and can tell you all about me."

"It isn't necessary. We are parsonage people, and we are accustomed to receiving men and women as worthy of our trust, until we find them different. We are glad to count you among our friends."

"Thank you, but--you see, Mr. Starr, this is a little different. Some day, Prudence and I will want to be married, and you will wish to be sure about me."

"Does Prudence know about that?"

"No," with a smile, "we haven't got that far yet. But I am sure she feels it. She hasn't--well, you know what I mean. She has been asleep, but I believe she is waking up now."

"Yes, I think so. Do you mind if I ask you a few questions?"

"No, indeed. Anything you like."

"Well, first, are you a Christian?"

"Not the kind you are, Mr. Starr. My parents were Christians, but I've never thought much about it myself because I was young and full of fun. I have never been especially directed to religion. I go to church, and I believe the Bible,--though I don't know much about it. I seldom read it. But I'll get busy now, if you like, and really study it and--try to come around your way. I know Prudence would make me do that." And he smiled again.

"Do you drink?"

"I did a little, but I promised Prudence this morning I would quit it. I never got--drunk, and I have not formed the habit. But sometimes with the boys, I drink a little. But I do not care for it, and I swore off this morning.--I smoke, too,--not cigarettes, of course. Prudence knows it, but she did not make me promise to quit that?" His voice was raised, inquiringly.

"Would you have promised, if she had asked it?" This was sheer curiosity.

"I suppose I would." He flushed a little. "I know I was pretty hard hit, and it was such a new experience that I would have promised anything she asked. But I like smoking, and--I don't think it is wicked."

"Never mind the smoking. I only asked that question out of curiosity. We're not as strait-laced as we might be perhaps. The only things I would really object to, are those things that might seriously menace your happiness, yours and hers, if the time does come. But the next question,--can you pass a strict physical examination?"

"Yes, I can. I'll go with you to your physician to-night if you like. I'm all right physically, I know."

"Tell me about your relations with your mother when she was living."

"She has been dead four years." Jerrold spoke with some emotion. "We were great chums, though her health was always poor. I wrote her three times a week when I was away from home, and she wrote me a note every day. When I was in school, I spent all my vacations at home to be with her. And I never went abroad until after her death because she did not like the idea of my going so far from her."

"Jerrold, my boy, I do not want to seem too severe, but--tell me, has there been anything in your life, about women, that could come out and hurt Prudence later on?"

Jerrold hesitated. "Mr. Starr, I have been young, and headstrong, and impulsive. I have done some things I wish now I hadn't. But I believe there is nothing that I could not explain to Prudence so she would understand. If I had thought beforehand of a girl like her, there are things I would not have done. But there is nothing, I think, that would really hurt, after I had a chance to talk it over with her."

"All right. If you are the man, God bless you. I don't suppose you are worthy of Prudence, for she is a good, pure-hearted, unselfish girl,--there could be none better. But the real point is just whether you will love each other enough!--I like your coming up here like this. I think that was very decent and manly of you. And, do you mind if I just suggest that you go a little slow with Prudence? Remember that she has been sound asleep, until this morning. I do not want her awakened too rudely."

"Neither do I," said Jerrold quickly. "Shall I go down now? The girls have invited me to stay for supper, and Prudence says I am to come back to-morrow, too. Is that all right? Remember, I'll be going home on Monday!"

"It is all right, certainly. Spend as much time here as you like. You will either get worse, or get cured, and--whichever it is, you've got to have a chance. I like you, Jerrold. Prudence judges by instinct, but it does not often fail her."

Prudence heard him running down the stairs boyishly, and when he came in, before she could speak, he whispered, "Shut your eyes tight, Prudence. And do not scold me, for I can't help it." Then he put his hands over hers, and kissed her on the lips. They were both breathless after that. Prudence lifted her lashes slowly, and gazed at him seriously. It was she who spoke first.

"I was never really kissed before," she whispered, "not really."

Then they sat in silence until Fairy announced that supper was ready. "But I won't promise it is eatable," she assured them, laughing.

"I wish I could go to the table, too," said Prudence, looking at her father wistfully, "I could lie on the old lounge out there."

"And have your supper on a tray, of course. Can you carry her, father?"

"I can!" volunteered Jerrold promptly. "I have done it."

"I think between us we can manage. We'll try it." And Prudence heroically endured the pain of being moved, for the sake of seeing Jerrold at the table with her parsonage family. For to her surprise, she realized that she could not bear that even a few minutes should pass, when she could not see the manly young face with the boyish mouth and the tender eyes!

Prudence, at last, was aroused from her slumber.

CHAPTER XIII
SHE ORDERS HER LIFE

Prudence, are you going to Aunt Grace's early in the summer, or late?" demanded Fairy.

"Oh, let's not talk of that now. There's plenty of time."

"No, there isn't. School will be out in a week, and Babbie wants to give a house party and have our little bunch at his home for a few days this summer. He wants to set the date, and I can't tell him when because I do not know when you are going to auntie's."

They sat around the breakfast table, Prudence and Fairy and their father, talking of the summer. The twins and Connie had long since excused themselves, and even now could be heard shouting gaily in the field beyond the old red barn.

Prudence looked restlessly from one to the other, when her sister insisted upon an answer.

"Why," she began, "I've about decided not to go to Aunt Grace's this summer."

Fairy rapped on the table with the spoon she held in her hand. "Don't be silly! You have to go. You've never had a vacation in your life, and father promised Aunt Grace on his reputation as a minister, didn't you, papa?"

"Yes, I promised all right."

"But, papa! I do not have to go, do I? A whole month,--oh, honestly, I do not want to."

"Why don't you? Last fall you were wild about it. Don't you remember dreaming----"

"Oh, but that was last fall," said Prudence, smiling softly, and unconsciously she lifted one hand to where a bulky letter nestled inside her dress. "I didn't know

I was going to sprain my ankle, and be so useless. It may be two weeks yet before I can walk on it."

"What has that got to do with it?"

"Do you really prefer to stay at home, Prudence?" queried her father. "The whole summer?"

Prudence blushed most gloriously. "Oh, well," she began slowly. Then she took the plunge recklessly. "Why, you see, father, Jerry lives with his aunt in Des Moines,--he told you that, didn't he? And they have quite a big house, and--he wants to take me and the twinnies to Des Moines in the car for a week or ten days. And Fairy will take care of you and Connie. And--if I can do that--I do not want any more vacation. I couldn't bear to stay at auntie's a whole month, away from you and the parsonage." She felt very guilty, for she did not add, as she was think-ing, "Besides, Jerry is coming every two weeks, and if I were away, we would miss a visit!"

Fairy laughed in an irritating, suggestive way, but Mr. Starr only nodded.

"I am sure you will not mind that, will you father? His aunt must be a perfectly good and nice woman, and--such a long drive in the auto, and--to see all over Des Moines." But Prudence paused guiltily, for she did not add, "With Jerry!" although the words were singing in her heart.

"That will be very nice indeed, and of course I do not object. It will be a forty years' delight and wonder to the twins! Yes, I will be glad to have you go. But you can still have your month at Grace's if you wish."

"But I do not wish," protested Prudence promptly. "Honestly, father, I'll write her the sweetest kind of a letter, but--oh, please do not make me go!"

"Of course, we won't make you go, you goose," said Fairy, "but I think you are very foolish."

"And you can go, Fairy," cried Prudence hospitably. "Aunt Grace loves you so, and you've worked so hard all year, and,--oh, yes, it will be just the thing for you." Prudence wished she might add, "And that will let me out," but she hardly dare say it.

"Well, when does your Des Moines tour come off? I must know, so I can tell Babbie about the house party."

"Let Babbie choose his own date. Jerry says we shall go whenever I say--I mean whenever you say, father,--and we can decide later on. Give Babbie first choice, by all means."

That was the beginning of Prudence's golden summer. She was not given to self-analysis. She did what seemed good to her always,--she did not delve down below the surface for reasons why and wherefore. She hadn't the time. She took things as they came. She could not bear the thought of sharing with the parsonage family even the least ardent and most prosaic of Jerrold's letters. But she never asked herself the reason. It seemed a positive sacrilege to leave his warm, life-pulsing letters up-stairs in a bureau drawer. It was only natural and right to carry them in her dress, and to sleep with them under her pillow. But Prudence did not wonder why. The days when Jerry came were tremulously happy ones for her,--she was all aquiver when she heard him swinging briskly up the ramshackle parsonage walk, and her breath was suffocatingly hot. But she took it as a matter of course. The nights when Jerry slept in the little spare bedroom at the head of the stairs, Prudence lay awake, staring joyously into the darkness, hoping Jerry was sound asleep and comfortable. But she never asked herself why she could not sleep! She knew that Jerry's voice was the sweetest voice in the world. She knew that his eyes were the softest and brightest and the most tender. She knew that his hands had a thrilling touch quite different from the touch of ordinary, less dear hands. She knew that his smile lifted her into a delirium of delight, and that even the thought of sorrow coming to him brought stinging tears to her eyes. But why? Ah, Prudence never thought of that. She just lived in the sweet ecstatic dream of the summer, and was well and richly content.

So the vacation passed, and Indian summer came. And the girls went back to their studies once more, reluctantly, yet unaccountably glad even in their reluctance. It is always that way with students,--real students. They regret the passing of vacation days, but the thought of "going back to school" has its own tingling joys of anticipation.

It was Saturday evening. The early supper at the parsonage was over, the twins had washed the dishes, and still the daylight lingered. Prudence and Jerry sat side by side, and closely, on the front porch, talking in whispers. Fairy had gone for a stroll with the still faithful Babbie. Connie and the twins had evidently vanished. Ah--not quite that! Carol and Lark came swiftly around the corner of the parsonage.

"Good evening," said Lark politely, and Prudence sat up abruptly. The twins never wasted politeness! They wanted something.

"Do you mind if we take Jerry around by the woodshed for a few minutes, Prue?"

"I'll come along," said Prudence, rising.

"Oh, no," protested Lark, "we do not want you,--just Jerry, and only for a little while."

Prudence sniffed suspiciously. "What are you going to do to him?" she demanded.

"We won't hurt him," grinned Carol impishly. "We had intended to tie him to a stake and burn him alive. But since you have interceded on his behalf, we'll let him off with a simple scalping."

"Maybe he's afraid to come," said Lark, "for there are two of us, and we are mighty men of valor."

"That's all right," Prudence answered defensively. "I'd sooner face a tribe of wild Indians any day than you twins when you are mischief-bent."

"Oh, we just want to use him a few minutes," said Carol impatiently. "Upon our honor, as Christian gentlemen, we promise not to hurt a hair of his head."

"Oh, come along, and cut out the comedy," Jerry broke in, laughing. "I'll be back in two minutes, Prue. They probably want me to shoo a chicken out of their way. Or maybe the cat has been chasing them."

Once safely around the corner, the twins changed their tactics.

"We knew you weren't afraid," said Lark artistically, "we were just teasing Prudence. We know we couldn't hurt you."

"Of course," emphasized Carol. "We want to ask a favor of you, that's all. It's something we can't do ourselves, but we knew you could do it, all right."

Jerry perceived the drift of this argument. "I see! I'm paid in advance for my service. What's the job?"

Then the twins led him to the woodshed. This woodshed stood about twenty feet from the back door of the parsonage, and was nine feet high in front, the roof sloping down at the back. Close beside the shed grew a tall and luxuriant maple. The lower limbs had been chopped off, and the trunk rose clear to a height of nearly twelve feet before the massive limbs branched out. The twins had discovered that by climbing gingerly on the rotten roof of the woodshed, followed by almost superhuman scrambling and scratching, they could get up into the leafy secrecy of the grand old maple. More than this, up high in the tree they found a delightful arrangement of branches that seemed positively made for them. These branches must be utilized, and it was in the act of utilizing them that they called upon their sister's friend for help.

"Do you see this board?" began Lark, exhibiting with some pride a solid board about two feet in length.

"My eyesight is quite unimpaired," answered Jerry, for he knew his twins.

"Well, we found this over by the Avery barn. They have a big scrap pile out there. We couldn't find anything around here that would suit, so we looked, over there. It's just a pile of rubbish, and we knew they wouldn't mind."

"Else you would not have taken it, eh? Anything like apples, for instance, is quite under the ban."

"Yes, indeed," smiled Lark. "We're too old to steal apples."

"Of course," added Carol. "When we need our neighbor's apples, we send Connie. And get nicely punished for it, too, I promise you."

"Quite so! And this exquisite board?"

"Well, we've found a perfectly gorgeous place up in the old tree where we can make a seat. It's quite a ways out from the trunk, and when the wind blows it swings splendidly. But it isn't very comfortable sitting on a thin limb, and so we want a seat. It's a fine place, I tell you. We thought you could nail this securely on to the limbs,--there are two right near each other, evidently put there on purpose for us. See what dandy big nails we have!"

"From the Avery's woodshed, I suppose," he suggested, smiling again.

"Oh, they are quite rusty. We found them in a sack in an old barrel. It was in the scrap heap. We're very good friends with the Averys, very good, indeed," she continued hastily. "They allow us to rummage around at will--in the barn."

"And see this rope," cried Carol. "Isn't it a dandy?"

"Ah! The Avery barn must be inexhaustible in its resources."

"How suspicious you are, Jerry," mourned Lark.

"I wish we were that way, instead of innocent and bland and trustful. Maybe we would get rich, too. This is the first time I ever really understood how you came to be a success in business."

"But you are quite wrong this time," said Lark seriously. "Old Mr. Avery gave me this rope."

"Yes, he did! Lark told him she was looking for a rope just exactly like this one, and then he gave it to her. He caught the idea of philanthropy right away. He's a very nice old gentleman, I tell you. He's so trusting and unsuspicious. I'm very fond of people like that."

"We thought when you had the board nicely nailed on, you might rope it securely to the limbs above. They are in very good position, and that will make it absolutely safe. Do you suppose you can do that, Jerry? Do you get seasick when you climb high?"

"Oh, no, high altitudes never make me seasick. I've a very good head for such purposes."

"Then suppose you get busy before it grows dark. We're in a great hurry. And we do not want Connie to catch us putting it up. It'll be such fun to sit up there and swing when the wind blows, and have poor Connie down beneath wondering how we manage to stick on. She can't see the seat from the ground. Won't it be a good joke on her?"

"Oh, very,---yes, indeed.--Well, let's begin.--Now, observe! I will just loop this end of the rope lightly about my--er--middle. The other end will dangle on the ground to be drawn up at will. Observe also that I bestow the good but rusty nails in this pocket, and the hammer here. Then with the admirable board beneath my arm, I mount to the heights of--Say, twins, didn't I see an old buggy seat out in the barn to-day? Seems to me----"

"Oh, Jerry!" The twins fairly smothered him. "Oh, you darling. You are the nicest old thing.--Now we can understand why Prudence seems to like you. We never once thought of the old buggy seat! Oh, Jerry!"

Then they hastily brought the discarded seat from the barn, and with the help of Jerry it was shoved up on the woodshed. From there, he lifted it to the lowest limb of the old maple, and a second later he was up himself. Then it was lifted again, and again he followed,--up, and up, and up,--the loose end of the donated rope trailing loose on the ground below. The twins promptly,--as promptly as possible, that is,--followed him into the tree.

"Oh, yes, we'll come along. We're used to climbing and we're very agile. And you will need us to hold things steady while you hammer."

And Jerry smiled as he heard the faithful twins, with much grunting and an occasional groan, following in his wake.

It was a delightful location, as they had said. So heavy was the leafy screen that only by lifting a branch here or there, could they see through it. The big seat fitted nicely on the two limbs, and Jerry fastened it with the rusty nails. The twins were jubilant, and loud in their praises of his skill and courage.

"Oh, Jerry," exclaimed Carol, with deep satisfaction, "it's such a blessing to discover something really nice about you after all these months!"

"Now, we'll just----"

"Hush!" hissed Lark. "Here comes Connie. Hold your breath, Jerry, and don't budge."

"Isn't she in on this?" he whispered. He could hear Connie making weird noises as she came around the house from the front. She was learning to whistle, and the effect was ghastly in the extreme. Connie's mouth had not been designed for whistling.

"Sh! She's the band of dark-browed gypsies trying to steal my lovely wife."

"I'm the lovely wife," interrupted Carol complacently.

"But Connie does not know about it. She is so religious she won't be any of the villain parts. When we want her to be anything real low-down, we have to do it on the sly. She would no more consent to a band of dark-browed gypsies than she would----"

Connie came around the corner of the parsonage, out the back walk beneath the maple. Then she gave a gleeful scream. Right before her lay a beautiful heavy rope. Connie had been yearning for a good rope to make a swing. Here it lay, at her very feet, plainly a gift of the gods. She did not wait to see where the other end of the rope was. She just grabbed what she saw before her, and started violently back around the house with it yelling, "Prudence! Look at my rope!"

Prudence rushed around the parsonage. The twins shrieked wildly, as there was a terrific tug and heave of the limb beside them, and then--a crashing of branches and leaves. Jerry was gone!

It did look horrible, from above as well as below. But Jerry, when he felt the first light twinge as Connie lifted the rope, foresaw what was coming and was ready for it. As he went down, he grabbed a firm hold on the branch on which he had stood, then he dropped to the next, and held again. On the lowest limb he really clung for fifteen seconds, and took in his bearings. Connie had dropped the rope when the twins screamed, so he had nothing more to fear from her. He saw Prudence, white, with wild eyes, both arms stretched out toward him.

"O. K., Prue," he called, and then he dropped. He landed on his feet, a little jolted, but none the worse for his fall.

He ran at once to Prudence. "I'm all right," he cried, really alarmed by the white horror in her face. "Prudence! Prudence!" Then her arms dropped, and with a brave but feeble smile, she swayed a little. Jerry took her in his arms. "Sweetheart!" he whispered. "Little sweetheart! Do--do you love me so much, my dearest?"

Prudence raised her hands to his face, and looked intensely into his eyes, all the sweet loving soul of her shining in her own. And Jerry kissed her.

The twins scrambled down from the maple, speechless and cold with terror,--and saw Prudence and Jerry! Then they saw Connie, staring at them with interest and amusement.

"I think we'd better go to bed, all three of us," declared Lark sturdily. And they set off heroically around the house. But at the corner Carol turned.

"Take my advice and go into the woodshed," she said, "for all the Averys are looking out of their windows."

Prudence did not hear, but he drew her swiftly into the woodshed. Now a woodshed is a hideously unromantic sort of place. And there was nothing for Prudence to sit on, that Jerry might kneel at her feet. So they dispensed with formalities, and he held her in his arms for a long time, and kissed her often, and whispered sweet meaningless words that thrilled her as she listened. It may not have been comfortable, but it was evidently endurable, for it is a fact that they did not leave that woodshed for over an hour. Then they betook themselves to the darkest corner of the side porch,--and history repeated itself once more!

At twelve, Jerry went up-stairs to bed, his lips tingling with the fervent tenderness of her parting kiss. At one o'clock, he stood at his window, looking soberly out into the moonlit parsonage yard. "She is an angel, a pure, sweet, unselfish little angel," he whispered, and his voice was broken, and his eyes were wet, "and she is going to be my wife! Oh, God, teach me how to be good to her, and help me make her as happy as she deserves."

At two o'clock he lay on his bed, staring into the darkness, thinking again the soft shy words she had whispered to him. And he flung his arms out toward his closed door, wanting her. At three o'clock he dropped lightly asleep and dreamed of her. With the first pale streaks of daylight stealing into his room, he awoke. It was after four o'clock. A little later,--just a few minutes later,--he heard a light tap on his door. It came again, and he bounded out of bed.

"Prudence! Is anything wrong?"

"Hush, Jerry, not so loud!" And what a strange and weary voice. "Come downstairs, will you? I want to tell you something. I'll wait at the foot of the stairs. Be quiet,--do not wake father and the girls. Will you be down soon?"

"In two minutes!"

And in two minutes he was flown, agonizingly anxious, knowing that something was wrong. Prudence was waiting for him, and as he reached the bottom step she clutched his hands desperately.

"Jerry," she whispered, "I--forgive me--I honestly-- Oh, I didn't think what I was saying last night. You were so dear, and I was so happy, and for a while I really believed we could belong to each other. But I can't, you know. I've promised papa and the girls a dozen times that I would never marry. Don't you see how it is? I must take it back."

Jerry smiled a little, it must be admitted. This was so like his conscientious little Prudence!

"Dearest," he said gently, "you have said that because you were not awake. You did not love. But you are awake now. You love me. Your father would never allow you to sacrifice yourself like that. The girls would not hear of it. They want you to be happy. And you can't be happy without me, can you?"

Suddenly she crushed close to him. "Oh, Jerry," she sobbed, "I will never be happy again, I know. But--it is right for me to stay here, and be the mother in the parsonage. It is wicked of me to want you more than all of them. Don't you see it is? They haven't any mother. They haven't any one but me. Of course, they would not allow it, but they will not know anything about it. I must do it myself. And father especially must never know. I want you to go away this morning before breakfast, and--never come again."

She clung to him as she said this, but her voice did not falter. "And you must not write to me any more. For, oh, Jerry, if I see you again I can never let you go, I know it. Will you do this for me?"

"You've been up all night, haven't you, dearest?"

"Yes,--I remembered, and then I couldn't sleep."

"What have you been doing all night? It is morning now."

"I walked up and down the floor, and pounded my hands together," she admitted, with a mournful smile.

"You are nervous and excited," he said tenderly. "Let's wait until after breakfast. Then we'll talk it all over with your father, and it shall be as he says. Won't that be better?"

"Oh, no. For father will say whatever he thinks will make me happy. He must not know a thing about it. Promise, Jerry, that you will never tell him one word."

"I promise, of course, Prudence. I will let you tell him."

But she shook her head. "He will never know. Oh, Jerry! I can't bear to think of never seeing you again, and never getting letters from you, and-- It seems to kill me inside, just the thought of it."

"Sit down here in my lap. Put your head on my shoulder, like that. Let me rub your face a little. You're feverish. You are sick. Go to bed, won't you, sweetheart? We can settle this later on."

"You must go right away, or I can not let you go at all!"

"Do you mean you want me to get my things, and go right now?"

"Yes." She buried her face in his shoulder. "If--if you stay in your room until breakfast time, I will lock you in, so you can not leave me again. I know it. I am crazy to-day."

"Don't you think you owe me something, as well as your father and sisters? Didn't God bring us together, and make us love each other? Don't you think He intended us for each other? Do you wish you had never met me?"

"Jerry!"

"Then, sweetheart, be reasonable. Your father loved your mother, and married her. That is God's plan for all of us. You have been a wonderfully brave and sweet daughter and sister, I know. But surely Fairy is old enough to take your place now."

"Fairy's going to be a professor, and--the girls do not mind her very well. And she isn't as much comfort to father as I am.--It's just because I am most like mother, you see. But anyhow, I promised. I can't leave them."

"Your father expects you to marry, and to marry me. I told him about it myself, long ago. And he was perfectly willing. He didn't say a word against it."

"Of course he wouldn't. That's just like father. But still, I promised. And what would the girls say if I should go back on them? They have trusted me, always. If I fail them, will they ever trust anybody else? If you love me, Jerry, please go, and stay away." But her arm tightened about his neck. "I'll wait here until you get your things, and we can--say good-by. And don't forget your promise."

"Oh, very well, Prudence," he answered, half irritably, "if you insist on ordering me away from the house like this, I can only go. But----"

"Let's not talk any more about it, Jerry. Please. I'll wait until you come down."

When he came down a little later, with his suitcase, his face was white and strained.

She put her arms around his neck. "Jerry," she whispered, "I want to tell you that I love you so much that--I could go away with you, and never see any of them any more, or papa, or the parsonage, and still feel rich, if I just had you! You--everything in me seems to be all yours. I--love you."

Her tremulous lips were pressed against his.

"Oh, sweetheart, this is folly, all folly. But I can't make you see it. It is wrong, it is wickedly wrong, but----"

"But I am all they have, Jerry, and--I promised."

"Whenever you want me, Prudence, just send. I'll never change. I'll always be just the same. God intended you for me, I know, and--I'll be waiting."

"Jerry! Jerry! Jerry!" she whispered passionately, sobbing, quivering in his arms. It was he who drew away.

"Good-by, sweetheart," he said quietly, great pity in his heart for the girl who in her desire to do right was doing such horrible wrong. "Good-by, sweetheart.

Remember, I will be waiting. Whenever you send, I will come."

He stepped outside, and closed the door. Prudence stood motionless, her hands clenched, until she could no longer hear his footsteps. Then she dropped on the floor, and lay there, face downward, until she heard Fairy moving in her room upstairs. Then she went into the kitchen and built the fire for breakfast.

CHAPTER XIV
SHE COMES TO GRIEF

Fairy was one of those buoyant, warm-blooded girls to whom sleep is indeed the great restorer. She slept soundly, sweetly, dreamlessly. And every morning she ran down-stairs so full of animation and life that she seemed all atingle to her finger-tips. Now she stood in the kitchen door, tall, cheeks glowing, eyes sparkling, and smiled at her sister's solemn back.

"You are the little mousey, Prue," she said, in her full rich voice. "I didn't hear you come to bed last night, and I didn't hear you getting out this morning. I am an abominably solid sleeper, am I not? Shall I get the maple sirup for the pancakes? I wonder if Jerry knows we only use maple sirup when he is here. I'm constantly expecting Connie to give it away. Why am I always so ravenously hungry in the morning? Goodness knows I eat enough--Why, what is the matter?" For Prudence had turned her face toward her sister, and it was so white and so unnatural that Fairy was shocked.

"Prudence! You are sick! Go to bed and let me get breakfast. Why didn't you call me? I'm real angry at you, Prudence Starr! Here, get out of this, and I will----"

"There's nothing the matter with me. I had a headache, and did not sleep, but I am all right now. Yes, bring the sirup, Fairy. Are the girls up yet?"

Fairy eyed her suspiciously. "Jerry is out unusually early, too, isn't he? His door is open. I didn't hear him coming down so he must have quite outdone himself to-day. He generally has to be called twice."

"Jerry has gone, Fairy." Prudence's back was presented to view once more, and Prudence was stirring the oatmeal with vicious energy. "He left early this morning,--I suppose he is half-way to Des Moines by now."

"Oh!" Fairy's voice was non-committal.

"Will you get the sirup now?"

"Yes, of course.--When is he coming back?"

"He isn't coming back. Please hurry, Fairy, and then call the others. The oatmeal is ready."

Fairy went soberly down cellar, and brought up the golden sirup. Then, ostensibly to call her sisters, she hurried up the stairs.

"Girls," she began, carefully closing the door of their room behind her. "Jerry has gone, and isn't coming back any more. And for goodness' sake, don't keep asking questions about it. Just eat your breakfast as usual, and have a little tact."

"Gone!"

"Yes."

"A lovers' quarrel," suggested Lark, and her eyes glittered greedily.

"Nothing of the sort. And don't keep staring at Prue, either. And do not keep talking about Jerry all the time. You mind me, or I will tell papa."

"That's funny," said Carol thoughtfully. "We left them kissing each other like mad in the back yard last night,--and this morning he has gone to return no more. They are crazy."

"Kissing! In the back yard! What are you talking about?"

Carol explained, and Fairy looked still more thoughtful and perturbed.

She opened the door, and called out to them in a loud and breezy voice, "Hurry, girls, for breakfast is ready, and there's no time to waste in a parsonage on Sunday morning." Then she added in a whisper, "And don't you mention Jerry, and don't ask Prudence what makes her so pale, or you'll catch it!"

Then she went to her father's door. "Breakfast is ready, papa," she called clearly. She turned the knob softly, and peeped in. "May I come in a minute?" Standing close beside him, she told him all she knew of what had happened.

"Prudence is ghastly, father, just ghastly. And she can't talk about it yet, so be careful what you say, will you?"

And it was due to Fairy's kindly admonitions that the parsonage family took the departure of Jerry so calmly.

"Fairy says Jerry took the morning train," said Mr. Starr, as they were passing the cream and sugar for the oatmeal. "That is too bad! But it is just the worst of being a business man,--one never knows when one must be up and away. And of course, one can not neglect business interests.--The oatmeal is unusually good this morning, Prudence." This was nothing short of heroic on his part, for her eyes upon her father's face were so wide and dark that the lump in his throat would not stay down.

That was the beginning of Prudence's bitter winter, when the brightest sunshine was cheerless and dreary, and when even the laughter of her sisters smote harshly upon her ears. She tried to be as always, but in her eyes the wounded look lingered, and her face grew so pale and thin that her father and Fairy, anxiously watching, were filled with grave concern. She remained almost constantly in the parsonage, reading very little, sitting most of her leisure time staring out the windows.

Fairy had tried to win her confidence, and had failed.

"You are a darling, Fairy, but I really do not want to talk about it.--Oh, no, indeed, it is all my own fault. I told him to go, and not come again.--No, you are wrong, Fairy, I do not regret it. I do not want him to come any more."

And Fairy worried. What in the world had happened to separate in the morning these two who had been kissing so frankly in the back yard the evening before?

Mr. Starr, too, had tried. "Prudence," he said gently, "you know very often men do things that to women seem wrong and wicked. And maybe they are! But men and women are different by nature, my dear, and we must remember that. I have satisfied myself that Jerry is good, and clean, and manly. I do not think you should let any foolishness of his in the past, come between you now."

"You are mistaken, father. Jerry is all right, and always was, I am sure. It is nothing like that. I told him to go, and not to come again. That is all."

"But if he should come back now----"

"It would be just the same. Don't worry about it, father. It's all right."

"Prudence," he said, more tenderly, "we have been the closest of friends and companions, you and I, from the very beginning. Always you have come to me with your troubles and worries. Have I ever failed you? Why, then, do you go back on me now, when you really need me?"

Prudence patted his shoulder affectionately, but her eyes did not meet his. "I do not really need you now, father. It is all settled, and I am quite satisfied. Things are all right with me just as they are."

Then he took a serious step, without her knowledge. He went to Des Moines, and had a visit with Jerry. He found him thinner, his face sterner, his eyes darker. When the office boy announced "Mr. Starr," Jerry ran quickly out to greet him.

"Is she all right?" he cried eagerly, almost before he was within hailing distance.

Mr. Starr did not mince matters. "Jerry," he said abruptly, "did you and Prudence have a quarrel? She declines to tell me anything about it, and after the conversations you and I have had, I think I have a right to know what has happened."

"Does she miss me? Does she seem sorry that I am away? Does----" His voice was so boyish and so eager there was no mistaking his attitude toward Prudence.

"Look here, Jerry, I want to know. Why are you staying away?"

"Won't Prudence tell you?"

"No."

"Then I can not. She made me promise not to tell you a word. But it is not my fault, Mr. Starr. I can tell you that. It is nothing I have done or said. She sent me away because she thinks it was right for her to do so, and--you know Prudence! It is wrong, I know. I knew it all the time. But I couldn't make her see it. And she made me promise not to tell."

In the end Mr. Starr went back to the parsonage no wiser than he left, save that he now knew that Jerry was really not to blame, and that he held himself ready to return to her on a moment's notice.

The Ladies of the Methodist church were puzzled and exasperated. They went to the parsonage, determined to "find out what's what." But when they sat with Prudence, and looked at the frail, pathetic little figure, with the mournful eyes,--- they could only sigh with her and go their ways.

The twins continued to play in the great maple, even when the leaves were fallen, "It's a dandy place, I tell you, Prudence," cried Carol. "Jerry didn't have time to put up the rope before Connie pulled him down, but we've fixed it ourselves, and it is simply grand. You can go up and swing any time you like,--unless your joints are too stiff! It's a very serious matter getting up there,---for stiff joints, of course, I mean. Lark and I get up easy enough."

For a moment, Prudence sat silent with quivering lips. Then she burst out with unusual passion, "Don't you ever dare climb up in that tree again as long as you live, twins! Mind what I say!"

Lark looked thoughtfully out of the window, and Carol swallowed hard. It was she who said gently, "Why, of course, Prue,--just as you say."

For the first time, Prudence had dealt with them harshly and unfairly. They knew it. There was neither sense nor justice in her command. But they did not argue the point. They kept their eyes considerately away from her, and buried themselves in *Julius Caesar*,--it must be remembered the twins are sophomores now. Five minutes later Prudence spoke again, humbly.

"I beg you pardon, twins,--that was a perfectly idiotic thing for me to say. Of course, you may play in the maple whenever you like. But be careful. You couldn't save yourselves in falling as--as men can."

"We won't play there if you want us not to," said Carol kindly.

"I do want you to play there," she answered. "It's a very nice place, and great fun, I know. I might try it myself if--my joints weren't so stiff! Now, go on with your Latin."

But Prudence did not pass under the maple for many weeks without clenching her hands, and shuddering.

The twins were not satisfied. They marveled, and wondered, and pondered over the subject of Jerry's disappearance. Finally they felt it was more than human flesh could stand. They would approach Prudence on the subject themselves. But they bided their time. They must wait until Fairy was safely out of the house. Fairy these days had an infuriating way of saying, "That will do, twins. You'd better go and play now." It enraged and distracted the twins almost to the point of committing crime.

They had made several artistic moves already. Professor Duke, of their freshman biology class, had written Carol a gay long letter. And Carol was enthusiastic about it. She and Lark talked of "dear old Duck" for two weeks, almost without pausing for sleep.

"I'm sure you would fall in love with him on the spot," Carol had said to Prudence suggestively.

Prudence had only smiled, evidently in sarcasm!

"Jerry was very nice,--oh, very nice,--but you ought to see our little Duck!" Carol rattled rashly. "I'm sure you wouldn't regret Jerry any more if you could just get hold of Duckie. Of course, his being in New York is an obstacle, but I could introduce you by mail."

"I do not care for Ducks," said Prudence. "Of course, they look very nice swimming around on the water, but when it comes to eating,--I'll take spring chicken every time."

Carol did not mention "Duck" again for three days.

But there came a day when Fairy was out in the country. Connie had gone driving with her father. The moment had arrived. The twins had their plan of campaign memorized, and they sauntered in to Prudence with a nonchalance that was all assumed.

"Prudence," Lark began, "we're writing a book."

"That's nice," said Prudence. Conversation languished. The subject seemed exhausted.

Carol came to the rescue. "It's a very nice book. It's a love-story, and perfectly thrilling. Larkie does the writing, but I criticize and offer suggestions."

"That's kind of you."

A pause.

"I'm going to dedicate it to Carol,--To my beloved sister, to whose kindness and sympathy, I owe all that I am,--or something like that," Lark explained hopefully.

"How proud Carol will be!"

A long pause.

"We're in a very critical place just now, though," Lark seemed to be commencing at the beginning once more. "We have our heroine in a very peculiar situation, and we can't think what to do with her next."

"How sad."

Another pause.

"We thought maybe you could help us out."

"I'm afraid not," Prudence smiled a little. "I haven't any imagination. Ask Fairy. She's strong on love-stories."

"Maybe if we explain the situation to you, you could give us a suggestion. It is like this: The young people have had all kinds of thrilling experiences, but they are not yet betrothed. But they are just on the point of getting there,--and something crops up all of a sudden! The hero goes dashing away, and returns no more. The heroine lies upon her silken couch, weeping, weeping. And no one knows what to do about it, because no one knows what has happened. What do you suppose could have sent the lover away like that?"

"Maybe he hasn't enough money for the heroine."

"Oh, yes,--he's very rich."

"Maybe he is already married."

"No, indeed. He's a bachelor."

"Maybe he didn't love her, after all."

Here Carol chimed in helpfully. "Oh, yes, he did, for we left him kissing her all over the back yard, and he wouldn't have done that if he hadn't loved her, you know."

Prudence's eyes twinkled a little, but her smile was sad.

"Now, what would you advise us to do?" inquired Lark briskly, feeling instinctively that Carol had explained too much.

Prudence rose slowly. "I think," she said very gently, "I think I would burn the book if I were you, and pay a little more attention to my studies."

Then she went up-stairs, and Carol told Lark sympathetically that they did not deserve an authoress in the parsonage when they didn't give her any more encouragement than that!

On the day before Christmas, an insured package was delivered at the parsonage for Prudence. A letter was with it, and she read that first.

"My dearest little sweetheart: I chose this gift for you long before I had the right to do it. I was keeping it until the proper moment. But the moment came, and went again. Still I want you to have the gift. Please wear it, for my sake, for I shall be happy knowing it is where it ought to be, even though I myself am banished. I love you, Prudence. Whenever you send for me, I am ready to come. Entirely and always yours. Jerry."

With trembling fingers she opened the little package. It contained a ring, with a brilliant diamond flashing myriad colors before her eyes. And Prudence kissed it passionately, many times.

Two hours later, she went quietly down-stairs to where the rest of the family were decorating a Christmas tree. She showed the ring to them gravely.

"Jerry sent it to me," she said. "Do you think it is all right for me to wear it, father?"

A thrill of hopeful expectancy ran through the little group.

"Yes, indeed," declared her father. "How beautiful it is! Is Jerry coming to spend Christmas with us?"

"Why, no, father,--he is not coming at all any more. I thought you understood that."

An awkward silence, and Carol came brightly to the rescue. "It certainly is a beauty! I thought it was very kind of Professor Duckie to send Lark and me a five-pound box of chocolates, but of course this is ever so much nicer. Jerry's a bird, I say."

"A bird!" mocked Fairy. "Such language."

Lark came to her twin's defense. "Yes, a bird,--that's just what he is."

Carol smiled. "We saw him use his wings when Connie yanked him out of the big maple, didn't we, Lark?" Then, "Did you send him anything, Prue?"

Prudence hesitated, and answered without the slightest accession of color, "Yes, Carol. I had my picture taken when I was in Burlington, and sent it to him."

"Your picture! Oh, Prudence! Where are they? Aren't you going to give us one?"

"No, Carol. I had only one made,--for Jerry. There aren't any more."

"Well," sighed Lark resignedly, "it's a pretty idea for my book, anyhow."

From that day on, Prudence always wore the sparkling ring,--and the women of the Methodist church nearly had mental paralysis marveling over a man who gave a diamond ring, and never came a-wooing! And a girl who accepted and wore his offering, with nothing to say for the man! And it was the consensus of opinion in Mount Mark that modern lovers were mostly crazy, anyhow!

And springtime came again.

Now the twins were always original in their amusements. They never followed blindly after the dictates of custom. When other girls were playing dolls, the twins were a tribe of wild Indians. When other girls were jumping the rope, the twins were conducting a circus. And when other girls played "catch" with dainty rubber balls, the twins took unto themselves a big and heavy croquet ball,--found in the Avery woodshed. To be sure, it stung and bruised their hands. What matter? At any rate, they continued endangering their lives and beauties by reckless pitching of the ungainly plaything.

One Friday evening after school, they were amusing themselves on the parsonage lawn with this huge ball. When their father turned in, they ran up to him with a sporting proposition.

"Bet you a nickel, papa," cried Carol, "that you can't throw this ball as far as the schoolhouse woodshed!--By the way, will you lend me a nickel, papa?"

He took the ball, and weighed it lightly in his hand. "I'm an anti-betting society," he declared, laughing, "but I very strongly believe it will carry to the schoolhouse woodshed. If it does not, I'll give you five cents' worth of candy to-morrow. And if it does, you shall put an extra nickel in the collection next Sunday."

Then he drew back his arm, and carefully sighted across the lawn. "I'll send it right between the corner of the house and that little cedar," he said, and then, bending low, it whizzed from his hand.

Lark screamed, and Carol sank fainting to the ground. For an instant, Mr. Starr himself stood swaying. Then he rushed across the lawn. For Prudence had opened the front door, and stepped quickly out on the walk by the corner of the house. The heavy ball struck her on the forehead, and she fell heavily, without a moan.

CHAPTER XV
FATE TAKES CHARGE

Four hours Prudence lay unconscious, with two doctors in close attendance. Fairy, alert but calm, was at hand to give them service.

It is a significant thing that in bitter anguish and grief, Christians find comfort and peace in prayer. Outsiders, as well as Christians, pray in times of danger and mental stress. But here is the big difference between the prayers of Christians and the prayers of "others." "Others" pray, and pray, and pray again, and continue still in the agony and passion of grief and fear. And yet they pray. But Christians pray, and find confidence and serenity. Sorrow may remain, but anguish is stilled.

Mount Mark considered this a unique parsonage family. Their liveliness, their gaiety, their love of fun, seemed a little inapropos in the setting of a Methodist parsonage.

"They ain't sanctimonious enough by half," declared old Harvey Reel, the bus driver, "but, by Jings! I tell you they are dandies!"

But as a matter of fact, every one of the family, from Connie up, had a characteristic parsonage heart. When they were worried, or frightened, or grieved, they prayed. Fairy passing up the stairs with hot water for the doctors, whispered to her father as he turned in to his own room, "Keep on praying, father. I can't stop now, because they need me. But I'm praying every minute between errands!" And Mr. Starr, kneeling beside his bed, did pray,--and the stony despair in his eyes died out, and he came from the little room quiet, and confident, and calm.

Connie had been unfortunate. In seeking a secluded corner to "pray for Prudence," she had passed the door of the dungeon, and paused. A fitting place! So she turned in at once, drawing the door after her, but leaving it a couple of inches ajar.

Then in the farthest and darkest corner, she knelt on the hard floor, and prayed, and sobbed herself to sleep. Fairy passing through the hall, observed the door ajar, and gave it a slight push. The lock snapped into place, but Connie did not waken.

Lark remained loyally with Carol until consciousness returned to her. As soon as she was able to walk, the two went silently to the barn, and climbed into the much-loved haymow. There they lay flat on the hay, faces downward, each with an arm across the other's shoulder, praying fervently. After a time they rose and crept into the house, where they waited patiently until Fairy came down on one of her numerous errands.

"Is she better?" they whispered. And Fairy answered gently, "I think she is a little better." Then the twins, in no way deceived, went back to the haymow again.

Fairy prepared a hasty supper, and arranged it on the kitchen table. She drank a cup of hot coffee, and went in search of her father. "Go and eat, dadsie," she urged. But he shook his head.

"I am not hungry, but send the girls to the table at once."

On their next trip into the house, Fairy stopped the twins. "Get Connie, and eat your supper. It's just a cold lunch, and is already on the kitchen table. You must help yourselves,--I can't come now."

The twins did not speak, and Fairy went hurriedly up the stairs once more.

"I do not think I can eat," said Carol.

"I know I can't," was Lark's reply.

"Won't Fairy make us? She'll tell papa."

"We'd better take away about half of this food, and hide it. Then she will think we have already eaten."

This novel plan was acted upon with promptitude.

"Where's Connie? She ought to eat something. We must make her do it."

"She probably cried herself to sleep somewhere. We'd better let her alone. She'll feel much better asleep and hungry, than awake and sorry for Prue."

So the twins went back to the haymow. When it grew dark, they slipped into the kitchen, and huddled together on, the woodbox beside the stove. And down to them presently came Fairy, smiling, her eyes tear-brightened.

"She is better!" cried Carol, springing to her feet.

"Yes," said Fairy, dropping on her knees and burying her face in Lark's lap, as she still sat on the woodbox. "She's better. She is better." Lark patted the heaving shoulders in a motherly way, and when Fairy lifted her face again it was all serene, though her lashes were wet.

"She is conscious," said Fairy, still on her knees, but with her head thrown back, and smiling. "She regained consciousness a little while ago. There is nothing really serious the matter. It was a hard knock, but it missed the temple. When she became conscious, she looked up at father and smiled. Father looked perfectly awful, twins, so pale, and his lips were trembling. And Prudence said, 'Now, father, on your word of honor, did you knock me down with that ball on purpose?' She spoke very low, and weak, but--just like Prudence! Father couldn't say a word, he just nodded, and gulped. She has a little fever, and the doctors say we may need to work with her part of the night. Father said to ask if you would go to bed now, so you can get up early in the morning and help us. I am to stay with Prudence to-night, but you may have to take turns in the morning. And you'll have to get breakfast, too. So father thinks you would better go to bed. Will you do that, twinnies?"

"Will we!" And Carol added, "Will you kiss Prudence good night for us, and tell her we kept praying all the time? Prudence is such a great hand for praying, you know."

Fairy promised, and the twins crept up-stairs. It was dark in their room.

"We'll undress in the dark so as not to awake poor little Connie," whispered Lark. "It's nice she can sleep like that, isn't it?"

And the twins went to bed, and fell asleep after a while, never doubting that Connie, in her corner of the room, was already safe and happy in the oblivion of slumber.

But poor Connie! She had not wakened when Fairy closed the dungeon door. It was long afterward when she sat up and began rubbing her eyes. She did not know where she was. Then she remembered! She wondered if Prudence-- She scrambled to her feet, and trotted over to the dungeon door. It was locked, she could not turn the knob. At first, she thought of screaming and pounding on the door.

"But that will arouse Prudence, and frighten her, and maybe kill her," she thought wretchedly. "I'll just keep still until some one passes."

But no one passed for a long time, and Connie stretched her aching little body and sobbed, worrying about Prudence, fearful on her own account. She had no idea of the time. She supposed it was still early. And the parsonage was deathly quiet. Maybe Prudence had died! Connie writhed in agony on the hard floor, and sobbed bitterly. Still she would not risk pounding on the dungeon door.

Up-stairs, in the front room, Prudence was at that time wrestling with fever. Higher and higher it rose, until the doctors looked very anxious. They held a brief consultation in the corner of the room. Then they beckoned to Mr. Starr.

"Has Prudence been worrying about something this winter?"

"Yes."

"Has she been grieving, and fretting for something?"

"Yes, she has."

"It is that young man, isn't it?" inquired the family doctor,--a Methodist "member."

"Yes."

"Can you bring him here?"

"Yes,--as soon as he can get here from Des Moines."

"You'd better do it. She has worn herself down nearly to the point of prostration. We think we can break this fever without serious consequences, but get the young man as soon as possible. She can not relax and rest, until she gets relief."

So he went down-stairs and over the telephone dictated a short message to Jerry. "Please come,--Prudence."

When he entered the front bedroom again, Prudence was muttering unintelligible words under her breath. He kneeled down beside the bed, and put his arms around her. She clung to him with sudden passion.

"Jerry! Jerry!" she cried. Her father caressed and petted her, but did not speak.

"Oh, I can't," she cried again. "I can't, Jerry, I can't!" Again her voice fell to low mumbling. "Yes, go. Go at once. I promised, you know.--They haven't any mother.--I promised. Jerry! Jerry!" Her voice rang out so wildly that Connie, down in the dungeon, heard her cries and sobbed anew, relieved that Prudence was living, frightened at the wildness of her voice. "Oh, I do want you--more than anybody. Don't go!--Oh, yes, go at once. I promised.--Father needs me." And then a piercing shriek, "He is falling! Connie, drop that rope!" She struggled up in the bed, and gazed wildly about her,--then, panting, she fell back on the pillows.

But Mr. Starr smiled gently to himself. So that was the answer! Oh, foolish little Prudence! Oh, sweet-hearted little martyr girl!

Hours later the fever broke, and Prudence drifted into a deep sleep. Then the doctors went downstairs with Mr. Starr, talking in quiet ordinary tones.

"Oh, she is all right now, no danger at all. She'll do fine. Let her sleep. Send Fairy to bed, too. Keep Prudence quiet a few days,--that's all. She's all right."

They did not hear the timid knock at the dungeon door. But after they had gone out, Mr. Starr locked the door behind them, and started back through the hall to see if the kitchen doors were locked. He distinctly heard a soft tapping, and he smiled. "Mice!" he thought. Then he heard something else,--a faintly whispered "Father!"

With a sharp exclamation he unlocked and opened the dungeon door, and Connie fell into his arms, sobbing piteously. And he did the only wise thing to do under such circumstances. He sat down on the hall floor and cuddled the child against his breast. He talked to her soothingly until the sobs quieted, and her voice was under control.

"Now, tell father," he urged, "how did you get in the dungeon? The twins----"

"Oh, no, father, of course not, the twins wouldn't do such a thing as that. I went into the dungeon to pray that Prudence would get well. And I prayed myself to sleep. When I woke up the door was locked."

"But you precious child," he whispered, "why didn't you call out, or pound on the door?"

"I was afraid it would excite Prue and make her worse," she answered simply. And her father's kiss was unwontedly tender as he carried her upstairs to bed.

Prudence slept late the next morning, and when she opened her eyes her father was sitting beside her.

"All right this morning, father," she said, smiling. "Are the girls at school?"

"No,--this is Saturday."

"Oh, of course. Well, bring them up, I want to see them."

Just then the distant whistle of a locomotive sounded through the open window, but she did not notice her father's sudden start. She nodded up at him again, and repeated, "I want to see my girls."

Her father sent them up to her at once, and they stood at the foot of the bed with sorry faces, and smiled at her.

"Say something," whispered Carol, kicking Lark suggestively on the foot. But Lark was dumb. It was Carol who broke the silence.

"Oh, Prudence, do you suppose the doctors will let me come in and watch them bandage your head? I want to begin practising up, so as to be ready for the next war."

Then they laughed, and the girls realized that Prudence was really alive and quite as always. They told her of Connie's sad experience, and Prudence comforted her sweetly.

"It just proves all over again," she declared, smiling, but with a sigh close following, "that you can't get along without me to look after you. Would I ever go to bed without making sure that Connie was safe and sound?"

Down-stairs, meanwhile, Mr. Starr was plotting with Fairy, a willing assistant.

"He'll surely be in on this train, and you must keep him down here until I get through with Prudence. I want to tell her a few things before she sees him. Bring him in quietly, and don't let him speak loudly. I do not want her to know he is on hand for a few minutes. Explain it to the girls, will you?"

After sending the younger girls down-stairs again, he closed the door of Prudence's room, and sat down beside her.

"Prudence, I can't tell you how bitterly disappointed I am in you."

"Father!"

"Yes, I thought you loved us,--the girls and me. It never occurred to me that you considered us a bunch of selfish, heartless, ungrateful animals!"

"Father!"

"Is that your idea of love? Is that----"

"Oh, father!"

"It really did hurt me, Prudence. My dear little girl, how could you send Jerry away, breaking your heart and his, and ours, too,--just because you thought us such a selfish lot that we would begrudge you any happiness of your own? Don't you think our love for you is big enough to make us happy in seeing you happy? You used to say you would never marry. We did not expect you to marry, then. But we knew the time would come when marriage would seem beautiful and desirable to you. We were waiting for that time. We were hoping for it. We were happy when you loved Jerry, because we knew he was good and kind and loving, and that he could give you all the beautiful things of life--that I can never give my children. But you thought we were too selfish to let you go, and you sent him away."

"But father! Who would raise the girls? Who would keep the parsonage? Who would look after you?"

"Aunt Grace, to be sure. We talked it over two years ago, when her husband died. Before that, she was not free to come to us. But she said then that whenever we were ready for her, she would come. We both felt that since you were getting along so magnificently with the girls, it was better that way for a while. But she said that when your flitting-time came, she would come to us gladly. We had it all arranged. You won't want to marry for a year or so, yet. You'll want to have some happy sweetheart days first. And you'll want to make a lot of those pretty, useless, nonsensical things other girls make when they marry. That's why I advised you to save your burglar money,--so you would have it for this. We'll have Aunt Grace come right away, so you can take a little freedom to be happy, and to make your plans. And you can initiate Aunt Grace into the mysteries of parsonage housekeeping."

A bright strange light had flashed over Prudence's face. But her eyes clouded a little as she asked, "Do you think they would rather have Aunt Grace than me?"

"Of course not. But what has that to do with it? We love you so dearly that we can only be happy when you are happy. We love you so dearly that we can be happy with you away from us,--just knowing that you are happy. But you--you thought our love was such a hideous, selfish, little make-believe that----"

"Oh, father, I didn't! You know I didn't!--But--maybe Jerry won't forgive me now?"

"Why didn't you talk it over with me, Prudence?"

"I knew you too well, father. I knew it would be useless. But--doesn't it seem wrong, father, that--a girl--that I--should love Jerry more than--you and the girls? That he should come first? Doesn't it seem--wicked?"

"No, Prudence, it is not wicked. After all, perhaps it is not a stronger and deeper love. You were willing to sacrifice him and yourself, for our sakes! But it is a different love. It is the love of woman for man,--that is very different from sister-love and father-love. And it is right. And it is beautiful."

"I am sure Jerry will forgive me. Maybe if you will send me a paper and pencil--I can write him a note now? There's no use waiting, is there? Fairy will bring it, I am sure."

But when a few minutes later, she heard a step in the hall outside, she laid her arm across her face. Somehow she felt that the wonderful joy and love shining in her eyes should be kept hidden until Jerry was there to see. She heard the door open, and close again.

"Put them on the table, Fairy dearest, and--leave me for a little while, will you? Thank you." And her face was still hidden.

Then the table by the bedside was swiftly drawn away, and Jerry kneeled beside her, and drew the arm from her face.

"Jerry!" she whispered, half unbelievingly. Then joyously, "Oh, Jerry!" She gazed anxiously into his face. "Have you been sick? How thin you are, and so pale! Jerry Harmer, you need me to take care of you, don't you?"

But Jerry did not speak. He looked earnestly and steadily into the joyful eyes for a moment, and then he pressed his face to hers.

The Codes Of Hammurabi And Moses
W. W. Davies

QTY

The discovery of the Hammurabi Code is one of the greatest achievements of archaeology, and is of paramount interest, not only to the student of the Bible, but also to all those interested in ancient history...

Religion   **ISBN:** *1-59462-338-4*   **Pages:132**
                                              MSRP $12.95

The Theory of Moral Sentiments
Adam Smith

QTY

This work from 1749. contains original theories of conscience amd moral judgment and it is the foundation for systemof morals.

Philosophy **ISBN:** *1-59462-777-0*   **Pages:536**
                                              MSRP $19.95

Jessica's First Prayer
Hesba Stretton

QTY

In a screened and secluded corner of one of the many railway-bridges which span the streets of London there could be seen a few years ago, from five o'clock every morning until half past eight, a tidily set-out coffee-stall, consisting of a trestle and board, upon which stood two large tin cans, with a small fire of charcoal burning under each so as to keep the coffee boiling during the early hours of the morning when the work-people were thronging into the city on their way to their daily toil...

Pages:84

Childrens   **ISBN:** *1-59462-373-2*   *MSRP $9.95*

My Life and Work
Henry Ford

QTY

Henry Ford revolutionized the world with his implementation of mass production for the Model T automobile. Gain valuable business insight into his life and work with his own auto-biography... "We have only started on our development of our country we have not as yet, with all our talk of wonderful progress, done more than scratch the surface. The progress has been wonderful enough but..."

Pages:300

Biographies/   **ISBN:** *1-59462-198-5*   *MSRP $21.95*

The Art of Cross-Examination
Francis Wellman

QTY

I presume it is the experience of every author, after his first book is published upon an important subject, to be almost overwhelmed with a wealth of ideas and illustrations which could readily have been included in his book, and which to his own mind, at least, seem to make a second edition inevitable. Such certainly was the case with me; and when the first edition had reached its sixth impression in five months, I rejoiced to learn that it seemed to my publishers that the book had met with a sufficiently favorable reception to justify a second and considerably enlarged edition. ..

Pages:412

Reference   ISBN: *1-59462-647-2*   *MSRP $19.95*

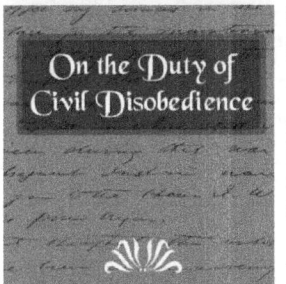

On the Duty of Civil Disobedience
Henry David Thoreau

QTY

Thoreau wrote his famous essay, On the Duty of Civil Disobedience, as a protest against an unjust but popular war and the immoral but popular institution of slave-owning. He did more than write—he declined to pay his taxes, and was hauled off to gaol in consequence. Who can say how much this refusal of his hastened the end of the war and of slavery ?

Law   ISBN: *1-59462-747-9*   **Pages:48**

MSRP $7.45

Dream Psychology Psychoanalysis for Beginners
Sigmund Freud

QTY

Sigmund Freud, born Sigismund Schlomo Freud (May 6, 1856 - September 23, 1939), was a Jewish-Austrian neurologist and psychiatrist who co-founded the psychoanalytic school of psychology. Freud is best known for his theories of the unconscious mind, especially involving the mechanism of repression; his redefinition of sexual desire as mobile and directed towards a wide variety of objects; and his therapeutic techniques, especially his understanding of transference in the therapeutic relationship and the presumed value of dreams as sources of insight into unconscious desires.

Pages:196

Psychology   ISBN: *1-59462-905-6*   *MSRP $15.45*

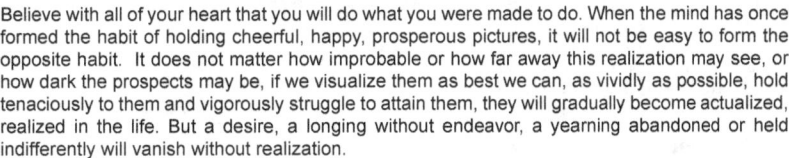

The Miracle of Right Thought
Orison Swett Marden

QTY

Believe with all of your heart that you will do what you were made to do. When the mind has once formed the habit of holding cheerful, happy, prosperous pictures, it will not be easy to form the opposite habit. It does not matter how improbable or how far away this realization may see, or how dark the prospects may be, if we visualize them as best we can, as vividly as possible, hold tenaciously to them and vigorously struggle to attain them, they will gradually become actualized, realized in the life. But a desire, a longing without endeavor, a yearning abandoned or held indifferently will vanish without realization.

Pages:360

Self Help   ISBN: *1-59462-644-8*   *MSRP $25.45*

www.bookjungle.com *email: sales@bookjungle.com fax: 630-214-0564 mail: Book Jungle PO Box 2226 Champaign, IL 61825*

QTY

The Rosicrucian Cosmo-Conception Mystic Christianity *by Max Heindel*   ISBN: *1-59462-188-8*   **$38.95**
The Rosicrucian Cosmo-conception is not dogmatic, neither does it appeal to any other authority than the reason of the student. It is: not controversial, but is: sent forth in the, hope that it may help to clear..   New Age/Religion Pages 646

Abandonment To Divine Providence *by Jean-Pierre de Caussade*   ISBN: *1-59462-228-0*   **$25.95**
"The Rev. Jean Pierre de Caussade was one of the most remarkable spiritual writers of the Society of Jesus in France in the 18th Century. His death took place at Toulouse in 1751. His works have gone through many editions and have been republished...   Inspirational/Religion Pages 400

Mental Chemistry *by Charles Haanel*   ISBN: *1-59462-192-6*   **$23.95**
Mental Chemistry allows the change of material conditions by combining and appropriately utilizing the power of the mind. Much like applied chemistry creates something new and unique out of careful combinations of chemicals the mastery of mental chemistry...   New Age Pages 354

The Letters of Robert Browning and Elizabeth Barret Barrett 1845-1846 vol II   ISBN: *1-59462-193-4*   **$35.95**
by Robert Browning and Elizabeth Barrett
   Biographies Pages 596

Gleanings In Genesis (volume I) *by Arthur W. Pink*   ISBN: *1-59462-130-6*   **$27.45**
Appropriately has Genesis been termed "the seed plot of the Bible" for in it we have, in germ form, almost all of the great doctrines which are afterwards fully developed in the books of Scripture which follow...   Religion/Inspirational Pages 420

The Master Key *by L. W. de Laurence*   ISBN: *1-59462-001-6*   **$30.95**
In no branch of human knowledge has there been a more lively increase of the spirit of research during the past few years than in the study of Psychology, Concentration and Mental Discipline. The requests for authentic lessons in Thought Control, Mental Discipline and...   New Age/Business Pages 422

The Lesser Key Of Solomon Goetia *by L. W. de Laurence*   ISBN: *1-59462-092-X*   **$9.95**
This translation of the first book of the "Lemegton" which is now for the first time made accessible to students of Talismanic Magic was done, after careful collation and edition, from numerous Ancient Manuscripts in Hebrew, Latin, and French...   New Age/Occult Pages 92

Rubaiyat Of Omar Khayyam *by Edward Fitzgerald*   ISBN:*1-59462-332-5*   **$13.95**
Edward Fitzgerald, whom the world has already learned, in spite of his own efforts to remain within the shadow of anonymity, to look upon as one of the rarest poets of the century, was born at Bredfield, in Suffolk, on the 31st of March, 1809. He was the third son of John Purcell...   Music Pages 172

Ancient Law *by Henry Maine*   ISBN: *1-59462-128-4*   **$29.95**
The chief object of the following pages is to indicate some of the earliest ideas of mankind, as they are reflected in Ancient Law, and to point out the relation of those ideas to modern thought.   Religiom/History Pages 452

Far-Away Stories *by William J. Locke*   ISBN: *1-59462-129-2*   **$19.45**
"Good wine needs no bush, but a collection of mixed vintages does. And this book is just such a collection. Some of the stories I do not want to remain buried for ever in the museum files of dead magazine-numbers an author's not unpardonable vanity..."   Fiction Pages 272

Life of David Crockett *by David Crockett*   ISBN: *1-59462-250-7*   **$27.45**
"Colonel David Crockett was one of the most remarkable men of the times in which he lived. Born in humble life, but gifted with a strong will, an indomitable courage, and unremitting perseverance...   Biographies/New Age Pages 424

Lip-Reading *by Edward Nitchie*   ISBN: *1-59462-206-X*   **$25.95**
Edward B. Nitchie, founder of the New York School for the Hard of Hearing, now the Nitchie School of Lip-Reading, Inc, wrote "LIP-READING Principles and Practice". The development and perfecting of this meritorious work on lip-reading was an undertaking...   How-to Pages 400

A Handbook of Suggestive Therapeutics, Applied Hypnotism, Psychic Science   ISBN: *1-59462-214-0*   **$24.95**
by Henry Munro
   Health/New Age/Health/Self-help Pages 376

A Doll's House: and Two Other Plays *by Henrik Ibsen*   ISBN: *1-59462-112-8*   **$19.95**
Henrik Ibsen created this classic when in revolutionary 1848 Rome. Introducing some striking concepts in playwriting for the realist genre, this play has been studied the world over.   Fiction/Classics/Plays 308

The Light of Asia *by sir Edwin Arnold*   ISBN: *1-59462-204-3*   **$13.95**
In this poetic masterpiece, Edwin Arnold describes the life and teachings of Buddha. The man who was to become known as Buddha to the world was born as Prince Gautama of India but he rejected the worldly riches and abandoned the reigns of power when...   Religion/History/Biographies Pages 170

The Complete Works of Guy de Maupassant *by Guy de Maupassant*   ISBN: *1-59462-157-8*   **$16.95**
"For days and days, nights and nights, I had dreamed of that first kiss which was to consecrate our engagement, and I knew not on what spot I should put my lips..."   Fiction/Classics Pages 240

The Art of Cross-Examination *by Francis L. Wellman*   ISBN: *1-59462-309-0*   **$26.95**
Written by a renowned trial lawyer, Wellman imparts his experience and uses case studies to explain how to use psychology to extract desired information through questioning.   How-to/Science/Reference Pages 408

Answered or Unanswered? *by Louisa Vaughan*   ISBN: *1-59462-248-5*   **$10.95**
Miracles of Faith in China   Religion Pages 112

The Edinburgh Lectures on Mental Science (1909) *by Thomas*   ISBN: *1-59462-008-3*   **$11.95**
This book contains the substance of a course of lectures recently given by the writer in the Queen Street Hall, Edinburgh. Its purpose is to indicate the Natural Principles governing the relation between Mental Action and Material Conditions...   New Age/Psychology Pages 148

Ayesha *by H. Rider Haggard*   ISBN: *1-59462-301-5*   **$24.95**
Verily and indeed it is the unexpected that happens! Probably if there was one person upon the earth from whom the Editor of this, and of a certain previous history, did not expect to hear again...   Classics Pages 380

Ayala's Angel *by Anthony Trollope*   ISBN: *1-59462-352-X*   **$29.95**
The two girls were both pretty, but Lucy who was twenty-one who supposed to be simple and comparatively unattractive, whereas Ayala was credited, as her Bombwhat romantic name might show, with poetic charm and a taste for romance. Ayala when her father died was nineteen...   Fiction Pages 484

The American Commonwealth *by James Bryce*   ISBN: *1-59462-286-8*   **$34.45**
An interpretation of American democratic political theory. It examines political mechanics and society from the perspective of Scotsman James Bryce   Politics Pages 572

Stories of the Pilgrims *by Margaret P. Pumphrey*   ISBN: *1-59462-116-0*   **$17.95**
This book explores pilgrims religious oppression in England as well as their escape to Holland and eventual crossing to America on the Mayflower, and their early days in New England...   History Pages 268

www.bookjungle.com *email: sales@bookjungle.com fax: 630-214-0564 mail: Book Jungle PO Box 2226 Champaign, IL 61825*

QTY

The Fasting Cure *by Sinclair Upton* ISBN: *1-59462-222-1* **$13.95**
In the Cosmopolitan Magazine for May, 1910, and in the Contemporary Review (London) for April, 1910, I published an article dealing with my experiences in fasting. I have written a great many magazine articles, but never one which attracted so much attention... New Age/Self Help/Health Pages 164

Hebrew Astrology *by Sepharial* ISBN: *1-59462-308-2* **$13.45**
In these days of advanced thinking it is a matter of common observation that we have left many of the old landmarks behind and that we are now pressing forward to greater heights and to a wider horizon than that which represented the mind-content of our progenitors... Astrology Pages 144

Thought Vibration or The Law of Attraction in the Thought World ISBN: *1-59462-127-6* **$12.95**
by William Walker Atkinson *Psychology/Religion Pages 144*

Optimism *by Helen Keller* ISBN: *1-59462-108-X* **$15.95**
Helen Keller was blind, deaf, and mute since 19 months old, yet famously learned how to overcome these handicaps, communicate with the world, and spread her lectures promoting optimism. An inspiring read for everyone... Biographies/Inspirational Pages 84

Sara Crewe *by Frances Burnett* ISBN: *1-59462-360-0* **$9.45**
In the first place, Miss Minchin lived in London. Her home was a large, dull, tall one, in a large, dull square, where all the houses were alike, and all the sparrows were alike, and where all the door-knockers made the same heavy sound... Childrens/Classic Pages 88

The Autobiography of Benjamin Franklin *by Benjamin Franklin* ISBN: *1-59462-135-7* **$24.95**
The Autobiography of Benjamin Franklin has probably been more extensively read than any other American historical work, and no other book of its kind has had such ups and downs of fortune. Franklin lived for many years in England, where he was agent... Biographies/History Pages 332

Name	
Email	
Telephone	
Address	
City, State ZIP	

☐ **Credit Card**   ☐ **Check / Money Order**

Credit Card Number	
Expiration Date	
Signature	

Please Mail to: Book Jungle
PO Box 2226
Champaign, IL 61825
or Fax to: 630-214-0564

ORDERING INFORMATION

web*: www.bookjungle.com*
email*: sales@bookjungle.com*
fax*: 630-214-0564*
mail*: Book Jungle PO Box 2226 Champaign, IL 61825*
or PayPal *to sales@bookjungle.com*

Please contact us for bulk discounts

DIRECT-ORDER TERMS

20% Discount if You Order
Two or More Books
Free Domestic Shipping!
Accepted: Master Card, Visa,
Discover, American Express